INVASION USA
BORDER
WAR

BOOK YOUR PLACE ON OUR WEBSITE AND MAKE THE READING CONNECTION!

We've created a customized website just for our very special readers, where you can get the inside scoop on everything that's going on with Zebra, Pinnacle and Kensington books.

When you come online, you'll have the exciting opportunity to:

• View covers of upcoming books

• Read sample chapters

• Learn about our future publishing schedule (listed by publication month *and author*)

• Find out when your favorite authors will be visiting a city near you

• Search for and order backlist books from our online catalog

• Check out author bios and background information

• Send e-mail to your favorite authors

• Meet the Kensington staff online

• Join us in weekly chats with authors, readers and other guests

• Get writing guidelines

• AND MUCH MORE!

**Visit our website at
http://www.kensingtonbooks.com**

INVASION USA
BORDER
WAR

William W. Johnstone

with

J. A. Johnstone

PINNACLE BOOKS
Kensington Publishing Corp.
www.kensingtonbooks.com

PINNACLE BOOKS are published by

Kensington Publishing Corp.
850 Third Avenue
New York, NY 10022

Copyright © 2006 William W. Johnstone and J. A. Johnstone

All rights reserved. No part of this book may be reproduced
in any form or by any means without the prior written con-
sent of the publisher, excepting brief quotes used in reviews.

All Kensington titles, imprints, and distributed lines are available at special quantity discounts for bulk purchases for sales
promotions, premiums, fund-raising, educational, or institu-
tional use.

Special book excerpts or customized printings can be created
to fit specific needs. For details, write or phone the office of
the Kensington special sales manager: Kensington Publishing
Corp., 850 Third Avenue, New York, NY 10022, attn: Special
Sales Department; phone 1-800-221-2647.

This book is a work of fiction. Names, characters, businesses,
organizations, places, events, and incidents either are the
product of the author's imagination, or are used fictitiously.
Any resemblance to actual persons, living or dead, events, or
locales is entirely coincidental.

PINNACLE BOOKS and the Pinnacle logo are Reg. U.S. Pat.
& TM Off.

ISBN 0-7860-1809-7

First Printing: September 2006

10 9 8 7 6 5 4 3 2 1

Printed in the United States of America

*"This will remain the land of the free
only so long as it is the home of the brave."*
—Elmer Davis

This is a work of fiction.
Unfortunately, events such as the ones
depicted in this novel occur all too often
along America's Southwestern borders in this day and age.

Dateline: Washington, D.C.

The U.S. State Department today issued its strongest warning yet regarding travel along the United States-Mexico border, urging American citizens not to cross the border into Mexico except in extreme emergencies.

"I was in Saigon. I was in Baghdad," said Jeffrey Parkhill, 52, an official in the Homeland Security Department and a retired colonel in the Marine Corps. "Nuevo Laredo and other Mexican border towns are rapidly becoming as dangerous as those cities were."

The Mexican government reacted quickly to the tough new travel advisory, accusing the U.S. authorities of over-reacting to the problem and attempting to undermine the Mexican economy. "Our military and police forces are engaged in a valiant effort to stem the tide of violence along the border and bring the wolves of the drug trade and other criminal activities to bay," the Mexican foreign minister said in a statement released in Mexico City.

Parkhill responded, "The Mexican government had a stake in such things when the country's economy depended to a large extent on tourism. Now the Mexican economy is built almost exclusively on the drug trade, and that's what has turned the border into a war zone."

Over the past several years, conditions along the U.S.-Mexico border have worsened as rival gangs such as the Sinaloa and Gulf cartels struggle to dominate the trafficking of illegal drugs. There have been hundreds of assassinations, the victims of which include numerous law enforcement officials, and Americans who venture across the border are prime targets for kidnapping. State Department officials say that this abduction epidemic is what prompted the latest, most stringent warning.

"An American's life isn't worth a plugged nickel on the other side of that river," said a police source in Laredo, Texas, who requested anonymity. "But what really worries me is what's going to happen when the killers who are running things over there start coming across the border. It hasn't happened yet, but borders don't mean anything to animals like that. . . ."

One

The Texas-Mexico border, upriver from Laredo

Even here, in the middle of nowhere, it was hard to escape from the lights. In the sky to the southeast, the stars were dimmed by the wash of illumination from Los Dos Laredos—the two Laredos, the American city of that name and its sister across the Rio Grande, Nuevo Laredo. Up here, the landscape on both sides of the border river was desolate, mostly uninhabited plains dotted with scrub brush, but always in the night sky was the reminder that civilization was not far off.

So-called civilization, thought Brady Keller as he crouched in the brush and waited. Sometimes he wondered just how far mankind had really progressed when somebody like him had to risk his life to keep a bunch of damn fools from injecting poison in their veins or sniffing it up their nose.

Brady was a man in his thirties wearing a dark blue flak jacket with the letters DEA displayed prominently on the back. The men scattered through the brush tonight were a combined force drawn from the Drug Enforcement Agency, the Border Patrol, and the Texas Rangers. They were members of a task force that had been trying for years, with limited success, to curb the drug traffic across the Mexican border. There were times when Brady felt like this was an unwinnable war, that they ought to just give up and let the animals take over.

But then he thought about all the men who had died in the effort to clean up the border, and knew that he and all the others like him couldn't give up. That would dishonor all the ones who had come before and made the ultimate sacrifice for their country.

Sure as hell, though, there were times when it seemed like the country didn't really give a damn. Brady thought of himself as a simple policeman, but he understood the law of supply and demand. If the cartels didn't have a voracious market for their drugs in the United States, they wouldn't be bringing them across the border. Maybe the public didn't really want this war to be won.

The politicians sure didn't. That included both the ones who whined about civil rights and bent over backward to protect the rights of criminals, even foreign criminals, and the others who were too tightfisted to commit the money and manpower necessary to truly shut down the drug trade. Even though he loved his country dearly, Brady often thought that its leaders had raised the practice of doing something in a half-assed manner to an art form.

The earphone tucked into his ear crackled, cutting into his musings. "Here they come," said the voice of Eduardo Corriente, the DEA agent in charge of tonight's operation, which had been set up following tips from several of the task force's sources. The radios were set on a special frequency that was jammed except for task force members, so that the enemy wouldn't know they were here.

Brady's grip tightened on the assault rifle in his hands. The dirt road in front of him ran from the Rio Grande to the railroad, about a mile behind the site of the ambush. A freight train had stopped back there on the rails, its crew working for the cartel. Those who couldn't be bought off were terrified into submission by horrible threats against their families. They had stopped the train, and when the trucks rendezvoused with it, an entire freight car would be filled with drugs headed west.

But that rendezvous would never take place. The task force would stop the trucks carrying the drugs before they ever reached their destination, and another group of agents would move in on the train itself and arrest the railroad workers who were working with the cartel. For tonight, at least, the poison's flow would be stopped.

But it was a mighty river, with many branches. . . .

Brady leaned forward as he heard the rumbling of heavy engines. He pulled the night-vision goggles down over his eyes, and as he peered through the brush that lined the road, the scene sprang into sharp, green-tinted relief.

Four big trucks with canvas covers over their backs rolled past Brady's position. Each truck would have some guards riding on it, probably armed with automatic weapons, but the task force numbered over forty men, also heavily armed, plus several jeeps. Brady was confident they could handle the smugglers.

"Go! Go!" Corriente yelled through the earphones. Brady surged to his feet, cradling the assault rifle against his chest, and along with several dozen other agents, he ran through the brush toward the road. At the same time, the jeeps roared out of the concealment of a clump of mesquites and blocked the road, forcing the driver of the lead truck to slam on his brakes.

As the trucks rocked to a halt, the agents surrounding them began shouting in Spanish for the drivers and the guards to get out with their hands above their heads. The men in the truck cabs didn't do any such thing, however. They stayed right where they were, and alarm began to gnaw at Brady Keller's guts.

The canvas covers on the backs of the trucks were suddenly thrown up, revealing not the tons of drugs the authorities had been expecting, but rather men in black hoods and commando garb, overlaid with body armor. Four men to each truck, two to each side, had bulky tanks strapped to their backs and carried some sort of apparatus. Brady barely had time to take in the sight and realize what it meant before long tongues of flame shot out from the nozzles of the outlandish gear and engulfed the members of the task force.

Flamethrowers . . . plain, old-fashioned flamethrowers. The members of the task force had been prepared for a gun battle, but not this. Men screamed and died horrible deaths as the fingers of hell closed around them.

Nor was that the only weapon being employed by the men on the trucks. Some of them threw grenades that burst in body-shredding explosions and sent bundles of torn flesh and blood that had been men flying into the air. Others wielded the sort of automatic rifles that the task force had been expecting, but now, in a matter of mere seconds, the agents were too disoriented and decimated to put up much of a fight.

One black-garbed fighter on the lead truck rested a rocket launcher on the top of the vehicle's cab and fired at the jeeps blocking the road. The rocket sizzled through the night, trailing fire behind it, and slammed into one of the jeeps, blowing it into a million pieces along with the men inside it. The force of the explosion toppled another jeep sitting close beside the one that was struck, and as men were thrown out of that vehicle, a hail of steel-jacketed slugs riddled them. The driver of the third jeep tried to back away hurriedly, but another rocket launcher was ready and flung its deadly missile through the night. The man at the wheel of the jeep screamed as the rocket impacted the hood just in front of him and consumed it in a ball of fire.

Brady hugged the ground to the side of the road. The assault rifle in his hands chattered as he fired instinctively toward the trucks. Somehow he had avoided a direct hit by the flamethrowers, although the hellish stream had come so close to him that the heat had blistered his skin even through his clothes. He had been blinded by the flash that had burst in his goggles during the split second before they had burned out. Now he ripped them off and tried to aim by the garish light of burning brush—and burning men.

The black-clad figures were jumping off the trucks, shooting as they came. Mopping up what was left of the task force. Bare minutes earlier, the Americans had been a group of proud, confident men, ready to bring justice to the brazen lawbreakers of the cartel.

They hadn't had a chance.

Moving like a wraith, one of the killers in black appeared beside Brady and kicked the assault rifle out of his hands. Brady rolled over and clawed at the pistol holstered on his hip, but before he could get it out the rifle in the enemy's hands blasted. Brady screamed as the bullet shattered his right elbow, flooding him with pain. He clutched his wounded arm with his left hand and lay there panting.

He expected to die at any second, but gradually he became aware that he was still alive. His elbow throbbed unmercifully, and his face stung where the skin had been blistered and cooked by the near miss with the flamethrowers. He couldn't see anything out of his right eye, and the vision in his left was blurred. It worked well enough, though, for him to see the menacing black-clad figure looming above him, rifle in hand.

He heard the crackle of flames and the screaming of wounded men. The gunfire had died away, and now there were only sporadic blasts. Brady felt sick to his stomach when he realized that after each shot, there was less screaming.

The killers were finishing off the task force members who had survived the ferocious counterattack. Tonight's ambush had been a trap, all right, Brady realized, but it had been he and his companions who were caught in it.

Finally, there were no more shots, no more screams. He was the last one left alive. He had no idea why he had been spared, but he prayed that they would let him live. Even in agony, life was so sweet that he didn't want to let go of it.

He had been raised on the border, down the Rio Grande valley in McAllen, and he spoke Spanish just as well as he did English. So he had no trouble understanding when the man standing over him called, "Here is the one you wished, Colonel."

They had kept him alive for a reason? Him in particular? That made no sense. But as Brady looked toward the lead truck and saw one of the black-clad figures remove the hood that covered his head, he began to understand.

The man was tall and powerful-looking, and the glare from the flames on both sides of the road lit up a face that was both handsome and cruel. Brady had never seen him before, not in person, but he had seen the one photo that the task force had, the picture that had been taken with a telephoto lens and had cost the agent who took it his life.

Colonel Alfonso Guerrero.

"Listen to me," Guerrero said in English. "You understand what I am saying? You know who I am?"

Brady managed to nod his head. It didn't matter to the killers who he was; they had kept him alive simply as a messenger boy.

"Tell the ones who sent you and your companions on this foolish errand that La Frontera now belongs to Los Lobos de la Noche. Tell them that if they interfere with our mission, they will die. All of them, every time. And if they continue to annoy me, their families will die as well. Can you remember that?"

Again, Brady nodded.

Guerrero said, "To be sure that you do not forget . . ." and nodded at the man standing over Brady.

The rifle in the man's hands blasted twice more, and Brady howled as the slugs shattered both kneecaps. His body arched and spasmed in agony.

"Of course," Guerrero continued, "you may bleed to death before help arrives, in which case I will have to send my message the next time you fools try to stop us. Really, it matters very little."

With that, Guerrero pulled the hood back over his head and turned away. His men climbed back onto the trucks, their job here done.

Brady lay on the sandy ground, awash in pain and only half-conscious. He heard the trucks pull away, and a few minutes later, more heavy vehicles rumbled past. Those would be the trucks carrying the shipment of drugs, he thought in the pain-wracked wasteland that was his mind. He was barely coherent enough to wonder if Guerrero's men had struck against the task force members waiting at the train as well. That seemed likely. Tonight had seen mass murder on two fronts.

Mass murder carried out by the self-appointed guardians of the drug trade, the mercenaries who hired themselves out to the cartel to carry out an orgy of death, destruction, and intimidation.

The men who now ruled La Frontera—literally, the frontier, that strip of land extending for miles on either side of the border—like a feudal kingdom. The men who called themselves Los Lobos de la Noche . . .

"The Night Wolves," Brady murmured, and those were his last words before oblivion claimed him.

Two

Angelina Salinas said, "Have you ever . . " and then leaned over to whisper the rest of the question into Shannon Horton's ear.

Shannon's face turned a bright red as she exclaimed, "Oh my God! Of course not. I wouldn't do *that*. It's . . . icky." She hesitated. "Have you . . . ?"

Angelina smiled knowingly.

Unwilling to let herself be one-upped that way, Shannon said hurriedly, "One time, though, Jimmy Dominguez and I . . ."

On the bus seat behind Angelina and Shannon, Laura Simms muttered to herself, "Children," and tuned out the rest of Shannon's lurid confession. She didn't care what Shannon and Jimmy had done together. Anyway, there was a good chance Shannon was making the whole thing up. The redheaded girl hated to think she was being left out of anything.

Laura reached down to the backpack at her feet and took out her copy of *The Once and Future King*. It had been one of her summer reading assignments for Advanced Placement English, and she hadn't quite finished it. Classes started the next day at Saint Anne's Catholic School, following today's annual junior/senior picnic at Lake Casa Blanca State Park, a short distance northeast of Laredo. Four buses carrying the small private school's students rolled up the highway toward the lake. For today, at least, they didn't have to wear the school uniforms; jeans were allowed. But not shorts.

And of course, the nuns had split up the boys and the girls, herding the separate groups onto two buses each. They would be allowed to mingle once they reached the park, but being together in the close quarters of the buses would be too much temptation for their overheated teenage hormones. At least, so the nuns believed. And considering the things that Angelina and Shannon were whispering to each other, the nuns might have been right.

Laura gritted her teeth and tried to concentrate on the words in her book. It was difficult to do, especially when Shannon giggled and said, "It was so big, I never—"

"Will you two sluts be quiet?" The words came out of Laura's mouth before she really thought about what she was saying. "I'm trying to read back here."

Angelina and Shannon turned around to glare at her. Shannon said, "Laura, you're the only person I know who would bring a book to a picnic."

"Nerd," Angelina muttered.

Laura looked down at the book again and gritted her teeth. She didn't care what they called her. She didn't.

She wanted to say that being a nerd was better than being a boy-crazy whore. But she couldn't. That would just make the others hate her that much more.

Angelina and Shannon went back to their conversation. Laura sighed as she realized that she had read the same paragraph at least four times. She gave up, sticking her bookmark back in the book and returning it to her back-pack. She looked up and down the aisle of the bus instead.

There were forty girls on this bus, all of them juniors and seniors, their ages ranging from sixteen to eighteen. Twenty-eight of them were Latinas. That was seventy percent, which Laura knew without having to think about it be-cause she did the math automatically in her head. Nine were Caucasian and three African-American. That was fairly representative of the population of Laredo, and Webb County. The actual figures skewed slightly higher Hispanic, as Laura knew because she had done a report on the demographics of La Frontera for her AP Govern-ment class the year before. The expenses involved in sending a child to private school tended to have an effect on the ethnic makeup of the student body, but with the population figures so predominantly Hispanic to begin with, they still comprised a large majority of the students.

Which meant, once you got past all the politically cor-rect, bureaucratic mumbo-jumbo that you had to put in reports for school, there were a lot of Mexican-American kids at Saint Anne's, a good number of whites, and a few blacks. Everybody spoke Spanish, of course, no matter what their race. You grew up bilingual in Laredo. In fact, Laura thought she spoke better Spanish than some of the Hispanic kids. The old Mexican culture still existed, but in these days of the Internet and cable TV, iPods and wi-fi, a Hispanic kid was more likely to be familiar with 50 Cent than with Flaco Jimenez, and any mention of Cantinflas would get you a blank look.

Laura's fair skin and blond hair—which was pulled back into a ponytail at the moment—didn't cause her any trouble with the other kids. Some of them didn't like her, but that was because she was smart and didn't try to con-ceal it. She told herself she didn't care. School wasn't a

popularity contest. One more year and she'd be gradu-
ated, ready to move on to college. If she could bump that
2350 SAT score up to a perfect 2400, Harvard wasn't out
of the question. . . .

Excited whoops from the girls on the left side of the
bus brought Laura out of her thoughts. She looked over
and saw a couple of pickups full of young men passing by
in the highway's left lane. They grinned and waved at the
girls staring out the bus's windows at them.

Shannon crossed the aisle, crowding in between other
girls until she reached the window. Then she reached
down, pulled the hem of her shirt out of her jeans, and
lifted the shirt, exposing her breasts in a lacy, pale green
bra just as the second pickup went by. The grins on the
faces of the young men got bigger.

Sister Katherine, who was driving the bus, looked
wide-eyed into the mirror and bellowed, "Sit down back
there! Everyone back in their seats! Shannon, what are
you . . . oh, my word! Shannon!"

The two pickups shot ahead and then cut back into the
right lane. They slowed. The bus was the last one in the
convoy of four, and Sister Katherine was notorious for
not being as heavy-footed as the nuns driving the other
buses. They were still in sight, but they had pulled ahead
quite a bit. The gap got bigger as the pickups slowed even
more and so did Sister Katherine. She probably didn't
want to pass them because that might set off another
round of hooting and flashing, Laura thought.

Something made her turn her head and look back,
some instinct inherited from her dad, perhaps. He had
been a cop before cancer had taken him five years earlier,
when Laura was twelve. A good cop, too, from everything she remembered about him. And she made an effort
not to forget, because she missed him fiercely. Her mom

was a lawyer and expected Laura to follow in her footsteps, which was one reason for going to Harvard, and Laura figured that in the end, that was what she would do.

But there was still a part of her that wanted to put on a badge, to take names and kick butt, but more than that, to help people and get the bad guys off the streets. It would probably never happen, but still . . .

In the meantime, she liked to think that she had at least some cop instincts, and that was why, when she looked out the rear window of the bus and saw four more pickups full of young men, she felt a sudden twinge of worry.

What was going on here?

Before she could do more than ask herself that question, two of the pickups behind the bus veered into the left lane and sped up.

"You girls get back in your seats!" Sister Katherine shouted. "I'm not joking! If you don't behave, as soon as we get to the lake I'll turn this bus around and go back! You'll miss the picnic!"

The warning had some effect on the girls. Most of those who had crossed the aisle moved back to their seats. As the second pair of pickups drew alongside the bus, Shannon leaned closer to the window, waggled her fingers at the young men, and said wistfully, "'Bye, boys."

Laura sat up straighter in her seat. The pickups had pulled up beside the bus, but they weren't going on. The drivers seemed to be matching their speed to Sister Katherine's. And the final two pickups had closed the gap so that they were right behind the bus. Six pickups in all, more than fifty men . . .

They had this bus full of teenage girls surrounded.

"Oh my God," Laura said softly as her heart began to hammer in her chest. "Oh my God."

She lifted her voice and started to call out, "Sister Katherine, there's something—"

But before she could finish, the front pickup that was beside the bus suddenly swerved toward it. A jolt shivered through the vehicle as the pickup's right front fender rammed into it. Sparks flew and metal shrieked. Several of the girls screamed in surprise and fear as Sister Katherine uttered an uncharacteristic but heartfelt, "Oh, *crap!*"

She fought desperately against the wheel as it tried to tear itself out of her hands. Before she could regain complete control, the pickup hit the bus again, and so did the other pickup racing alongside. Lights flared redly just ahead as the driver of the pickup immediately ahead of the bus slammed on his brakes. Sister Katherine was forced to brake violently, too. The girls were thrown forward in their seats.

Most of them were screaming now. Laura pushed herself back up and rubbed her left wrist, which throbbed a little because she had used it to brace herself against the seat in front of her. Before she could steady herself again, she was thrown out of her seat to the floor as the bus left the paved surface of the road and bounced across the rougher right-of-way next to the highway. Luckily, this was a very flat stretch of terrain, and there was nothing to the side of the highway for hundreds of yards except open ground with a few mesquites and some other scrubby brush.

Luck probably had nothing to do with it, Laura thought as she tried to pull herself back onto her seat. The men in the pickups had chosen this spot to make their move. They wanted a place where they could force the bus off the road and yet minimize the chance of the big vehicle crashing.

Think like a cop, she told herself, think like a cop. Why were they doing this? The men in the pickups were all Latinos. Across the border, Nuevo Laredo was practically ruled by gangs of lawless, mostly young Latinos. Kidnappings were common, and how much more audacious could you get than to kidnap an entire busload of teenage girls from a private school, most of whom had parents who would be willing to pay ransoms for them?

But things like that happened on the *other* side of the border, not here. Not in the United States. Not in *America*.

Laura bit back a sob as the bus continued to careen across the sandy ground, gradually slowing. Clouds of dust swirled around it. Laura tried to remain calm, tried to force herself to think rationally, but when you came right down to it, she was still a seventeen-year-old girl.

And she was scared shitless.

Three

The bus finally rocked and skidded to a halt a hundred yards off the highway. Four of the pickups had followed it, and now surrounded it as the cloud of choking dust began to dissipate.

Inside the bus, Laura coughed and blinked watering eyes. She thought she had heard a couple of explosions in the distance as the bus careened out of control, but wasn't sure about that. It was hard to be sure about anything with all the screaming and crying going on.

Glass shattered. A sound like very loud, very rapid hammering filled the bus. Laura had heard automatic weapons fire often enough in action movies to recognize it now. She threw herself to the floor again and shouted, "Get down! Everybody get down!"

She clapped her hands over her ears in an attempt to shut out the chaos. The men were going to kill all of them, she thought hysterically. They were going to storm onto the bus and machine-gun the girls.

That made no sense. Why would they do such a horrible thing?

Laura lifted her head as the bus door was jerked open.

A man in jeans and a black T-shirt, with a black hood pulled over his head and an automatic rifle in his hands, lunged up the steps and onto the bus. Sister Katherine, half out of the driver's seat, swatted at him with her open hands and shouted incoherently. Ruthlessly, the man drove the butt of the rifle into her face and knocked her back across the seat, shutting her up. Then he fired a burst into the roof of the bus, and the deafening racket shocked the screaming girls into sudden silence.

"Quiet!" he shouted in English. "All of you be quiet and don't move! You're all right. We won't hurt you if you do as you're told."

Laura doubted that.

"Angelina Salinas!" the hooded man called. "Angelina, where are you?"

That shocked Laura almost as much as anything else that had happened. What sort of connection could these awful men have with Angelina?

That meant, too, that this wasn't a random kidnapping. What was going on here?

Think like a cop. No matter how scared you get, Laura told herself, keep thinking like a cop.

She looked around. Most of the girls were lying in tumbled heaps in the aisle, where they had been thrown during the wild ride. Angelina and Shannon were there, right in front of her. Shannon was crying, quietly but hysterically. Angelina just looked stunned. She hadn't responded to the man's mention of her name.

"Damn it," the man said, obviously growing impatient. "I'm looking for Angelina Salinas."

Laura thought about standing up and saying that she was Angelina. That made her think of an old movie she had seen, where a bunch of guys all stood up and claimed to be somebody named Spartacus. The difference was that nobody else on this bus would claim to be Angelina, and by doing so she might just get shot.

She stayed where she was.

"Angelina!" the man bellowed.

Finally, Angelina lifted her head, despite Laura hissing at her to stay down, and what she said then stunned Laura into silence.

"D-daddy?" Angelina asked.

The man reached up and pulled the hood off his head. He was older than the men who had been riding in the backs of the pickups, in his forties at least. His thick dark hair was touched with silver, and his lean face was handsome in a very dangerous way. But his eyes were as dark and cold as a snake's, even when he smiled and said, "*Sí, chiquita*, your *papá* has come for you."

He started down the aisle toward her, the automatic rifle swinging easily in his hands, as if he carried it every day. The girls lying in the aisle recoiled and crawled out of his way, making a path for him.

"No," Angelina whispered, then she cried out urgently, "No!" and twisted around frantically, trying to get away. She shoved the sobbing Shannon aside and came up on her hands and knees.

Before she could crawl more than a foot, the man loomed over her and reached down to hook an arm around her. He pulled her up against him. She screamed and jerked around and tried to fight him. "Angelina!" he said. "Angelina, stop it! I will not hurt you!"

"No! No, I can't be with you! Mama said!" She took a choking, gasping breath. "You're not supposed to even come within five hundred yards—"

His laugh stopped her, and from Laura's vantage point on the floor, she thought he looked crueler and more evil than ever. "Gringo law!" he practically spit, contempt dripping from the words. "Since when did gringo law mean anything to Colonel Alfonso Guerrero? It will never keep me away from my little girl!"

With that, he started dragging her toward the front of the bus.

Maybe he would just take Angelina and leave the rest of them alone. Laura felt bad for having that thought, but she couldn't help it. Maybe all the man wanted was Angelina . . . his daughter, if he was telling the truth. Maybe this nightmare would be over soon.

But then the man reached the door, and before he stepped down out of the bus, taking the still-struggling Angelina with him, he said to someone outside, "Take the rest of the girls and put them in the trucks."

Hope vanished, heart sank, terror welled up. That turmoil of emotions filled Laura, clogging her brain, making her heart pound, causing her stomach to clench sickly. This couldn't be happening.

Men in black shirts and black hoods, men carrying pistols and rifles, poured onto the bus, and the girls began shrieking in terror again as they were grabbed and dragged toward the door. One by one they were taken prisoner.

Laura bolted up from the floor. She knew she wasn't thinking straight, but it might be better if they shot her instead of whatever else it was they had in mind for her. She hit the bar that opened the bus's rear, emergency door.

If this wasn't an emergency, she had never seen one.

The door flew open and she leaped out into space, throwing her hands in front of her to catch herself when she hit the ground. But she didn't land on the ground because strong, mostly bare, brown arms closed around her, catching her in midair.

Of course Guerrero had put some of his guys behind

the bus. He wouldn't go to this much trouble and then leave the emergency exit unguarded.

Laura's muscles spasmed. She couldn't stop the tears that ran down her face as she tried to tear herself free from the grips of the men who held her. No matter how hard she struggled, she couldn't get loose. Finally, after long seconds that seemed even longer than they really were, she subsided. She couldn't get away, but she could look around and record every detail in her mind, just in case she ever got to tell the story of what was happening on this horrible day.

For one thing, there were a *bunch* of bad guys. Sitting in the back of pickups, grinning and waving, they hadn't looked so bad, nor seemed so numerous. But now, clad in their black hoods and brandishing weapons, their numbers seemed overwhelming, especially when they were matched against teenage girls. The bus had been emptied out by now, and there were enough of the men so that every girl was being held tightly and there were kidnappers left over.

Laura turned her head toward the highway. Any hope that help might come from that direction disappeared when she saw the columns of black smoke rising from several burning vehicles. The men had blown up the rest of the sparse traffic along the road, using God knows what, grenades or rocket launchers or something.

But the other buses were still up ahead somewhere, and surely by now the people on them had noticed that the last bus wasn't behind them anymore. They had to see the smoke, and they would be calling 911.

That was why Guerrero wasn't wasting any time. "Get them in the trucks!" he ordered again. He still had an arm around Angelina's waist. She had stopped fighting him and now just stood there sobbing futilely.

The kidnappers dragged the girls toward the pickups.

Some of the girls struggled until the men holding them hit them in the head, stunning them and making them cooperate. Laura saw blood running down the faces of both Billie Sue and Aubrey Cahill, twins who had been Laura's friends since third grade. Their captors had slapped them around.

Only one man had hold of Laura now, but he was too strong. When he shoved her toward the same pickup where Billie Sue and Aubrey had been placed, along with Shannon and several other girls, all she could do was go along with what he wanted. She didn't want to get hit.

She had to keep her mind clear so that she could take advantage of any opportunity to escape that came along.

She climbed onto the open tailgate and scuttled forward, wedging herself among the other girls crowded into the bed of the truck. Some of them were sobbing while others looked almost catatonic with fear. Laura bit her lip and kept her eyes open alertly, fighting down her own terror as it tried to rise inside her.

All the girls had been crammed into the backs of two of the pickups. As the tailgates slammed shut, Guerrero shouted in Spanish, "Cover them up and move out!"

But the bus wasn't completely empty. As men moved forward with large canvas tarps, Sister Katherine staggered out of the wrecked vehicle, having regained consciousness from the blow that had knocked her out.

"Stop this!" she cried as she held out her hands toward Guerrero. "Please! You can't do this! Let these innocent children go!"

"I cannot do that, Sister," Guerrero told her. "They must go with us."

"For the love of God! Please!"

With Angelina still huddled against him, Guerrero smiled, lifted the rifle, and fired it one-handed, just a single short burst that stitched into Sister Catherine's body and tossed her backward onto the steps leading up into the bus. Sister Katherine jerked and twitched and then lay still, and after a moment blood began to pool on the bottom step and drip to the sandy ground beneath it.

Laura's eyes were wide with horror as she saw that terrible sight, and then it was suddenly cut off from view as the men threw the tarps over the pickup beds. The coverings had bungee cords attached, and in a matter of seconds they were lashed down securely. The girls couldn't see anything, and the air rapidly grew hot and stifling.

Laura felt the lurch as the pickup she was in roared into motion. She could tell from the way the tires bounced and jounced across the landscape and continued to do so that they weren't going back toward the highway. They were going across country. The truck's transmission growled. It had four-wheel drive, Laura thought, and could go almost anywhere, on-road or off. Since they had left the highway behind, they had to be headed east, but there wasn't anything for fifty or sixty miles in that direction.

They wouldn't continue east, she told herself. Soon they would turn south, and then eventually west again, and somewhere downriver from Laredo they would cross the border. It was only a guess, but she felt confident in it. After doing what they had done, these men couldn't afford to stay on the American side of the river.

They—and their prisoners—were headed to Mexico.

Four

Little Tucson, Arizona—twenty miles
from the border
Tom Brannon wheeled the dolly through the open back door of Brannon Auto Parts in downtown Little Tucson. Four cases of assorted spark plugs were stacked up on the dolly. Tom put a hand on the top one to steady the stack, and let the dolly tip forward so that the cases rested on the tile floor of the storeroom. He pulled the dolly out from under them and in a habitual gesture, ran a hand over his graying, close-cropped sandy hair.

It felt good to be working again.

It felt good to be *normal* again.

Long months had passed since the horrific battle that had brought an orgy of death and destruction to Little Tucson. Shattered glass had been replaced, bullet-pocked walls has been patched and repainted, bloodstains had been scrubbed up off the sidewalks and the street. People didn't even talk much about the time when Mara Salvatrucha, the vicious gang of drug smugglers and criminals composed mostly of Central Americans, had crossed the border and declared war on one sleepy little American town. All that was in the past. Better to forget about it.

But Tom Brannon couldn't forget. He had spearheaded the effort to defeat the brutal and quite possibly insane Ernesto Luiz Montoya and his bloodthirsty M-15 *compañeros*. He had seen loved ones die, including his own parents, and he had dealt out death with his own hands. A man couldn't just put that behind him, even if he wanted to.

Tom didn't want to forget. He didn't want to blind himself to the fact that there was evil loose in the world, and that sometimes, for the sake of all that was good and right, decent men had to stand up to that evil and do their best to defeat it. That might not be convenient. It might not be expedient. It might not even be, God help us all, the politically correct thing to do.

But it had to be done, and if people forgot that fact, they ran the risk of forgetting how to stand up to evil in the first place.

So, no, Tom would never forget the battle of Little Tucson and everything that had come before it . . . but sometimes it was mighty nice to put all those memories aside for a while and just be a husband and a father and a businessman again.

Louly Parker, who managed the auto-parts store for him, came into the storeroom, looked at the cases of spark plugs, and said, "Good. I was afraid we were going to run out before we could restock."

"Nobody gets in too big a hurry to buy spark plugs," Tom said.

Louly gave him a skeptical look. "Are you kidding? These days everybody's in a hurry for everything. Even if it's one of your regular customers who comes in here and you're out of something, you know where he's going to head . . . straight to the edge of town."

"SavMart."

"That's right. And when he sees the prices they've got there, he's never going to come back here."

Tom didn't bother arguing with her. He knew she was right. Loyalty only went so far, especially when folks had to work so hard just to make ends meet. If it hadn't been for the fact that the average American citizen had to work almost half the year just to pay all of his or her various tax bills, SavMart might not have ever gotten such a stranglehold on the nation's economy.

On the other hand, Tom had definite mixed emotions about the retail giant. Old Hiram Stackhouse, the founder of SavMart himself and one of the richest men in the country, had come to Little Tucson to help out in the town's time of trouble. And Tom liked him. Stackhouse was free enterprise and the American dream personified.

"Well, we'll keep the doors open as long as we can. Might just surprise you."

"I could use a pleasant surprise," Louly said.

She was in her mid-twenties, a tall, pretty young woman with red hair that came halfway down her back. Tom, who was old enough to be her daddy, thought of her as a sort of surrogate daughter, which always made him feel a little guilty because he already had a daughter of his own whom he loved dearly. But Lisa didn't live in Little Tucson anymore, and he saw Louly just about every day. They were friends as much as they were boss and employee.

The bell over the front door jangled. Tom motioned toward the front of the store and told Louly, "Maybe there's your surprise now. You go see about it and I'll stock these spark plugs."

"Okay." She vanished into the front of the store.

Tom cut open one of the boxes, picked it up, and carried it to the long, heavy-duty metal shelves behind the counter where inventory was kept. Brannon Auto Parts was old-fashioned. Customers came to the counter and asked for what they needed, and the clerk got it from the shelves and rang it up. The system meant that folks had to actually speak to each other, and often they would slow down and talk about other things, gossip mostly, and for that amount of time everybody involved escaped, at least temporarily, from the exhausting pace of modern life.

But only temporarily. Little Tucson wasn't Mayberry, after all. Hell, Mayberry probably had its own SavMart by now. Probably a SuperSavMart.

Louly fetched a set of brake shoes for the customer and rang them up on the old cash register that was really just a glorified money drawer. The fellow had just left the store when the cell phone in the pocket of Tom's faded blue work shirt buzzed. He walked over to the counter, set down the half-empty case of spark plugs, and pulled out the phone.

"Hello?"

"Tom." He heard his wife Bonnie's voice, sounding flat and strained. Something was wrong. "Turn on the TV."

A portable television sat at the end of the counter next to the wall. It didn't get used much; mostly it was on for college football games on Saturday afternoons during the fall and baseball games during the summer. Tom had teased Louly once about using it sometimes to watch her "stories"—but only once. Now he said to Bonnie, "Hang on," and then clicked the TV on. The sound was off, but as the picture came up he saw a shot of what looked like desert country somewhere. In the distance something was burning, with a column of black smoke rising from it. He couldn't make out what it was.

Louly came over, looked at the TV screen, and said, "Is it the Middle East?"

Tom didn't answer her. He flipped the channel twice but got the same shot each time, telling him that all three networks were using the same video feed. One of the channels had a graphic superimposed on the screen underneath the blazing whatever-it-was, though. The graphic read LIVE—LAREDO, TEXAS.

"What is it you wanted me to see?" he asked Bonnie. "Whatever this is is going on in Texas."

Louly leaned toward the screen suddenly and said, "My God! Is that a *school bus* that's on fire?"

It was indeed a school bus, Tom saw as his eyes narrowed. He could make it out, now that he knew what he was looking for. That must have been a terrible accident.

"It's Laura," Bonnie said into his ear.

"Laura?" he repeated, as for a second he couldn't think of who Bonnie was talking about.

"Kelly's girl."

Tom felt his heart lurch. Kelly was Bonnie's sister, and Laura was Kelly's daughter, and they lived in—

Laredo, Texas.

"Oh, no," Tom said in a hushed voice. "Was she in that wreck?" The way the bus was burning like an inferno, he didn't see how anyone could have survived such a terrible crash.

Although, he suddenly wondered, how had the bus crashed? It looked like it was out in the middle of some open ground somewhere, with nothing around it.

"It's not a wreck," Bonnie said, her voice trembling. "Laura's been kidnapped."

"Turn it up," he snapped at Louly. "Turn the sound up."

Louly turned the knob, and a female newscaster's well-modulated voice said, ". . . some details starting to come in now. Jeremy Hernandez works for our affiliate in

Laredo and is on the scene. Jeremy, what can you tell us about this terrible attack?"

The scene stayed the same, but a man's voice picked up the report. "Paulette, the Webb County Sheriff's Office hasn't provided an official statement yet, but sources tell us that it appears this school bus, which you can see burning, was forced off the road as it was carrying some students from Saint Anne's Catholic School to a picnic today at Lake Casa Blanca State Park. As the bus was being attacked, several other vehicles passing by on the highway were attacked as well, and blown up by what appears to have been some sort of rockets."

"Then this attack was carried out by terrorists, Jeremy?" the woman asked.

"Not the sort that you're thinking of, Paulette. From what I'm hearing, one of the gangs from Nuevo Laredo was responsible for this atrocity."

A different man's voice said, "This is Kevin Webster, Jeremy. What about the students on the bus?"

"We, ah, don't know yet, Kevin, but I've been told unofficially that none of them were on the bus when it blew up. Evidently, they were taken off and something was done with them before the bus was destroyed. Only one body was found with the bus, and it was tentatively thought to be that of the driver, one of the nuns from Saint Anne's School. And while this hasn't been confirmed either, I've been told that there were at least nine fatalities on the highway, in the other vehicles that were attacked."

"So we have at least ten people killed and a busload of students missing?"

"That's right, Kevin."

"Jeremy," the female newscaster said, "these students . . . boys or girls? Or both?"

"Girls, Paulette. I'm told that they were all juniors and seniors."

Louly looked shocked as she watched the news coverage. Tom supposed that he did, too, but somehow, there was a part of him that wasn't all that surprised. To the people of Laredo, and to those newscasters sitting safe somewhere in a network news bureau in New York or Los Angeles, it was hard to believe that a band of criminals would be daring enough to invade the United States and carry out such an atrocity.

They had already forgotten what had happened in Little Tucson.

He reached out and changed the channel, getting the same picture but a different set of talking heads, in this case superimposed in a small box in a corner of the screen. These newscasters evidently had better sources than Jeremy Hernandez.

"—the work of a notorious Mexican gang known as Los Lobos de la Noche. An e-mail supposedly from the leader of the gang claiming responsibility for the kidnapping and murders stated that the missing students were all right and would not be harmed. The motive for the kidnapping is not known, but it's assumed that ransom will be demanded for the safe return of the students, many of whom come from well-to-do families. We've had no word about actual ransom demands being made as of yet—"

Tom turned the sound down and brought the cell phone back to his ear. "Bonnie, are you there?"

"I'm here, Tom," she said, and he could tell that she had been crying. She would be watching the same thing on TV that he was.

"I'm sure Laura's okay," he said, trying to sound as reassuring and comforting as he could. "If . . . if those girls have been taken for ransom, the kidnappers won't hurt them—"

"You heard what they said on TV," Bonnie cut in. "It's a gang that took them. A gang like M-15. You saw what they did here, Tom. You know what . . . animals like that are capable of . . ."

Bonnie's voice trailed off in a series of wracking sobs.

"I'm coming home," Tom said into the phone. "I'll be there in just a little while." He broke the connection and looked at Louly.

She nodded and waved him toward the door. "I'll take care of the store."

"Thanks. One of Bonnie's nieces was on that bus."

"My God." She touched Tom's arm. "I'm sure she'll be all right."

"That's what I tried to tell Bonnie," he said grimly, "but all she can think about is what happened here. She knows that men like that . . . they'll do anything."

"They're not men," Louly said. "They're monsters."

And remembering what had happened when Little Tucson was invaded by the same sort of gang, Tom couldn't argue with her about that.

Five

The middle-aged black man held out his hand and said, "John Holland."

Sheriff Phil Garza shook Holland's hand. "Are you from the FBI, Mr. Holland?"

"State Department."

Garza's pale eyebrows rose a little in surprise.

Holland saw the reaction and went on. "This matter impacts the relationship between the United States and Mexico, so the secretary thought it would be a good idea to have someone on the scene."

"You got here in a hurry," Garza commented. "It's only been a couple of hours."

"I was at a trade conference in Houston," Holland explained. "I choppered over." He took a deep breath. "What have you got?"

The other man in the office, Saul Jimenes, said, "Maybe it would be better if we waited, so we only have to go over everything once."

Holland turned and looked at him coolly. "And you are, sir . . . ?"

"Jimenes. Chief of Police in Laredo."

It was Holland's turn to raise his eyebrows. "I thought this incident occurred outside of the city limits."

"It did," the stocky Jimenes replied. "But all the local law-enforcement agencies are cooperating and pooling our intelligence concerning these so-called Night Wolves."

"Ah, yes," Holland said with a slight smile. "Los Lobos de la Noche. A rather melodramatic name, don't you think?"

"There's nothing melodramatic about their actions," Sheriff Garza said. "They're probably the most dangerous group in northern Mexico."

"They're a gang?"

Garza tried not to sigh. Holland was determined to go ahead and get his briefing one way or the other, whether the FBI and the Texas Rangers were on hand yet or not.

"They're *not* a gang in the sense that you're using the word, Mr. Holland. They're not one of the drug cartels. They *work* for the largest of the drug cartels."

"Doing what? Smuggling heroin and cocaine?"

"No. They protect the drug smugglers. They wage war against other cartels. They assassinate law enforcement and military officials who represent a threat to the cartel they work for." Garza took a deep breath. "In other words, the Night Wolves are like a gun, Mr. Holland. The cartel points them at whoever gets in their way . . . and pulls the trigger."

Holland's forehead beneath his thinning hair creased in a frown. "But that doesn't really make any sense. A bunch of teenage girls couldn't have done anything to cause trouble for a drug cartel . . . could they?"

Garza shook his head. "Not that we've been able to figure."

Jimenes spoke up again. "The Night Wolves are mercenaries. Money is always their primary objective. Their actions could have been motivated by something as simple as holding the girls for ransom. Ransom kidnappings happen all the time in Nuevo Laredo . . . throughout all of Mexico, for that matter. And Americans are always prime targets." The chief of police gave a short, humorless bark of laughter. "It seems there's a feeling below the border that all Americans are rich."

Holland pursed his lips. "What about these particular girls? *Are* their families wealthy?"

"We're still working on getting information about all of them," Garza said. "Right now we have mostly just their names. We've contacted their families, and officers from my department and from the Laredo Police Department will be interviewing them. But all that's just getting started."

A knock sounded on the door of Garza's office. He called for whoever it was to come in, and a man and a woman entered. The man wore the uniform of the Texas Rangers, including the neatly shaped straw Stetson, which he took off as he came into the room. He was about thirty, slender, with close-cropped dark hair.

The woman's hair was short, too, but it was the color of fresh honey. She wore a dark blue conservative skirt and blazer. She spoke first, saying, "Sheriff Garza? I'm Sharon Morgan, from the San Antonio office of the FBI."

Garza tried not to frown. "I was expecting Special Agent in Charge Willis. We spoke on the phone—"

"SAC Willis was unavoidably detained in San Antonio," Morgan said, breaking in. "He asked me to take his place and do whatever I can to assist you until he arrives later."

Garza nodded. "All right. I'm pleased to meet you, Agent Morgan." He looked at the Ranger. "And it's good to see you again, Roy. Wish it was under better circumstances."

Before the Ranger could respond, Morgan turned to him and said, "Wait a minute. When we introduced ourselves out in the hall, you said you were Sergeant Rogers. Your name is Roy Rogers?"

The lawman smiled tolerantly. "Rodgers, with a D in the middle of it. Old family name. There were Roy Rodgerses in Texas a long time before Leonard Slye ever took the name."

"Okay," Morgan said. "When they sent me down here from Quantico, I should have figured that I'd wind up working with a cowboy."

Rodgers's eyes narrowed slightly, but he didn't say anything and the polite smile remained on his lips.

Garza tried to ignore the instinctive dislike he felt for the woman. "We've got approximately forty missing girls to find," he said. "Everybody sit down and let's figure out how to do it."

Morgan frowned in annoyance at the sharp tone in the sheriff's voice, but she took one of the empty chairs. Rodgers looked down at the floor to hide the grin that flashed briefly over his boyish face. Holland and Jimenes just looked worried.

When they were all seated, Morgan looked over at Holland and said, "I didn't catch your name."

"John Holland. State Department."

She looked a little impressed by that. Garza got the feeling it was the first time she had been impressed by anything here in Texas.

Saul Jimenes introduced himself as well and then said, "We were just talking about Los Lobos de la Noche."

"What's that?"

Quickly, Garza went over the same explanation he and Jimenes had given Holland concerning the Night Wolves. He concluded by asking, "No offense, Agent Morgan, but how long have you been working in the San Antonio office?"

"Since last week," Morgan snapped. "If that's your way of telling me that I'm not up to speed, Sheriff, I promise you, I'm well aware of it."

"It's just that we've had a combined federal and state task force working in this area for quite a while now, trying to interdict the drug traffic—"

"The Rio Grande Ambush," Morgan said. "I've heard of it, of course. How many men were killed?"

"All of them but one," Holland said grimly.

The repercussions of that terrible night three months earlier had been felt all the way to Washington, D.C. Heads had rolled, figuratively, in the DEA, which had had the primary responsibility for setting up the operation that had backfired and gotten several dozen men killed. It had been one of the darkest times for law enforcement in recent years, and the whole thing was made even worse by the knowledge that someone connected with the task force—someone who was supposed to be one of the good guys—had to have betrayed them and tipped off the cartel about what was supposed to go down.

Cross and double cross, Garza thought, and in the end good men had died. Some of them, he knew, had been friends of Rodgers from the Rangers. The youthful-looking lawman's face had grown grim at the reminder.

"So this Night Wolf gang was connected with that debacle?" Morgan asked.

Garza didn't correct her about the status of the Night Wolves. He said, "The lone survivor of the ambush reported that the leader of the Night Wolves, Colonel Alfonso Guerrero, was there that night."

"Colonel?" Holland repeated. "Am I to understand that this is a military unit of some sort?"

"That's how they started out," Jimenes said.

"What's really bad," Rodgers said quietly, "is that we

trained a lot of them right here on American soil . . .
including Guerrero."

Morgan frowned and said, "You're going to have to
explain that."

"Some years ago, the Mexican army decided to form a
special unit to deal with drug smuggling and gang violence
along the border," Garza said. "They recruited some of the
best men from within their ranks and put together . . . I
guess you could call it a commando group. And they made
arrangements with our military and the Drug Enforcement
Agency to bring them over to the States and give them the
special training they needed."

"But these men worked *against* the drug trade, you said."

Garza nodded. "For a while. They even did some damage
to the cartels. Then some of the drug lords got the bright
idea that it would be easier to buy the commandos off,
rather than fighting them."

"They deserted from the Mexican Army?" Morgan asked.

"That's right. This Colonel Guerrero was in charge of the
unit. The largest cartel got to him first, and when he went over
to their side, his junior officers went, too, and then the rest of
the group. They deserted en masse about five years ago.
Since then they've recruited other members from the cartel
and have trained them in the commando tactics they use."

"It sounds like you know a lot about them, Sheriff."

Holland spoke up. "It's my understanding that the DEA
has been able to infiltrate agents into the cartels to provide intelligence."

"That's right," Garza said. "As a matter of fact, we know
quite a bit about the Night Wolves. But knowing what they
do and being able to stop it are two different things."

"You had no idea they were going to attack that school
bus and kidnap those girls?"

Garza shook his head. "None at all."

"So what do we do now?"

"I have all my available manpower searching throughout the county for any sign of them," Garza said.

Jimenes added, "And my men are sweeping Laredo."

"And the Rangers are standing by to help in the search," Rodgers said.

Morgan looked around at the men. "But what if they're not on this side of the border anymore? What if they've crossed into Mexico?"

Garza felt a little sick to his stomach as he said, "Then we'll have to rely on the Mexican police and military to find them."

"We can't intrude on their jurisdiction or interfere with their internal affairs," Holland said quickly. "The secretary made that quite clear when I spoke to him on the phone from the helicopter."

"Can the Mexican authorities be trusted?" Morgan asked.

Garza, Jimenes, and Rodgers exchanged uneasy looks. After an awkward moment of silence, Garza said, "Some of them are honest. But they've got their work cut out for them. There have been five different chiefs of police in Nuevo Laredo in the past eighteen months."

"What, they keep quitting because the job's so hard?"

"They keep getting killed," Jimenes said. "The cartels place bounties on the heads of honest policemen, and the Night Wolves are happy to collect." He grunted. "I've been told by informants that Phil and I both have targets on our backs, too, but nobody's come after us yet."

"They want to assassinate American officers, too?" Morgan sounded as if she could hardly believe that. "What is this, a goddamn war zone?"

"I think you're beginning to understand the problem, Agent Morgan," Garza said softly.

Six

That ride in the back of the pickup was the most hellish experience so far in Laura's young life. Crowded in so that there was no room to move, no light except that which filtered in around the edges of the tarp, incredible heat and not enough air. Most of the girls were crying, too. Laura felt like some sort of animal that had been herded into a truck to be carried off to the slaughterhouse.

She could only pray that wouldn't wind up being her fate.

Every time she closed her eyes she saw again that horrible moment when the man called Guerrero had lifted his rifle and fired almost point-blank at Sister Katherine. His face had held no emotion at all when he pulled the trigger. It was as hard and cold as stone. Laura could barely believe that he was Angelina Salinas's father.

And yet Angelina had called him "Daddy," and Guerrero had acted toward her with a certain solicitousness that could be regarded as paternal. Even though Laura had gone to school with Angelina for five years—Angelina had started at Saint Anne's during sixth grade—she didn't know that much about the other girl's family life. She had seen Angelina's mother, an attractive, somewhat tense woman, at numerous school functions, but now that she thought about it, Laura couldn't remember ever seeing Angelina's dad.

Evidently, there had been a good reason for his absence from Angelina's life. One of her comments had made it sound like her mother had a restraining order against him, or something like that.

But as Guerrero had put it, what did gringo law mean to him?

To keep her mind off the physical ordeal, Laura forced herself to think. If the kidnappers demanded ransom, could her mother pay? Kelly Simms made a decent, upper-middle-class living as a lawyer, but she wasn't filthy rich by any means. And the medical bills from her late husband's illness had been significant, even with insurance covering some of them. If the kidnappers demanded some ungodly amount for Laura's safe return—a million dollars, say, or even half a million—Kelly probably wouldn't be able to come up with it.

And would it matter even if she did? A lot of times, Laura recalled, kidnappers killed their victims almost right away, even before ransom demands were made, just to simplify things for themselves. It was entirely possible that Guerrero and his men would take the girls out somewhere in the Mexican desert and murder all of them, then leave their bodies there for the buzzards and the coyotes. The thought made her shudder.

Somebody clutched at her, and instinctively Laura tensed to fight back if she was attacked. But it was only Shannon. The redhead pressed her face against Laura's shoulder and sobbed. "Oh, Laura, what's going to happen to us? What are they going to do to us?"

Probably kill us all, Laura thought, but she didn't say that because she didn't want Shannon wailing in her ear. Instead, she said, "We'll be fine. They wouldn't dare hurt us."

"They . . . they killed Sister Katherine! They'd do anything! They're evil bastards!"

Laura couldn't argue with that, and it wouldn't do any good to point out that Shannon hadn't thought the young men were so bad when she was waving and flashing her tits at them.

It was hard to tell time under such miserable conditions, but Laura thought at least an hour had passed since the attack on the school bus. The pickup had turned several times and she had no idea what direction they were going now. Sometimes from the sound of the tires, it seemed like they were on rough gravel roads. At other times, the pickup bounced across open ground and brush scraped against the side. Finally, the truck turned again and the ride grew smoother, and from the hum of the tires Laura could tell that they were on a paved road again.

The ride was fairly short from there. The pickup turned and rattled across something that Laura tentatively identified as a cattle guard. The road was no longer paved, but it wasn't too rough, either. A dirt road, then, instead of gravel. The dust that rose from the wheels and seeped into the pickup bed through small openings, making some of the girls cough, confirmed the guess.

With a squeal of brakes, the pickup rocked to a halt. Most of the girls who were crying sniffled, wiped the backs of their hands across their noses, and swallowed any further sobs. An air of tension and dread spread swiftly through the prisoners. The long ride had been miserable enough, but now that they had stopped, there was no telling what their captors would do next.

Laura heard the men moving around at the side of the pickup and squeezed her eyes shut. Sure enough, the bungee cords were unfastened and the tarp thrown back, and blinding sunlight hammered down, bringing gasps from a few of the girls.

The light that came through her eyelids had been bright enough to force her eyes to start adjusting, so she was able to see a little. The pickup was parked inside some sort of courtyard with high adobe walls around it. The sound of an electric motor caught her attention, and she looked around to see a heavy wooden gate sliding shut. Men who held automatic rifles stood next to the gate. There was a guard post on top of the wall where several other men were stationed, and what looked to Laura's inexperienced eyes like a heavy machine gun was mounted there.

They were in a fortress of some sort.

Four pickups were parked in the courtyard, the two containing the prisoners and two more full of the men who had captured them. They had taken their hoods off and didn't seem to care that their faces were exposed to the prisoners. Laura didn't know if that was a good sign—or a bad one.

A couple of men unlatched the tailgates and lowered them, then stepped back and brandished their weapons. "Get out," one of the men ordered in Spanish.

Slowly, shakily, the girls began to climb out of the pickups. They had been crowded in so tightly that some of them had trouble standing now on legs that had gone to sleep. The girls around them had to grasp their arms and hold them up.

Laura slid out of the truck and stood with Shannon, Billie Sue, Aubrey, Carmen Hinajosa, and Stacy Wells. None of them were what could be called good friends with each other, Laura thought. Shannon was a slut, Billie Sue and Aubrey were obsessed with clothes and makeup and things like that, Carmen hung with the other Latinas and played soccer, and Stacy was black and usually kept to herself, pretty much like Laura did. The fact that they were grouped together now was pure chance. Most of the girls were huddled together in bunches of six or eight.

Some of the gun-wielding men lined up facing each other, forming a path of sorts that led to a wooden door in the far wall of the courtyard. One of the men opened the door while another man gestured with his rifle and said gutturally, "In there."

The girls closest to the door hesitated, and Laura couldn't blame them. The opening was dark and scary and there was no way of knowing where it led. It wouldn't be someplace good, though, that was pretty sure. But when their captors scowled and raised the guns a little, the girls marched forward reluctantly, between the two rows of men and through the dark door.

When it came time for Laura and the girls with her, they had no choice but to go.

Actually, getting out of the blazing sun was a relief of sorts, she discovered as she moved into a corridor with arched doorways on both sides. Those openings had doors with iron bars on them, and the men herded the girls into the cells on the other side of the barred doors, one group of six or eight into each chamber.

Laura sensed an air of antiquity about this place, as if it had been here for a couple of hundred years or more. The thick adobe walls kept the air cool inside. The only windows were narrow and also blocked by iron bars. As they moved into their cell, Laura realized that the room reminded her of the small chambers in old missions she had visited, the rooms where priests had once lived.

There were no men of God here in this place today. Men of the Devil, more likely.

They slammed the barred doors shut. Laura could look

across the corridor and see some of the other girls in an identical cell. The room where she and her companions were measured about twelve by twelve feet. One wall had a barred window in it, but it was too high to reach. Six rolled-up sleeping bags were propped in a corner. The only other furnishing was a large wooden bucket, and Laura felt queasy as she realized what it was there for.

Shannon went to the door, clutched the bars, and called, "Hey! Hey, you can't keep us locked up like this!" Laura wasn't sure where she found the courage to do something like that. Maybe anger was finally overcoming her fear.

Laura was mad, too, but she didn't have the nerve to challenge their captors like that. "You guys better let us out of here," Shannon went on. "You're gonna be in a shitload of trouble."

"Shannon," Laura said, "maybe you'd better be quiet. . . ."

Too late. One of the men sauntered over to the door, smiled through the bars at Shannon, and then pointed his rifle at her. She recoiled, backing away from the door so fast that she lost her balance, tripped, and sat down hard on the concrete floor.

"Stop your chirping, little redbird," he said to Shannon in English. "A bird that sings too much becomes annoying." He held up his left hand, loosely clenched. "A bird in the hand is soon silenced."

He closed his hand into a hard fist. Shannon gulped. The man's meaning was unmistakable.

He laughed and stepped away from the door. The men moved off down the corridor, talking quietly among themselves and occasionally laughing. Laura could make out some of the words, but not enough to get any real sense of the conversation.

Anyway, they were probably talking about what was

going to happen to the prisoners, and Laura wasn't sure she wanted to know. They would find out soon enough.

Shannon climbed to her feet and rubbed both hands on her butt, which was probably bruised from sitting down so hard on the concrete. "What the hell is this place, anyway?" she muttered.

"It looks like part of an old mission," Carmen said, echoing the same thought that had occurred to Laura earlier. "At one time these were probably the priests' cells."

Shannon frowned. "The old priests were kept locked up?"

"That's just what they called them," Laura said. "Those barred doors were probably added later." Carmen nodded in agreement.

"What are they going to do to us?" Billie Sue Cahill suddenly asked in a voice that shook with hysteria. "Are they going to rape us?"

None of the other girls answered her. That fear of being raped had been there all along in each of them, right along with the fear of being killed.

Into the tense silence, Laura finally said, "I don't think they're going to do anything to us right now except keep us prisoner. They put sleeping bags in here for us. That means we'll be here for a while."

"They could still rape us," Billie Sue said.

"They could, but it might make it more difficult for them to collect ransom for us."

"Is that why they grabbed us?" Shannon asked.

Laura shrugged. "I don't know for sure. But there are kidnappings for ransom all the time in Nuevo Laredo. They're in the paper nearly every day."

"We weren't in Nuevo Laredo," Stacy said, speaking up for the first time since they had been put in here. "We were on our way to the park!"

"I know," Laura said. "I guess those men don't care which side of the border they're on."

"My family can't pay a big ransom," Carmen said. "My dad works two jobs just to pay my tuition to the school!"

Laura had no answer for that. She didn't even know for sure yet if ransom was the goal of their captors.

All she knew for sure was that she was locked up and scared half out of her wits and that she wanted to go home.

Home, she thought.

She had never known that the word could sound so good.

Seven

By the time he reached his house about a mile outside
Little Tucson, Tom Brannon was already thinking about
what to do next. His wife Bonnie and her younger sister
Kelly were very close. They traded e-mails just about
every day and spoke on the phone at least once a week.
During all the trouble with M-15, Kelly had offered to
come out to Arizona, but Bonnie had persuaded her to stay
home. It would have been dangerous, for one thing, and
for another, Kelly had her daughter Laura to take care of.

Now Laura was the one in danger.

Tom pulled his F-150 into the garage and got out. By
the time he reached the door that led from the garage into
the kitchen, it was open and Bonnie was there, her face
streaked with tears.

"I have to go, Tom," she said by way of greeting. "I have
to go down there."

Tom drew her into his arms. "I know," he said quietly
as he held her and felt the little shudders running through
her. "We'll both go."

She lifted her head to look at him, and she didn't have

to raise her eyes much since she was almost as tall as he was. "But the store—"

"Louly can look after the store. It's not like we're swamped all the time these days, anyway. The store will be fine."

Bonnie managed to smile. "Thank you, Tom. When can we leave?"

"As soon as you're ready. I'll call the airport in Tucson and find out if there are any direct flights from there to Laredo later today."

"There are," Bonnie said. "I already checked on it. There's a Southwest Airlines flight that leaves at four o'clock this afternoon."

Tom thought about it and nodded. "We can make it. I'll start packing."

"I already started on that, too."

Tom grinned. His wife knew him awfully well.

But then, she ought to, considering how long they had been married. They'd been together a long time and raised two kids who were now grown and on their own. They even had a couple of grandkids, although you'd never know by looking at her that Bonnie Brannon was old enough to have grandchildren. Tall and slender, she had been quite a tomboy as a youngster, and still had a little of that coltish quality about her. Her thick brown hair had only a few streaks of gray in it, and she wore it longer than most women her age, which also made her look younger. Tom thought she was the most beautiful woman he had ever seen, which was only natural considering that he'd been married to her for decades.

He followed her into the bedroom to help her finish up the packing. As he opened a drawer to take out some underwear and socks, he saw the deadly little automatic nestled among them and wished that he could put it in the suitcase and take it with him, too.

But of course in this day and age, there was no way he could get on an airplane carrying a gun or even toting one in his luggage. He would never make it through security. He would just have to go to Laredo unarmed. He told himself that would be all right.

After all, he was just going down there to offer moral support. It wasn't like he was going to *need* a gun while he was there.

After making arrangements with one of the neighbors to feed their dogs, Tom and Bonnie put their bags in the pickup and headed for Tucson, some seventy-five miles to the northeast. It was only a little after one o'clock, so they had plenty of time to make the flight. Tom swung back into Little Tucson to pick up some hamburgers for them to eat on the way. Bonnie insisted that she wasn't hungry and was too worried about Kelly and Laura to eat, but the smell of the burgers changed her mind.

From there they drove straight to Tucson International Airport, on the south side of the city. It had been a while since Tom had flown anywhere, but the process hadn't gotten any more efficient or less annoying. Endless lines, endless security checkpoints with metal detectors and X-ray machines, and the whole hurry-up-and-wait mentality were still prevalent. In this dangerous day and age, such inconveniences were just something people had to put up with.

Finally they were on the airplane, winging eastward toward Texas. They lost an hour on the way, crossing from the Mountain Time Zone to the Central. It was early evening, nearly seven o'clock Laredo time, when they landed, but at this time of year the sun was still fairly high in the sky.

Between the driving, the hassle at the airport, and then the time in the air, they had lost touch with what was going on. While Bonnie took out her cell phone to call Kelly, Tom watched one of the television sets playing in the terminal, hoping to catch some news. Maybe there would be a report that the kidnapped girls had been rescued.

That proved not to be the case. The story was still big news, of course, but there didn't seem to be many fresh developments since the reports Tom had seen earlier in the day. The girls were still missing, and the local police, the Texas Rangers, and the FBI were coordinating efforts to locate them. The death of the nun who had been driving the bus, one Sister Katherine, had been confirmed, as had eleven more fatalities from the vehicles that had been blown up on the highway at the time of the attack. So the death toll was up to an even dozen now, with exactly forty girls, all of them either juniors or seniors at Saint Anne's, missing. All the kids who had been on the other buses involved in the field trip had been accounted for.

So from the looks of things, Tom mused, this one bus had been targeted by the kidnappers. It was the last one in the group, and according to information gathered from the other drivers, it had fallen behind considerably before disappearing. Of course, it hadn't disappeared at all, but at first that was what the others had thought. They had suspected a breakdown or something like that, so when they reached the state park that was their destination, one of the nuns had gone back after unloading the kids who had been on her bus.

By that time, the attack was over and smoke was rising from the wreckage of the various vehicles littered over the landscape. Within a half hour, emergency vehicles from all over the city and county had converged on the scene, all of them much too late to do any good.

Tom had gleaned all that background from the news reports by the time Bonnie joined him again. "I talked to Kelly," she said grimly. "They haven't heard anything, no ransom demand, nothing. And I had to talk to some woman FBI agent, too. She had the nerve to tell me that we should turn around and go back home!"

Even under the circumstances, Tom managed to smile a little. He said, "I don't imagine that suggestion went over too well."

"It sure as hell didn't. Come on." Bonnie marched toward one of the car-rental desks. Tom followed her.

When they had rented a car and piled their bags into the trunk, they left the airport, heading for the nice residential neighborhood on the edge of Laredo where Kelly Simms lived. Tom knew that Kelly was fairly well-to-do, but by no stretch of the imagination could she be considered rich.

When they reached the street where Kelly lived, Tom had to slam on the brakes. Plastic barricades had been set up in the street, leaving an opening barely big enough for a single vehicle, and that opening was blocked by a Laredo police car. A fairly large crowd had gathered. A satellite uplink truck with a local TV station's logo painted on it was parked at the side of the road.

"Vultures," Bonnie muttered when she saw the TV truck. "I'm surprised there aren't more of them here."

"There are forty missing girls," Tom pointed out. "There probably aren't enough local news crews to stake out the homes of all of them." He paused. "Wait until tomorrow, when all the ones from San Antonio and elsewhere get here."

Many of the people standing on the sidewalks, the lawns, and in the street were probably Kelly's neighbors, people who were concerned about her—in addition to having some of the same morbid curiosity that infected nearly everyone human. They stayed back, already knowing by now that they couldn't get any closer. Tom drove past them, well aware of their curious stares, and eased the rented car up to the barricades.

One of the cops, a young Latino, came over as Tom rolled down the car window. "Sorry, sir, you'll have to turn around and go back," he said as he lifted a hand. "No admittance to this street right now."

"My name is Tom Brannon," Tom said. He handed the cop his and Bonnie's Arizona driver's licenses. "This is my wife, Bonnie. Kelly Simms is her sister."

The cop frowned as he studied the licenses. "They didn't tell us anything about family coming. Hold on a minute while I check with my lieutenant."

He unclipped a walkie-talkie from his belt and turned away to speak into it for a moment. The walkie-talkie crackled a reply, and the cop nodded despite the fact that whoever was on the other end couldn't see him. He said something else and then returned the walkie-talkie to his belt.

Motioning to another cop who stood beside the police car that blocked the opening in the barricades, he called, "Sid! Let these folks through!" Then he turned to Tom, handed him the driver's licenses, and went on. "Okay, the lieutenant said to let you come up to the house."

"Thanks." Tom drove carefully through the opening and past the police car.

"I don't really understand all this hoopla," Bonnie said. "Kelly didn't do anything wrong. Why is the place crawling with police?"

"I guess the cops think the kidnappers might try to contact her, and they want to be on hand if that happens, to try to get any leads."

"Like the kidnappers are just going to waltz up here and deliver their ransom demand in person? That's insane!"

Tom smiled wryly. "Standard operating procedure doesn't always make sense."

Several police cars and several unmarked cars were parked in front of Kelly's house, a red-brick colonial that might have seemed out of place in this semiarid, almost frontier landscape if not for the fact that most of the other houses along the street were the same sort. Tom parked the rental car by the curb, and as he and Bonnie got out, a couple of uniformed officers came across the lawn toward them.

"Mr. and Mrs. Brannon?" one of the cops said. "Come on inside."

Even though it was early evening, the afternoon heat lingered in the air. Accompanied by the cops, Tom and Bonnie stepped into the foyer of the house and cool air washed over them. The central air-conditioning unit was cranked up high. Tom immediately had the sense that there were a lot of people in the house, but it was strangely quiet, almost hushed, as if they were in a church.

Straight ahead down a short hallway, past a pristine, seldom-used living room, was the large, dark-paneled den where under normal circumstances Kelly and Laura spent most of their time. A fireplace took up most of one wall; a big-screen TV dominated another. Several people sat on a large chocolate brown sofa, Bonnie's sister Kelly among them.

As Tom and Bonnie came into the room, Kelly stood up and ran toward them, throwing herself in Bonnie's arms. Kelly was seven or eight years younger than Bonnie, with blond hair that fell around her shoulders and a delicate prettiness that had just about vanished because of the emotional strain she was under. Her eyes were red with recently shed tears. She wore a fashionable skirt and blouse, conservative yet elegant, and Tom wondered if she had been in court when she got the word about the kidnapping.

As the sisters hugged, Kelly babbling out frightened, barely coherent words and Bonnie trying to reassure and comfort her, one of the other women in the room came toward Tom. She said, "Mr. Brannon?"

Tom nodded. "That's right."

"I'm Special Agent Sharon Morgan of the FBI. No offense, Mr. Brannon, but you and your wife shouldn't be here. I told your wife as much when she called."

Tom frowned. This woman rubbed him the wrong way. "My wife just wants to help her sister get through this, Agent Morgan. We won't interfere with your investigation in any way."

"Really, Mr. Brannon?" Morgan's voice lowered, and she went on. "Or do you intend to come in here and screw everything up and get a bunch of people killed, the way you did in Little Tucson?"

Eight

The room was huge, with heavy, overstuffed furniture and thick carpets. Whoever lived here would not want for creature comforts. It was a sybaritic oasis in the middle of the ancient mission.

Built in 1762, the mission had served the farmers in the area as well as travelers on their way to Villa de San Augustín de Laredo, some twenty miles to the north on the Rio Grande. In time, the mission was abandoned as more churches were built in Laredo and then later, after the Treaty of Guadalupe Hidalgo established the Rio Grande as the boundary between the United States and Mexico, in Nuevo Laredo, the new town that sprang up on the south side of the river. The mission itself, as well as the outbuildings and the surrounding compound, had fallen into disrepair. No tourists wanted to come and see it. It was too far across the border, off the beaten track. So it sat unused, a place of God that evidently even El Señor Dios had turned His back upon.

Then Los Lobos de la Noche had found it, and made it their home.

Money, of course, could accomplish almost anything.

The mission was repaired, and modern furnishings were moved into the long barrackslike building that had once housed the peons who worked the mission's garden plots. The red-tile roof was repaired, and then satellite dishes sprouted on it. Heavy compressors hummed as central air-conditioning units pumped cool air into the big mission building itself. The stables were converted into a motor pool. In a matter of months, the old mission was transformed. Now, instead of being home to humble priests who wished only to spread the word of God, it was occupied by the deadliest, most dangerous fighting force in all of northern Mexico, the Night Wolves, and their leader, Colonel Alfonso Guerrero.

So why, wondered Guerrero, if he had all this power, was he being defied by one seemingly helpless young girl who weighed barely one hundred pounds?

"How dare you say such things to me?" he thundered at her as they stood in Guerrero's luxurious private quarters. His face was dark with the rage he struggled to control. "I am your father! You should respect me!"

Angelina's chin jutted out defiantly and her hands were clenched into fists at her side. "If you really loved me, you wouldn't have dragged me off that bus and murdered poor Sister Katherine!" she said. "You wouldn't have kidnapped me and all my friends!"

"You were not kidnapped," Guerrero grated between clenched teeth. "I have told you . . . I liberated you from your mother's captivity."

She crossed her arms over her heaving chest and turned away from him. Her stubborn stance weakened a little, though, as she said quietly, "I want to go home."

"Impossible," Guerrero snapped. "If I returned you to your mother now, she would take you far away, where I would never see you again. I know that she already planned to do so, later this year."

"That's her right," Angelina murmured. "The court gave her custody of me."

"An American court," Guerrero said with a sneer. "Its rulings mean nothing to me."

"Oh?" She looked back over her shoulder at him. "Is that why you stayed away for five years and didn't even try to see me?"

"I saw you." Guerrero's voice suddenly softened. "When your soccer team played for the championship of its league when you were thirteen, I was there. You never saw me, but I was there."

She half turned. "You were?"

Guerrero nodded. "I would have congratulated you after your team won, but your mother would have seen me and caused trouble. Just as she always does and tries to keep us apart."

Angelina stiffened again, her momentary unbending gone, and Guerrero knew he had overplayed his hand. She wouldn't tolerate anything bad being said about her mother—that bitch. He could have had her assassinated any time he wanted to. With a nod of his head he could have ordered a bomb planted in her car, or something as simple as a high-powered rifle bullet through her head. It was no more than Rebecca Salinas deserved for abandoning him, abandoning his name, and stealing his daughter, his only child, away from him.

Somehow, though, he didn't think Angelina would be swayed by the argument that she should be grateful to him because he hadn't had the bitch killed.

"What are you going to do with me?" Angelina muttered after a moment.

"Keep you here with me and love you, of course."

"I'm about to start my last year of high school. I'm almost eighteen, an adult."

"I will have the finest tutors brought in. You can continue your education." He ignored her statement about almost being an adult. It was beneath consideration.

"Will you send me to college next year?"

"Of course. To the university in Mexico City."

"With guards to watch me twenty-four hours a day, so that I can't run away?"

"Yes," Guerrero said. "Mexico City is not as dangerous a place as Nuevo Laredo, but you will still need bodyguards. Even though few men would dare to harm the child of Colonel Alfonso Guerrero. You will be safe, I promise you."

"What about all my friends?" Angelina demanded. "Will they be safe, too?"

Guerrero's features hardened. "Do not concern yourself with them. You would have been leaving them before the year was over, anyway. Have you not told them that?"

"I . . . I didn't say anything to anybody about moving. I kept hoping Mom would change her mind and not take that job in Chicago."

Guerrero shook his head. "Your mother is a very stubborn woman. Once she makes up her mind about something, there is no swaying her. She would have taken you away from your home and friends in the middle of your last year of school, and never given your feelings a second thought if they interfered with her desires."

Angelina covered her face with her hands and began to sob.

Although he hated to see his daughter cry, Guerrero felt a surge of carefully concealed satisfaction. He was getting through to her, making her realize just how cruel and unfeeling her mother really was. He would never cause his beautiful *chiquita* such pain. Soon she would see that.

Carefully, Guerrero crossed the room toward her, not moving too fast or too aggressively. He wanted to take her into his arms and hug her, comfort her as he had when she was a little girl and she had fallen and skinned her knee. He knew that would be unwise, though. Better to move slowly. He touched her shoulder lightly, patted it for a second, and then withdrew his hand.

"It will be all right," he said. "You will see, Angelina. This is a new beginning for us."

She lowered her hands from her tear-streaked face and asked again, "What about all the other girls?"

Guerrero took a deep breath. "They will be fine," he said. "Soon they will be back safe with their families."

Laura had claimed one of the sleeping bags for her own, placed it behind her, and sat down on the concrete floor, leaning back on the sleeping bag propped against the adobe wall. She didn't know what was going to happen, but pacing back and forth nervously, the way Billie Sue and Aubrey were, wasn't going to solve anything. Stacy followed Laura's example and sat down beside her. After a while, Carmen did likewise. Shannon stood at the door, gripping the bars and peering out of the cell.

After a while, Stacy said quietly, "If they were going to just kill us, they would've done it already, wouldn't they?"

"I think so," Laura said, and Carmen nodded in agreement.

"So they're keeping us alive for a reason."

"I guess. Ransom is still the best bet."

"My father can pay ransom," Stacy said slowly, "as long as it's not too much."

"Mine can't," Carmen said. "I'm doomed."

Laura said, "Not necessarily. Maybe they just plan to ask for ransom for the girls whose families can afford it."

"And what will they do with the others?" Carmen asked bleakly. "Send us to some whorehouse to work for them?"

Laura frowned. She hadn't thought about that. Like the others, she had a general fear of being raped, but it hadn't occurred to her that their captors could turn them into . . . prostitutes. Looking at the situation logically, though, it made sense. The girls were young, most of them were reasonably attractive, a few were even beautiful. And a good percentage of them were probably virgins, although Laura didn't know that for sure about anybody except herself. Of course, some of them definitely weren't virgins—hello, Shannon, Laura thought with a faint, grim smile—but still they would undoubtedly fetch a good price from the proprietor of some Mexican whorehouse.

Laura closed her eyes. It didn't do any good to speculate about what was going to happen to them. They were prisoners, helpless captives stuck off God knows where, and nobody was coming to get them. The kidnapping had been carried out with ruthless military precision. Guerrero and his men weren't careless. Laura was sure they would have covered their trail. By now all of Laredo would know that they were missing . . . but no one would have the slightest idea where to find them.

"Hey!" Shannon suddenly said to someone outside the cell. "Hey, you, come here."

Laura wanted to tell her to shut up. Drawing attention to themselves couldn't be a good thing right now. And yet drawing attention to herself was what Shannon did. It was as natural to her as breathing.

One of the guards came over. He was fairly tall and not too old, somewhere between twenty and twenty-five,

Laura guessed. Handsome, too, with his thick dark hair and olive skin. His black T-shirt was stretched over well-developed muscles. He had an automatic rifle slung over his left shoulder.

"What is it you want?" he asked in reasonably good English.

"What I *want* is to get the hell out of here," Shannon said. "What I'll settle for right now is something to eat and drink. We've been locked up in here for a long time, and you haven't given us anything."

That was true. Laura's mouth was dry, and her stomach cramped occasionally from hunger.

"Someone will bring food and drink soon," the guard said.

"You can't go get something for us now?" Shannon asked.

The young man shook his head. "I must stay here, as ordered."

Shannon leaned against the bars. "What's your name?"

He hesitated, obviously unsure whether he should answer or not. Finally he said, "My name is Ricardo."

"Like Ricky Ricardo on *I Love Lucy*?" Without waiting for him to answer, Shannon went on. "I'm gonna call you Ricky, okay? Ricky, I'm *really* hungry and thirsty, and if you were to help us out, I'd appreciate it so much. You just don't know how grateful I'd be."

Shannon was going to be disappointed, Laura thought. She wasn't going to be able to manipulate this man with her patented blend of innocence and sexiness, the way she did with high school boys—

"I will see what I can do," Ricardo said.

And as he hurried off, Shannon turned and grinned at Laura, as if she knew exactly what the other girl had been thinking.

Nine

Tom's eyes narrowed angrily as he stared at Special Agent Morgan. "What do you know about Little Tucson?"

"I know you were right in the thick of that mess out there a while back. You were the one who started that so-called Patriot Project. It was illegal, you know."

Tom shook his head. "That's not what the courts said. Every lawsuit that was brought against us was thrown out. Anyway, what's an FBI agent doing siding with the ACLU?"

"Who said I was siding with the ACLU?" Morgan snapped. "I just know that it's not right for civilians to take the law into their own hands."

"Tell that to the Founding Fathers."

"People like you always bring up the Founding Fathers. That was a long time ago. The country was a lot different place then. You get a bunch of crackpot vigilantes running around now, all it'll lead to is anarchy and mob violence . . . just like what happened in Little Tucson."

"There were no crackpots in the Patriot Project," Tom said. People who preached tolerance the most usually had the least tolerance when it came to other folks' opinions.

We weeded out the troublemakers and we had as many Hispanic members as we did Anglos. And there was no mob violence."

"Half the town was shot up, and dozens of people were killed."

"Only because M-15 declared war on us, and we had to defend ourselves."

"And don't get me started on Hiram Stackhouse," Morgan went on, ignoring him. "Congress should investigate him and his operation for antitrust violations, not to mention racketeering."

Tom's frown deepened. As a small-business owner, he had plenty of reasons to be less than happy with Stackhouse and SavMart, but the idea of the government cracking down on a business simply because it was successful, well, that just wasn't right.

But then, the government punished success all the time, he reminded himself. All you had to do was take a good look at the income tax laws to see that.

None of which mattered a damn right now or had anything to do with Laura's kidnapping. Tom forced himself to remain calm, and said, "Look, my wife and I came down here to help my sister-in-law get through this. That's all."

"Just keep your nose out of our investigation," Morgan said.

Tom looked around and saw that Bonnie and Kelly were sitting on the sofa, Kelly talking in low tones. Not wanting to intrude, Tom moved over to the side of the room and sat down in an armchair. For now, he would just stay out of the way.

Morgan went back to talking to a small group of uniformed cops and other men in plainclothes. They might be FBI agents or detectives from the Laredo PD.

A man wearing a white shirt, dark jeans, a string tie, and a white Stetson came into the room. His alert gaze lit on Tom. Tom took note of the holstered automatic on the man's hip and the badge fastened to his belt. The man pulled up another chair and sat down next to him. Politely, he asked, "Who might you be, sir?"

"Tom Brannon," Tom introduced himself. He nodded toward the sofa. "My wife is Mrs. Simms's sister. We flew in from Arizona to be with her."

The man nodded and stuck out a hand. "Roy Rodgers, Texas Rangers."

Tom couldn't help but smile. The Ranger saw the reaction, chuckled tolerantly, and held up his other hand to forestall whatever Tom was about to say.

"King of the Cowboys, I know. In this case, Rodgers has a D in it."

"Still seems appropriate somehow," Tom said as he shook hands with the man.

"Brannon, Brannon . . ." Rodger mused. "That name seems familiar, too." His eyebrows rose as he obviously made the connection. "You say you're from Arizona?"

"That's right."

Rodgers let out a low whistle. "I don't reckon there's a lawman in the country who didn't hear about all the trouble out there. You folks had your hands full."

"Yes, but the illegal alien traffic in the area has fallen off dramatically, and the bad guys steer clear of Little Tucson most of the time."

"Imagine that," Rodger said with a grin he didn't bother to conceal. "Honest citizens stand up for what's right and defend themselves, and the bad guys start steering clear of them. I don't reckon we need a five-year, fifteen-billion-dollar government study to figure *that* one out."

Tom returned the grin, sensing a kindred spirit in the

Ranger. He nodded toward Morgan and said, "The FBI lady over there didn't seem to feel the same way."

"Her head's still stuck inside the Beltway. This is Texas."

Those three words seemed to sum it up. Quietly, Tom asked, "Do you know any more about this kidnapping than what's been talked about on the news?"

Rodgers hesitated, then said, "I'm not sure I could discuss it, even if I did, but as a matter of fact . . . no. Everything we know has been leaked to the media already."

"On purpose?"

"Not by the Texas Rangers," Rodgers said sharply. "I don't know where the leaks came from."

"The Feds, more than likely."

Rodgers shrugged.

"I didn't mean any offense by that question, Ranger," Tom said. "Can you tell me anything about the kidnappers?"

"Los Lobos de la Noche," Rodgers said. "As big a bunch of bad-asses as you'll find anywhere, Mr. Brannon. I don't want to add to your worry about your niece, but those are some really dangerous men."

"I'd say a dozen people killed is proof enough of that."

"Tip of the iceberg. The Night Wolves have been responsible for hundreds of murders over the past five years. They work for one of the cartels trying to take over all the drug smuggling in the region."

"So most of the time it's bad guys killing other bad guys," Tom guessed.

"Exactly. That's not to say we've turned a blind eye to it. The Rangers, the DEA, the Border Patrol, local authorities . . . we've all been trying to put a stop to the war, especially when it spills over onto American soil. Haven't had much luck so far, though."

Tom leaned forward in the chair and clasped his hands

together. "This kidnapping—could it have anything to do with the war between the cartels?"

"Don't see how. This strikes me as more of an independent operation by Guerrero and his men."

"Guerrero?"

"Colonel Alfonso Guerrero. He's the head honcho of the bunch." Quickly, Rodgers sketched in the background of the Night Wolves and their leader. Tom listened intently, his amazement growing as the story unfolded. To think that such a vicious gang could have been trained in this country, by American military and law-enforcement personnel . . . it boggled the mind how something with such a good purpose could have gone so bad.

Tom asked, "What if there's a connection between one of the girls on that bus and a rival cartel?"

"We've thought about that," Rodgers admitted. "We're looking into the background of all the girls—that's one reason we're here now—but no link has surfaced yet." He looked at Tom with added interest. "That's the sort of question a cop would ask. What is it you do again, out there in Arizona?"

"I own an auto-parts store. Have for years. Never worked as a cop or anything like that, but my best friend for years was the sheriff of Sierrita County."

Rodgers nodded. "I remember. He got hurt real bad in all that trouble, didn't he?"

"Yeah," Tom answered shortly. Buddy Gorman would never be the same again, that was for sure.

The Ranger said, "I've got a favor to ask of you, Mr. Brannon."

"Sure. What is it?"

"When you talk to the media—and you *will* have to talk to the media before this is over, you can count on that—I'd appreciate it if you'd keep any speculation to yourself. We don't want to tip off anybody on the other side to what we're thinking."

Tom said, "I'll watch what I say."

"Thanks. I've got a hunch that we'll need all the help we can get."

Tom looked at Special Agent Morgan across the room. "I don't think everybody feels that way."

Rodgers said, "Remember what I said about Texas."

Tom frowned. He knew that Rodgers wasn't telling him it was all right to take the law into his own hands. Even here in the Lone Star State, which was proud of its wild-and-woolly past, vigilantes weren't encouraged.

But Rodgers wasn't too proud to listen to what a civilian had to say, either, Tom sensed.

"Do you think the girls have been taken across the border?" Tom asked.

"Seems likely. Guerrero knows that we can't follow him across the Rio Grande. That would create too much of a political stink, from Washington to Mexico City." Rodgers sighed softly. "Was a time when the Rangers didn't let something like an easily forded river stand between them and doing what was right."

"What about the Mexican authorities? Can you count on them for any help?" Tom recalled that officials of the Mexican government had pitched a hissy fit about the Patriot Project, while sitting on their hands and refusing to do anything about the illegal immigration problem themselves.

"We can count on them to *say* they're doing everything they can." Rodgers's meaning was clear—the Mexicans weren't going to go after Guerrero.

"So I guess we wait."

"Yeah." The frustration was plain in the Ranger's voice, which explained why he was talking so bluntly to this civilian. "We wait."

"The kidnappers are bound to call sooner or later," Tom said hopefully, gesturing toward the table on the other side of the room where an FBI technician with headphones on sat beside a laptop computer and several other pieces of audio and electronic equipment. When the kidnappers called with their ransom demand, everything that was said would be recorded, digitized, traced, and analyzed out the wazoo.

"We can hope that they call, but I'm not sure," Rodgers said. "They work for a cartel that smuggles billions of dollars' worth of drugs across the border every year. The amount of ransom they can collect from a job like this doesn't amount to much compared to that."

The more Tom thought about it, the more the same feeling had come over him. This wasn't about the money.

There had been something—someone—on that school bus that the Night Wolves wanted.

Ten

Ricardo was true to his word. He came back to the cell about fifteen minutes later carrying a tray of sandwiches and a six-pack of bottled water. Two more guards were with him. They motioned the girls away from the bars. One of them unlocked the door and then stood back. He and the other man trained their automatic rifles on the girls while Ricardo opened the door. He stopped just inside the cell and placed the sandwiches and the water on the floor, then stepped out quickly and clanged the door shut.

"Thank you, Ricky," Shannon said sweetly as she smiled at him. "If there's ever anything I can do for you, you just let me know."

The young man looked vaguely embarrassed. "Make the water last," he advised. "There will be no more for you until morning."

Then he and the other guards moved away down the corridor.

As Laura, Shannon, and the other girls tore hungrily into the sandwiches, they heard the doors of the other cells opening and closing. Obviously all the prisoners were getting their supper.

The sandwiches were just peanut butter and jelly, but they tasted wonderful after the long day with nothing to eat. The girls sat around on their sleeping bags and ate, and when they were finished, Carmen said, "Well, it wasn't really a picnic, but I guess it'll have to do."

"And it wasn't really what you'd call a hearty meal, so I guess we haven't been condemned yet," Stacy put in with a smile, surprising Laura. She didn't think she had ever heard Stacy make a joke before.

Shannon took a sip of her water and said, "Don't worry, they won't let us starve. I'll see to that."

"What do you mean?" Aubrey asked.

"Didn't you see how I've got that guy Ricky wrapped around my finger? He'll do anything I want."

"Yeah?" Carmen said. "Then tell him to let us out of here and take us home."

"Well . . . he'll do anything I want within reason."

"That's what I thought."

Shannon's face flushed with anger. "Listen, bitch, I got us those sandwiches, didn't I?"

"They were going to feed us anyway. Ricardo said so."

"Yeah, well, you don't know when they would have gotten around to it, do you? All I know is I smiled at him, and we had food and water."

Carmen glared at her for a moment before muttering, "Don't call me bitch."

"Why not? How do you say it in Spanish? *Puta?*"

"No, that's you, a whore."

Both girls started to get up. Laura was between them. "Stop it, both of you!" she said. "We're in enough trouble. We can't afford to be fighting among ourselves."

"Then tell her to keep her slutty mouth shut," Carmen grumbled.

Shannon tossed her hair and said, "This slutty mouth of mine may be the only thing that keeps us alive."

"Oh, I don't doubt that your mouth will get a workout—"

"That's enough!" Laura said. "Just stop it."

Billie Sue said, "Who made the nerd the boss?"

"Don't you know?" Laura shot back at her. "Nerds run the world. Ever heard of Bill Gates?"

"He's got something to do with . . . computers, right?" Laura rolled her eyes.

"Don't be a dumb-ass," Aubrey said. "Bill Gates invented the Internet."

"I thought that was some old politician guy."

"No, he invented the information superhighway."

"That's the same thing as the Internet, isn't it? Anyway, you're thinking of the guy who was in that old movie *Love Story*."

"The guy who used to be married to Farrah Fawcett invented the Internet?"

"Who's Farrah Fawcett?"

"The one who was all stoned and acting crazy on David Letterman's show one night."

"That was Courtney Love."

"She's the one who got up on his desk and flashed him."

"No, no, you're thinking about Drew Barrymore."

Laura bit back a scream. She had the horrible feeling that some valuable brain cells were dying just from listening to this.

There was no light in the cell, so when the sun went down and the last of its glow faded from the high window, darkness closed in. As frightened as the girls had been during their captivity so far, the darkness made it worse. They weren't able to distract themselves by arguing about who had invented the Internet or just how slutty Shannon really was, so all they could think about as they huddled there in the thick shadows was what was going to happen to them. None of them expected it to be anything good. The cell grew a little chilly, too, as the heat of the day dissipated quickly once the sun went down in this desert landscape.

After a while, though, no matter how scared and cold and lonely they were, exhaustion began to take its toll. Laura heard soft snores coming from a couple of the girls in her cell. She couldn't tell which ones were asleep, but it didn't really matter. She felt her own eyelids getting heavy, and her head drooped forward as she continued to sit up. She wanted to stay awake, so she wouldn't be taken by surprise if any shit came down. If she spread the sleeping bag on the floor and stretched out on it, she knew she would be asleep in minutes.

Despite her intentions, she dozed off anyway. When a sudden noise woke her, she was slumped on her side, her arms wrapped around the rolled-up sleeping bag as she used it as a pillow.

She wasn't sure what had roused her from sleep, but a second later a man yelled in Spanish, "Watch out! She has a gun!"

Somewhere down the corridor, shots blasted out, the reports deafeningly loud as they echoed back from the thick adobe walls. The muzzle flashes lit up the cells with their brief, hellish glare. A man shouted in pain. Running footsteps slapped against the concrete floor.

Laura and her companions were all awake now. They scooted back against the wall as far as they could and huddled there, trying to stay out of the line of fire even though they didn't know exactly where the line was.

A flashlight snapped on, its beam of light lancing through

the darkness. Laura squinted against the brightness. The beam darted here and there and then froze, pinning a girl against the heavy door at the end of the corridor, just outside the cell where Laura and the others were locked up. The girl was fumbling at the door, trying to get it to open, when the light hit her. She twisted around and brought up the pistol in her other hand.

Laura recognized the girl as Rosa Delgado, another senior. Rosa wore only a pair of pink panties. There was a smear of what looked like blood across her bare breasts.

In that frozen instant, Laura knew what must have happened. Some of the men had taken her out of the cell and started to have some fun with her, probably tearing her clothes off until she was nearly naked.

But in his animal lust, one of the bastards had been careless, and Rosa had grabbed his gun and shot herself free of their clutches. Unfortunately, there was nowhere to run, no way to escape. She was trapped in the beam of the flashlight, pinned against the heavy wooden door that barred the way out of the corridor.

"Drop the gun, girl!" a man yelled in Spanish.

Rosa didn't drop the gun. She kept pointing it at them. The barrel shook. Rosa didn't say anything. Her eyes were wide with terror and hysteria.

But then she grew calm suddenly and a look of resolve appeared on her face. She turned the gun around.

"Rosa, no!" Laura screamed.

The girl ignored her. Rosa opened her mouth, put the barrel of the gun in it, and pulled the trigger.

The blast threw her back against the door behind her. A huge mass of blood and brains and bone fragments splattered the wood, leaving a grisly, irregular splotch on the door. Rosa bounced off and pitched forward, landing in a limp sprawl on the concrete.

All the girls in the cells were screaming now. Laura joined in, unable to control the horror. The girls clutched at each other and practically crawled in each other's laps as they desperately tried to escape the nightmare.

But there was no escape—short of what Rosa Delgado had just done. This was their life now, for however long it lasted.

Heavy footsteps in the corridor made the girls in the cells recoil even more. Several men stepped into the reflected glow of the flashlight, which was now shining on Rosa's body. One of the guards, an older man with a mustache, turned his head and looked into the cell at the terrified prisoners. "You see what happens?" he said to them. "This one did not have to die. All she had to do was cooperate, and she would still be alive. It'a damned shame."

"The colonel—" one of the other men began.

"The colonel cares only about the one he keeps with him," the older man snapped. He jerked a thumb toward the door to the courtyard. "Take her out and dispose of her." Then, with his thumb sticking up and his index finger extended to make a gun, he pointed at Laura and the other girls and said, "Learn from this, eh? Be good girls. You will live longer that way." His thumb snapped down as if he had fired.

Then he stalked off, leaving the other men to take care of Rosa's corpse.

One of them, Laura noted even in her stunned state, was the young man who called himself Ricardo. His face was drawn and pale in the glow of the flashlight, and as he looked down at Rosa, Laura saw the same sort of shock in his eyes that she was feeling. He lifted his gaze and suddenly it locked with hers, and she felt something go through her like an electric shock. It wasn't love at first sight or anything stupid like that. Under these horrible circumstances, nobody could even think about such a thing. It was a spark of empathy, a shared moment of revulsion and horror at the fate that had overtaken Rosa Delgado. A fate that might well be in store for all the captives, sooner or later.

And Ricardo didn't like that idea, any more than Laura did.

Then he tore his eyes away, and she sensed that he deliberately didn't look at her again. Because he was afraid to? She wondered. Because he sensed the same sort of connection that she had in that fleeting moment?

The chances were overwhelming that in the end it wouldn't make a bit of difference. But as the men picked up Rosa Delgado's limp body and carried it out and Ricardo followed them, flicking one last glance back at the cell where Laura was held captive, she allowed herself for the first time since this ordeal had begun to clutch at a tiny shred of hope. . . .

Eleven

Ricardo Benitez leaned against the adobe wall and took a deep drag on the joint, drawing the smoke into his lungs and holding it there for a long moment before he allowed it to trickle slowly out of his mouth. A calmness spread through him, soothing him and dulling the clamor of alarm that had threatened to overwhelm his brain. This was good weed. He needed something right now to keep him focused on the job at hand.

He needed something to keep him from thinking too much about those girls . . . especially the blonde.

The redhead would be the biggest annoyance, smiling at him and flaunting her ripe young body and promising all sorts of things in her coy voice without ever actually promising anything at all. But he was confident that he could handle her, even though in a moment of weakness he had given in to her flirting and fetched the sandwiches and water for the prisoners.

No, it was the quiet blond one who represented the greatest threat to him. When their eyes had met, during that terrible moment after Rosa's death, Ricardo had seen intelligence there, a keenness of intellect that not even fear could totally conceal. More than that, he had sensed the courage in her, too, and was drawn to it. She would fight to the very end, and she probably possessed more aptitude for such a battle than even she herself dreamed of.

Maybe the other girl's suicide would serve a purpose. Maybe it would convince the blonde to cooperate and not to fight. Ricardo hoped so.

Otherwise, sooner or later she would be trouble, and he didn't want to be forced into the position of having to make a decision he didn't want to make.

Ricardo inhaled another lungful of the marijuana smoke and looked up at the stars floating in the night sky above the old mission. They seemed more brilliant than ever tonight. It was wrong somehow for something so beautiful to shine down on a scene of such evil.

Several men tramped toward the wall surrounding the mission compound. They were returning from the grim chore of burying the dead girl. An unmarked grave in the desert would be her final resting place. Sun and wind and the passage of time would erase all signs, and no one would ever know where Rosa Delgado lay. Her clothes would be burned, and the identification that had been taken from her purse and that had given her captors her name would be disposed of as well. It would be as if she had never been here.

Eventually, that would be true for all of them. He knew from listening to them talk that they thought they had been kidnapped for ransom, as happened so often along the border. Guerrero's e-mail had teased the American authorities with that possibility without actually saying as much. Just like the captives, the law-enforcement personnel on the other side of the border would assume that they were dealing with a simple kidnapping.

In reality, though, none of them would ever go home.

They would be sold into what was once quaintly known as white slavery and shipped off, dispersed to brothels throughout Mexico where they would live out their lives pleasuring the men who paid their owners for the privilege. A terrible existence, but they would still be alive, at least for a while.

The money that the Night Wolves would make from all of this would be a mere pittance compared to what they made working for the cartel. But the colonel had to justify his actions some way, and as long as he turned a profit for his men, neither they nor his employers could complain.

All because of one girl . . . the girl Colonel Guerrero had taken off the bus and kept with him ever since. It was rumored among the men that she was his daughter, but Ricardo didn't know that for sure.

If it was true, it would be a nice bit of knowledge to have. One never knew when even the smallest bit of leverage might come in handy.

Ricardo lounged against the wall as he smoked. His rifle was tucked under his arm. As the men from the burial detail came up to the gate, one of them said, "You should have come with us, Ricardo. One more man to dig would have made the job go faster."

"It was not my job," Ricardo said. "You four were the ones who decided to rape the girl on her first night here. It was fitting for Major Cortez to assign her burial to you." Cortez was Colonel Guerrero's *segundo,* a grizzled military veteran who was the oldest member of Los Lobos de la Noche.

"What does it matter if it was her first night here?" one of the other men demanded angrily. "All of them will be raped before we're through with them."

Ricardo smiled thinly. "You're just upset, Pablo, because it was your gun the señorita grabbed. The colonel will not be pleased with you when Major Cortez tells him about the incident."

The man called Pablo snarled a curse and stepped toward Ricardo. He still had a shovel in his hands, and for a second it seemed he was going to strike the younger man with it.

Ricardo moved slightly, and the rifle was no longer held negligently under his arm. It was in his hands, ready to fire, with the barrel pointed toward Pablo.

Still muttering curses, Pablo turned away and went through the gate into the compound.

"That one hates you," one of the other men said to Ricardo.

He replied, "The opinion of such a dog means nothing to me."

"Are you coming in?"

"In a minute." Ricardo stayed where he was as the others filed inside. He had been detailed to stand guard over the burial. Now that it was finished, he was off duty for the night. He could go to his room and sleep. . . .

Or he could return to the wing of the mission where the girls were being held and look through the bars again at that blond one.

With a jerk of his head, Ricardo forced that idea out of his thoughts. He couldn't afford to weaken and do something foolish now.

Not after all the time and effort he had put into this assignment.

He had started out as a mule, one of the drug runners for the cartel. Getting the job hadn't been all that difficult. He had gone into a Nuevo Laredo bar that was frequented by a known mule, picked a fight with the man, and then killed him as they fought with knives in the alley behind the place. That had displeased the people the man worked for, until Ricardo offered to take his place in the distribution chain. Since he was responsible for the man's death, that was the way of the cartel.

He wasn't supposed to kill the mule, just injure him badly enough to take him out of circulation for a while. But plans hatched in a well-lit office where a ceiling fan stirred the hot air meant very little in a dark alley that stank of garbage and shit. The garish glow from a neon sign was the only light that filtered into the alley, and in that glow Ricardo had seen the knife in the other man's hand coming at his throat. He had reacted the only way he could—instinctively and fatally.

From there he had worked hard, done his job well, kept his mouth shut. His rise in the organization was steady, if not spectacular.

No, "spectacular" had waited for the ambush laid by members of the rival cartel, the ambush that had been sprung as Ricardo and a couple of his fellow mules had been driving a pickup full of drugs across an isolated river ford. Suddenly the air was full of bees buzzing around them—deadly, steel-jacketed bees. The man behind the wheel of the pickup lurched forward, his head practically exploding as several slugs smashed into it. Blood and brains splattered all over the inside of the cracked windshield.

Ricardo was sitting in the middle of the seat. The man on his right, by the passenger door, died in the early seconds of the ambush, too. Suddenly alone, Ricardo did the only thing he could. He bent low, reached across the body of the man who had been driving, and opened the door. A hard shove sent the corpse tumbling out of the pickup. Staying hunched over in the seat, Ricardo punched his foot against the accelerator, stuck the MAC-10 machine gun he had been given out the window, and fired blindly as the truck surged ahead.

He was driving almost blindly, too, risking only an occasional glance through the blood-smeared windshield. Then the glass shattered under the fusillade of lead, showering him with razor-sharp shards. Luckily he was able to close his eyes in time to keep any of the glass splinters from getting into them, although his face was scratched up pretty bad. He ignored the stinging pain and kept going, the machine gun chattering in his left hand as he gripped the steering wheel with his right. The previous driver's blood and brains made the wheel slippery, but Ricardo ignored that, too.

Then he was through the ambush and roaring away from the river, although a bullet had found the pickup's radiator and it was destined to go only another mile before giving out. That mile was enough, though. He was able to rendezvous with the cartel's men who were supposed to meet him on the American side of the river. He heard them talking about it later, about how they had seen the bullet-riddled truck approaching, apparently driving itself, and how surprised they had been when the pickup lurched to a halt and a young man, covered with blood and with broken glass in his hair and embedded in his cheeks, had crawled out with an empty machine gun in his hand.

A story like that gets around. It hadn't been very long after that when a tall, powerful-looking man had come to see him in Nuevo Laredo and introduced himself as Colonel Alfonso Guerrero. Ricardo knew who the colonel was, of course, and when Guerrero asked him if he would be interested in joining Los Lobos de la Noche, there was a genuine catch in Ricardo's voice as he replied that this was the proudest day of his life.

* * *

The joint was down almost to the end now. Ricardo took one last drag on it and then pinched out the glowing ember. He slipped the roach into the pocket of his T-shirt.

Six months had passed since he was invited to join the Night Wolves, and during that time, he had hardly left this compound south of Nuevo Laredo. He hadn't gone along the night that the Wolves ambushed the American task force on the other side of the Rio Grande, and he hadn't been part of the force today that had crossed the border to attack the school bus and capture the girls who were on it. He didn't think it was because Guerrero didn't trust him—*Dios*, he hoped that wasn't the case!—but rather because he was still relatively new to the group.

That was all right with Ricardo. He could do a lot of things—hell, he had already done a lot of things to get to where he was—but he wasn't sure he could pull the trigger and kill American lawmen. He knew damned well he couldn't kill a bunch of teenage girls, and he was fervently thankful that the blood of that poor nun wasn't on his hands.

Or was it? He had known that Guerrero was about to pull off something major, and he had done nothing. He knew the fate that the colonel had in mind for the captives, too, and unless something unforeseen happened, he would be forced to stand by and do nothing to stop *this* atrocity, as well.

Because he couldn't. He had bigger goals. The lives of a few dozen people were as nothing compared to the death toll that the Night Wolves took on an annual basis. Factor in the tens of thousands of deaths caused each year by the drug traffic—if the number wasn't even higher than that, perhaps in the hundreds of thousands—and it quickly became clear that those poor girls might have to be sacrificed for the greater good. Ricardo's goal, his job, was nothing less than the destruction of Los Lobos de la Noche and the crippling of the cartel they worked for.

Ricardo Benitez looked out across the desert where the silver starlight shone on the lonely grave where Rosa Delgado lay, and he murmured, "I'm sorry." He meant it, too.

But there was nothing he could have done to prevent her death.

Being an undercover agent for the American Drug Enforcement Agency came first.

Twelve

Agent Morgan left the Simms house a short time after Tom and Bonnie arrived there, taking most of the other agents and detectives with her. There were other kidnapping victims, thirty-nine of them, in fact, and Morgan intended to touch base with all of their families before the night was over. There was no telling where the break in the case might come.

But it *would* come. She was sure of that, and said so before she left. Criminals always slipped up sooner or later.

Tom was glad to see Morgan go. She hadn't really accomplished anything while Tom was there.

Bonnie persuaded Kelly to go lie down for a while. Tom was left sitting in the den with a couple of officers from the Laredo Police Department and the technician who was still monitoring his equipment in case the kidnappers called. After a while, Tom went over to the table and introduced himself to the man.

"Pete Yarnell," the technician said as he shook hands with Tom.

"Are you an FBI agent, too, Mr. Yarnell?" Tom asked.

"That's right," Yarnell said. He was in his thirties, but

premature hair loss had left him mostly bald. "Not usually a field agent, you understand. Most of the time I work in the lab at our San Antonio office."

"I thought the FBI lab was back in Virginia or somewhere like that."

"Well, the main one is, of course. But every office has lab facilities of its own."

Tom nodded. "If the kidnappers call, do you think you'll be able to tell anything from the recording you make of it?"

"All we can do is try," Yarnell said, "but the filtering and enhancement software we have is state-of-the-art." He patted the laptop computer that was sitting on the table, the gesture almost as fond as if he had been petting the head of a favorite dog.

Tom leaned forward in his chair. "You can pick up any background noises and things like that?"

"Absolutely."

"I don't suppose there's any chance you could let a civilian . . . say, me . . . listen to such a call after you recorded it?"

Yarnell frowned. "Of course not. That would be interfering in FBI business."

"It's my niece who's been kidnapped, along with all those other girls. Naturally, I want to do anything I can to help. Maybe I could hear something—"

"Not without a court order, Mr. Brannon," Yarnell said firmly, "which I seriously doubt you'd be able to get." The agent's tone softened a little. "Besides, they haven't called yet, and we don't know that they will."

"They have to, if they're going to make a ransom demand. They have to get in touch somehow."

Yarnell shrugged. Like everybody else, he seemed to assume that the girls had been kidnapped for ransom—

but so far there was absolutely no proof of that, Tom realized. The only contact had been the lone e-mail from Colonel Guerrero, claiming that the girls were safe. From that, everybody had jumped to the conclusion that Guerrero would be back in touch again later with his demands. That was the way these things always went.

So what were the authorities doing in the meantime? Waiting. Waiting for something to happen. Nobody was actually out *looking* for the girls.

Tom's misgivings grew stronger as he turned those thoughts over in his mind. He recalled his earlier conversation with the Texas Ranger and the possibility that Guerrero had had some reason besides ransom for kidnapping the girls. Maybe everybody was playing it all wrong. Maybe Guerrero was counting on the authorities biding their time and waiting for ransom demands, when actually he had other plans.

But what?

Tom didn't know, but he figured the tension in his gut was trying to tell him something. He was no cop. He was just an average guy—but an average guy who had been through the fire, an average guy who had stared into the very face of evil and madness and come to the realization that you couldn't always count on monsters to do what you expected.

You couldn't reason with them, either. In the end, all you could do was kill them.

Bottom line, though, he didn't really know anything. Like everybody else involved in this case, he was just as far away as ever from figuring out where the kidnapped girls were being held.

And as that thought went through his head, Tom felt his gut tense again. Why was he even thinking about such things? It wasn't like he could do anything to help rescue the girls. A whole horde of law enforcement personnel was already on that job. He was just a civilian, he reminded himself again, a guy who owned an auto-parts store.

He couldn't help but remember, though, what a difference a bunch of common people had made in Little Tucson. Just your average, everyday Joes and Janes who had risen up against evil and driven it back to where it had come from. It was foolish for people to sit on their butts and assume that somebody else—usually the government—would take care of them.

More than foolish, sometimes that attitude was downright deadly.

It was a long night, and contrary to the old saying, things didn't look a bit better in the morning.

The telephone in Kelly Simms's house had rung several times, prompting a surge of hope, fear, and adrenaline each time, along with a burst of frantic activity from Pete Yarnell as he got ready to tape the conversation, but on each occasion, when Kelly answered, the caller proved to be only a member of the media looking for a quote. After the last call, Kelly had slammed the phone down with a heartfelt comment about goddamn bloodsucking vultures.

Tom Brannon couldn't have agreed more.

He didn't know how much sleep Kelly had finally gotten. Judging by the haggard look of his sister-in-law's face, not much. Bonnie was exhausted, too. She had stayed in Kelly's bedroom all night, sitting up in a chair while Kelly tried to get some rest. Bonnie had dozed in the chair, but only fitfully.

Yarnell and the cops had been awake all night. They were on duty.

Tom figured he had gotten more sleep than anyone else,

because eventually he had gone off to the guest room and crawled into bed. Given those circumstances, he thought it was only fitting that he prepare breakfast the next morning. When he got up, he spoke briefly to Bonnie and Kelly as they sat in the living room, then went into the kitchen. He started a fresh pot of coffee and rummaged through the cupboards and refrigerator. Soon he had pancakes cooking in one pan and bacon and sausage sizzling in another.

Yarnell came into the kitchen, yawning prodigiously. Tom looked at him and said, "Coffee should be ready. Help yourself and I'll have something for you to eat in a few minutes."

"Thanks," Yarnell muttered as he poured himself a cup of coffee.

"Heard from your boss this morning?"

"Special Agent Morgan?" Yarnell shook his head. "Nope. I imagine she was pretty busy all night, checking in with all the victims' families and following up on any leads." He summoned up a faint smile. "She may not be the most likable agent I've ever known, but she's a hard worker. Seems to be, anyway, in the time she's been down here."

"She's new to the San Antonio office?"

"New to the Bureau, period. Relatively speaking."

"She's not *that* young," Tom pointed out.

"She used to be a lawyer. Federal prosecutor in Washington, D.C. Scuttlebutt is that she lost some big case on a technicality and got so disgusted with the courts that she quit and decided to go into our end of the job instead."

Tom hadn't heard anybody use the word "scuttlebutt" in a long time. He thought it was a perfectly good word and was glad to know that it hadn't been completely forgotten.

He wasn't surprised to hear that Morgan had been a lawyer, either. That explained, at least partially, her combative and superior attitude.

"I shouldn't be gossiping like this," Yarnell said.

"Your tongue was loosened by the smell of bacon and pancakes."

"Oh, yeah," Yarnell agreed. "They smell great. Where'd you learn to cook, Mr. Brannon?"

"Just something I picked up in my bachelor days and haven't completely forgotten. I guess it comes back to you, like riding a bicycle. . . . You want sausage or bacon?"

"Uh . . . both?"

With a grin, Tom piled sausage, bacon, and pancakes on a plate and set them on the table in front of Yarnell. Tom took syrup and butter—real butter, not that greasy stuff made from soybean oil—from the refrigerator and put them on the table, too.

"Thanks," Yarnell said. "You're a lifesaver."

Tom turned away so the agent wouldn't see the frown that appeared on his face, replacing the grin. He wished that what Yarnell had said was true. He wished there was something he could do to save the lives of Laura and all the other girls who had been on that bus.

Bonnie came into the kitchen and smiled at Tom. "I thought I smelled coffee," she said.

He poured a cup for her, fixed her a plate of food, and then sat down to eat, too. It was a little awkward, the married couple sitting at the table with the FBI agent, who was almost a stranger to them.

The awkwardness vanished a moment later when Tom heard voices in the living room, and Kelly began shouting angrily, "You're not doing anything to find them! You're not doing *anything*!"

"Oh my God," Bonnie said as she got quickly to her feet. "What now?"

Tom and Yarnell stood up, too, as a voice that Tom recognized as belonging to Special Agent Sharon Morgan said sharply, "Take it easy, Mrs. Simms. It's not going to do anybody any good for you to have hysterics."

"Hysterics?" Kelly repeated as Tom, Bonnie, and Yarnell reached the short hallway between kitchen and living room. "I'll show you hysterics, you cold-blooded bitch!"

They burst into the living room just as Kelly threw herself at Morgan, ready to claw her eyes out. The FBI agent caught Kelly's wrists neatly, twisted them, hauled Kelly around, and forced her right arm up behind her back in a hammerlock. A few steps away, the two uniformed cops who had spent the night there looked on, tired, befuddled, and clearly unsure what they ought to do in this situation.

"Relax, Mrs. Simms," Morgan said. "You don't want a dislocated shoulder on top of your other troubles."

Bonnie said, "Let her go!" and started toward Kelly and Morgan. Tom grabbed her around the waist, holding her back. She cried, "Damn it, Tom, let me go!"

Tom was tempted. But even though Bonnie was athletic and in top shape, she was still older and lacked the hand-to-hand combat training that Morgan had no doubt received at the FBI Academy. He said, "Agent Morgan, why don't we all stand down, and you can tell us what's going on here." He hadn't heard Morgan come into the house this morning, but obviously the agent hadn't brought good news.

Morgan let go of Kelly's arm and gave her a little push that sent her forward a step. At the same time, Tom let go of Bonnie, and his wife rushed forward to hug her sister. "My God," Bonnie said to Kelly, "what's happened?"

"They're not even going to *look* for Laura and the other girls!" Kelly said as tears coursed down her face.

Tom stared grimly at Morgan. "Is that true?"

Morgan adjusted the blazer she was wearing this morning, despite the fact that it would be hot in Laredo before the day was over. "I didn't say that we weren't going to continue searching," she said. "But for the time being, the Mexican authorities are going to take the lead in the investigation."

Tom felt his heart sink. His talk with Rodgers the night before had only confirmed what his instincts had already told him—the Mexican authorities couldn't be counted on for anything except stonewalling. Too many of them had been paid off or scared off—or both.

"Why?" Tom demanded. "Why turn things over to the Mexicans?"

Morgan shrugged. "Because that's where it appears the girls were taken. The Rangers and the Border Patrol were able to follow the tracks of the vehicles that left the scene of the attack on the bus. They made a wide circle around Laredo, mostly cross-country, and then crossed the river at a ford north of Falcon International Reservoir that's known to the Border Patrol."

"If it's a crossing that the Border Patrol knows about, why didn't they have anybody watching it?" Tom asked.

"There was no time. Guerrero and his men got there first."

"What about after that? Did they follow the tracks across the river?"

"Of course not." Morgan sounded shocked that he would even suggest such a thing. "We have no jurisdiction in Mexico."

Tom's teeth grated together. He remembered Rodgers's comment about a time when the Rangers wouldn't have let a thing like that stop them. Now bureaucracy and political red tape had tied the hands of anybody who just wanted to do what was right.

"We asked the Mexican government for permission to fly in their airspace so that helicopters could cross the border and carry on the search," Morgan went on. "That permission was denied, of course. We have to respect international boundaries. We've passed along all the information we have to the Mexican authorities, and they assure us that they will carry out a search with all due diligence."

In other words, Tom thought bitterly, they were abandoning those poor girls to the mercies of Los Lobos de la Noche, the Night Wolves.

"Did they ever call?" Bonnie asked hollowly. "Have there been any ransom demands to any of the families?"

Morgan shook her head. "There's been no further communication with the kidnappers."

Nor would there be, Tom realized. His gut told him that Guerrero had never intended to ransom any of the girls. He had taken them, and he wasn't going to give them back.

And according to Special Agent Sharon Morgan—and by extension, the United States government—there wasn't a damned thing anybody could do about it except to rely on the Mexican authorities for help that would never come. Not a damned thing . . .

Tom Brannon took a deep breath and felt something inside him turn cold and hard, like steel.

They would just see about that.

Thirteen

The two cops were sent on their way. Yarnell would remain on duty at the Simms house until another FBI lab tech arrived to relieve him. Although it seemed from Morgan's attitude that she shared Tom's belief the kidnappers would not be in touch, as long as that possibility remained, they had to be prepared for it.

The barricades had been removed from the street, and most of the media were gone. A few reporters remained, as did the satellite uplink truck, but if there was no news here, they would probably leave before the day was over, too.

After all, the story was almost twenty-four hours old now. It was already losing its news value.

The breakfast Tom had prepared was ruined. He didn't care. He didn't have much of an appetite anymore. As he sat quietly in the living room with Bonnie and Kelly, he turned over his options in his mind.

It was easy to be gung-ho, easy to say to yourself, *By God, I'm going down there into Mexico and finding those girls and bringing them back! And I'll kick Colonel Alfonso Guerrero's ass while I'm doing it!* Figuring out a way to accomplish either of those noble objectives was another thing entirely.

To start with, he couldn't do it by himself. He could handle himself in a fight pretty well—the events in Little Tucson had proven that—but one man against a hundred or more highly trained commandos just wouldn't work. All he could accomplish by going it alone would be to get himself killed, probably before he ever got anywhere close to those missing girls.

He couldn't count on any help from the FBI. If Morgan knew what he was thinking about, she'd probably arrest him and claim it was for his own good. Other agencies of the federal government—the Border Patrol, the DEA, folks like that—wouldn't be able to provide any assistance, either. Some of the individual agents might sympathize with him, but their hands were tied by the reams of red tape, not to mention the attitude of the current administration that it was more important to curry favor with the scum of the world than it was to protect American citizens.

The only one who *might* be willing to give him a hand was Roy Rodgers, the Texas Ranger captain. And there was only so much Rodgers could do.

There were other people, though, who had a bigger stake in this than the law enforcement agencies that were involved. Those people were the families of the missing girls. They had the biggest stake of all—the lives of their loved ones.

That was where he needed to start, Tom decided—the families of the other girls.

He left the living room and walked out onto the front porch of the house. The morning newspaper was there, as he had hoped it might be. Nobody had thought to bring it into the house.

As he bent to pick it up, several reporters charged across

the lawn like bull elephants who had just spotted a guy in a peanut costume. Tom straightened, thought about darting back into the house, but decided against it. He didn't want to be rude—and besides, he might be able to turn this encounter with the minions of the press to his advantage.

"Sir?" one of the reporters called. "Sir, could we ask who you are? Are you a family member? Do you have any information about the kidnapping? Has there been a ransom demand?" The other two reporters were shouting variations on the same questions.

Tom smiled at them as he unrolled the rubber band from the newspaper. "My name is Tom Brannon," he said. "I'm Mrs. Simms's brother-in-law."

"Do you have any new information?"

"I'm sorry, I can't discuss the case," Tom said with a shake of his head. "You'll have to talk to Special Agent Sharon Morgan of the FBI." He opened the newspaper to the front page and saw the banner headline that read GANG INVADES TEXAS. Quickly, his eyes scanned down the page, hoping to see a list of the names of the kidnapped girls. There wasn't one, though, just a mention in the lead story that their identities were being withheld because of the paper's policy of not naming juveniles in its stories. Tom thought that was a good policy, but not this time. It meant he would have to work a little harder to get the ball rolling.

"What can you tell us about Mrs. Simms? How is she holding up?"

"Kelly's a strong woman," Tom said. "Of course she's upset and worried about her daughter, but at least she has her sister and me here to give her some support." He paused as if an idea had just occurred to him, then went on. "You know, it might be a real good thing if the families of all the missing girls could get together. That way they'd be able to help each other get through this."

The reporters scribbled furiously in their notebooks. They could get behind the idea of assembling the families of the victims. It would make a great story.

He started to turn toward the door. A reporter asked quickly, "Do you have any other comment, Mr. Brannon?"

Tom paused. "No, only that we're hoping and praying for Laura's safe return, and of course for all the other girls, too. I just hope somebody will do something to bring that about."

He ignored the other questions they called after him as he went inside. He hoped he had gotten his message across.

There was a good chance he would know before the morning was over.

Morgan got back there first. She stormed into the house, confronted Tom, and demanded angrily, "What the hell did you think you were doing when you talked to those reporters?"

"Just answering the media's questions honestly, Agent Morgan," Tom replied, his voice cool. "That's what a good citizen's supposed to do, isn't it?"

"A good citizen keeps his damn mouth shut," Morgan snapped. "Your comments were reported on TV less than an hour ago, and already we're getting calls from the families demanding a meeting with all of them at the same time."

Tom shrugged. "Sounds like a good idea to me. That way you only have to explain once why you're going to just let those girls rot down in Mexico."

He could tell that Morgan wanted to punch him. She couldn't do it, though, with both Bonnie and Kelly sitting there watching, along with the young Asian man who had shown up a short time earlier to relieve Pete Yarnell.

Before Morgan could do anything more than glare

murderously at Tom, Roy Rodgers arrived, walking into the room with his white Stetson in his hand. He didn't look happy, either.

"Mr. Brannon, didn't we have a talk about what you should and shouldn't say to the media?" the Ranger asked.

Tom turned toward him. "I didn't give out any details of the investigation. I just referred the reporters to Agent Morgan. I didn't say a word about how those poor girls are being abandoned down there below the border."

"We haven't abandoned them," Morgan said through clenched teeth. "We're working through proper channels on locating and rescuing them."

Tom folded his arms across his chest. "We both know proper channels don't work in Mexico."

"What about the idea of that comment about getting all the families together?" Rodgers asked.

From the sofa next to Kelly, Bonnie said, "I think that's a good idea. We're all scared. It'll help people to get through this if they're sharing it with someone else."

"Impossible," snapped Morgan. "It would just be a media circus. We don't need that."

Rodgers's anger seemed to ease somewhat. He rubbed his chin as he frowned in thought, and after a moment he said, "You know, that might not be such a bad thing, Agent Morgan. You've interviewed all the families separately, haven't you?"

"You know I have. That's why I haven't slept in over twenty-four hours."

"If you put all those folks together, maybe something would come out that hasn't so far . . . like a reason the girls were kidnapped in the first place."

"We know why they were kidnapped. Ransom—"

"Wouldn't amount to a hill of beans where the Night Wolves are concerned. Mr. Brannon and I talked about this yesterday. It seems to us that there may be something else behind the whole thing."

The fact that the Ranger seemed to be taking Tom's side in the argument didn't endear either of them to Morgan. She glowered at them for a long moment, but finally said, "This is your state. As long as you don't interfere with the Bureau, you can do whatever you want."

"Much obliged," Rodgers replied dryly. He turned to Kelly and went on. "Mrs. Simms, I'll see what I can do about arranging a get-together like Mr. Brannon talked about."

"Thank you, Ranger," Kelly said. "I . . . I think we should do anything that might help."

"Yes, ma'am." Rodgers looked at Tom. "Let's go talk in the kitchen, Mr. Brannon."

Tom followed the Ranger into the kitchen while Morgan left the house after curtly instructing the FBI technician to remain at his post in case the kidnappers called. By this time, Tom was convinced that was a forlorn hope, and he suspected that Morgan was, too. She wasn't going to do anything that went against government policy, though.

Maybe Rodgers wasn't quite that inflexible. He put his hat on and thumbed it to the back of his head, then leaned a hip against the kitchen counter. "Is that coffee I smell?" he asked.

"Yeah, I've been keeping it warm. We had some breakfast earlier, but it got ruined when Agent Morgan showed up and announced that the investigation was being turned over to the Mexican authorities."

"I sort of figured you'd heard about that. Otherwise, you wouldn't have come up with the idea of getting all the families together to agitate for the government to do something."

Tom got a cup and poured coffee for Rodgers, using

the action to keep his face turned away while a smile played over it. "Is that what you think I'm doing?" he asked as he handed the cup to the Ranger.

"At the very least. I don't know what else you might have in mind, Mr. Brannon, but I do know you make me a mite nervous."

"Why don't you call me Tom? Mr. Brannon was my father."

"Who was murdered by that gang out in Arizona," Rodgers said, not pulling any punches. "A gang you wound up practically annihilating."

"*They* attacked *us.*"

"Just like Los Lobos de la Noche attacked your family here by invading this country and kidnapping your niece." Rodgers took a sip of the hot coffee. "You know how much shit you could get into by doing something the federal government doesn't want you to do?"

"I'm not saying I plan to do anything . . . but if I get in trouble with the government, at least I'll still be alive." Tom's voice hardened. "We don't even know if those girls are alive, and if they are, how long they'll stay that way. We don't know anything, and the Feds want to abdicate their responsibility and turn everything over to people who won't do squat. How can we just abandon those girls like that?"

"Nobody wants to abandon them. There are issues. . . ."

"Political issues."

Rodgers shrugged. "Certain folks think it would look mighty bad to the rest of the world if we sent troops and planes and choppers across the border into Mexico."

"Even if it was to rescue American citizens who had been taken there by force?"

"The reason doesn't matter. The world already thinks we're a bunch of imperialist warmongers. Washington doesn't want to give them any more ammunition to use against us."

"You know what I think, Captain?" Tom asked softly. "I don't really give a shit what the rest of the world thinks of us. I want my niece back safe and sound, and the families of all those other girls want them back safe and sound, and right now, that's all any of us really care about."

For a long moment, Rodgers didn't say anything. Then, finally, he nodded and said slowly, "I know. And I don't blame you for feeling that way. That's why there's a man I think you ought to meet."

Fourteen

Laura's sleep was haunted by dreams. She saw Sister Katherine thrown backward by the bullets striking her body; she saw the way all the muscles in Rosa Delgado's body went limp as the nerve impulses ceased flowing from the destroyed brain. She saw these pictures painted in the dark red of blood, the thick black of night, the stark flashes of death from the muzzle of a gun. Even though she was asleep, she wept from the tragedy of the dreams as they played out, and in the morning when she woke, she felt the dried tears on her cheeks.

The knowledge that those were not just dreams, that those terrible things had really happened, crowded in on her brain and made her breath catch in her throat. If someone had forced her to be honest about it, she would have had to admit that she never particularly cared for Sister Katherine. The nun was strict, domineering, bossy, and had never really seemed to like the girls and boys who went to school at Saint Anne's. And Rosa Delgado was little more than a name and a face to Laura. She knew the other girl when she saw her in the hall, but they hardly ever spoke. In fact, once Laura thought about it, she realized that the last words she had spoken to Rosa before the frantic cry the night before had occurred the previous spring, during gym class, when Laura had asked her to throw back an errant basketball.

Despite that, Laura wept for them, and she hated the men who had killed them, and if some divine Providence had placed a machine gun in her hands at that moment and provided the opportunity, she would have blasted the living shit out of the bastards without a second's hesitation.

She sat up and rubbed her eyes with the heels of her hands as fresh tears threatened to well up. Although she couldn't have said why, she felt that it was important not to sit around and mope and cry. She didn't want her captors to see her like that.

Dawn light stole into the cell from the high window. The day before, the rays from the setting sun had entered that window, telling Laura the cell was located on the west side of the building—wherever the building was. That meant the morning light was reflected, not direct, and that softened it. When Laura, who seemed to be the only one awake, looked around at the faces of the other girls, she didn't see terror etched there, as it had been the previous day. She saw exhaustion. She saw wet streaks on their faces, too. She wasn't the only one who had been crying in her sleep.

Quietly, she got to her feet and went over to the bucket in the corner, glad that she could use it before the others were awake. When she was finished, she walked over to the door and leaned against it, grasping the iron bars. She looked directly across the corridor into the opposite cell. The window in it was red with the sunrise, but its occupants still slept. Laura knew all of them, too, but again, none of them could be considered close friends.

They were closer now. If they survived, they would share a bond of terror and danger and hope that would always link them, no matter how much physical distance lay between them. She suspected that people in prisoner-of-war camps and political prisons felt the same way. Maybe men in regular prisons did, too, although she thought that it might be different there. Criminals always had a certain isolation about them, an inability to connect properly with other people and the society around them. And despite their constant protestations of innocence, most of them were there because they really had done something bad, something that showed that in the end they didn't really give a damn about anybody except themselves.

She was thinking too much. She had a habit of doing that. But it helped to keep the fear at bay—the fear that pushed at her brain when she looked at the ruddy glow in the window across the way and knew it was entirely possible she would never see another sunrise.

When somebody tugged at her jeans, she shrieked and grabbed the bars hard, as if she wanted to try to climb the door.

"Geez, don't have a hissy fit," Shannon said from the floor, where she was still lying in her sleeping bag. "It's just me."

Laura's scream had disturbed the slumber of the other girls. They were starting to stir around as she said to Shannon, "Why did you grab me like that?"

"I just wanted to know if you can see Ricky anywhere."

"Is that all you can think about? Some guy?"

"I thought maybe he'd bring us some breakfast."

Shannon had a point there. Ricky had delivered their supper the night before. It wasn't unreasonable to think that he might bring breakfast this morning. Laura looked along the hallway as much as she could, though, and then shook her head as she looked down at Shannon.

"I don't see any of them."

Shannon sat up and ran her fingers through her red hair. "You think maybe they're all gone?"

"I doubt it. I'll bet there are guards around. They're just not here in the corridor because they know we can't get out of these cells."

The next few minutes proved Laura right. She heard a key rattle in the lock of the door between this cell block and the rest of the building, and a moment later it swung open. By now all the girls were awake, and Shannon had stood up to join Laura at the door.

A couple of men carrying rifles came through the door first, followed by Ricardo, or Ricky as Shannon called him. He pushed a cart that had platters of sandwiches and six-packs of water on it. "Breakfast, ladies," he said with an attempt to make his voice cheerful, at least.

Laura just looked at him emotionlessly, unwilling to give him the satisfaction of responding to his phony cheerfulness. Shannon smiled brightly, though, and said, "Hello, Ricky. I knew you wouldn't forget about us."

"Small chance of that," he said.

"Does that mean you've been thinking about me?"

Laura gritted her teeth and tried not to roll her eyes at the flirtatious tone of Shannon's voice.

"Step back, please," Ricardo said. "Away from the door."

The two men with him hefted their rifles to emphasize the request that was really a command.

Laura and Shannon moved back, and the other girls in the cell, who were still lying on their sleeping bags, scooted against the wall. Ricardo unlocked the door and opened it enough to put a plate of sandwiches and a six-pack of water in plastic bottles on the floor. Then he hurriedly closed the door and relocked it, almost like he was afraid the occupants of the cell were ravenous beasts who might leap at him.

And of course, where Shannon was concerned, he might actually have something to worry about. . . .

Hunger and thirst pushed that thought out of Laura's brain. As the girls in the other cells were given their breakfast, Laura and her companions fell on the peanut butter and jelly sandwiches. This diet was going to get awfully old, but at least it would keep them alive.

Shannon ripped the plastic rings that held the bottles together off the six-pack of water and tossed them aside. The girls had thrown the empty bottles from the night before into a corner, along with the plastic rings that had been on them. As Laura sat down to eat her sandwich and sip at her bottle of water, she looked at the rings Shannon had just discarded. After a moment, with a faint frown creasing her forehead, she picked them up and studied them. When she finished eating, she idly twisted the rings, which gave her a strip of plastic about seven inches long. She held it by each end and pulled hard.

Then she untwisted the rings, smoothed them out, folded them into a small bundle, and slipped them into the pocket of her jeans. A few minutes later, she snagged the other set of plastic rings from the corner and squirreled it away, too.

As Ricardo pushed the empty cart past the cell after passing out breakfast to all the other girls, Shannon jumped to her feet and called, "Ricky! Ricky, wait a minute."

Ricardo paused and cast a quick glance at the two men with him. "I cannot stop and talk to you," he said to Shannon. "It is not allowed."

"Sure you can," she said. "It won't hurt, just for a minute, will it?" She pouted. "Pretty please."

Laura couldn't stop the eye roll this time. The urge was just too strong.

"There is nothing I can do for you," Ricardo said in a low,

intense voice. "Make it easier on both of us, Señorita, and do not even ask."

"I'm not asking you to let us go or anything. I just want a little company."

Ricardo shook his head and said curtly, "Sorry." He turned away from the cell, opened the door and pushed the cart out.

Shannon stared after him, a look of disbelief on her face.

"What's the matter, Shannon?" Carmen asked. "Not used to having a boy say no to you?"

Shannon turned away from the bars and glared at Carmen. "That's right, boys don't usually run away from me like they do from you, you Mexican dyke."

Carmen scrambled to her feet. "Just because I haven't put out for half the guys in school doesn't mean I'm a lesbian."

"Yeah, well, I'm just sayin'. . . . You soccer girls hang around with each other all the time, and God knows what goes on in the locker room. . . . I bet it gets all slick and steamy in there sometimes, doesn't it, Carmen?"

With a growled curse, Carmen launched herself at Shannon, knocking the redhead back against the cell door. Carmen tried to get her hands around Shannon's throat as Shannon screamed and fought her off.

Laura and Stacy grabbed Carmen at the same time and pulled her back. Shannon took advantage of the opportunity to reach out and rake her fingernails down Carmen's face. Carmen howled in pain.

While Stacy hung onto Carmen, Laura got between them. She drove an elbow into Shannon's midsection. "Stop it, you two!" she said. "Have you gone crazy?"

"I'm not a lesbian!" Carmen cried. "And I'm not a Mexican! I was born in Laredo. I'm as much an American as she is!"

"What's the matter, *chica*?" Shannon asked with a sneer. "Don't you think brown is beautiful anymore?"

Laura turned her head to glare at Shannon. "Shut up! This isn't helping anything."

From where she sat on the floor, Billie Sue said in a small, pathetic voice, "Nothing's going to help us. We're doomed." She and her sister Aubrey put their arms around each other and started crying.

"You don't know that," Laura said as she stayed between Carmen and Shannon. "Giving up and fighting among ourselves isn't going to make things any better, though. People are bound to be looking for us. Somewhere out there, there's someone who's going to help us."

"You really believe that, Laura?" Shannon asked bleakly.

"Yeah. Yeah, I do."

"Well, you just cling to that hope, then, and you keep on clinging to it while fifty of those bastards take turns raping you, and when they're done you just tell yourself that everything's going to be all right . . . right up until the time when they cut your throat and dump your body in an unmarked grave." Shannon's façade of control had slipped, and all her terror had come out in the shakily voiced words. "You just keep up the act, okay, and see what it gets you in the end."

And with that she slumped to the floor, put her hands over her face, and joined Billie Sue and Aubrey in sobbing pathetically.

Laura looked at Carmen and Stacy. They weren't crying, but they looked like they wanted to. Laura wanted to, as well. But she wouldn't let that happen. She hoped because she had to. She believed because she had to. If she gave up, she would collapse and wouldn't be any good to anybody, most of all to herself.

It was the twenty-first century, long past the time of heroes, if such an era had ever really existed in the first place. Now it was an age of pragmatism, of the bottom line on one hand, and political correctness on the other. No longer was there a place for a knight in shining armor or a cowboy who rode to the rescue. To place any faith in the idea that someone would actually do the right thing and display any real courage and selflessness—well, that was just setting yourself up for a fall.

But something deep inside Laura's soul refused to give up hope. Sooner or later, help would come.

And in the meantime, it was up to her and her companions to remain strong and do whatever they could to help themselves get out of this mess.

Because the day would come, she told herself—a day of reckoning. . . .

Fifteen

Tom didn't know what the Texas Ranger had in mind, but he was willing to play along with Rodgers and find out. He caught a moment alone with Bonnie and told her that he was going somewhere with Rodgers for a little while.

"We shouldn't be gone long," he said, "and you can call the cell phone if you need to get hold of me."

Bonnie frowned. "But where are you going?"

"I'm not sure. I think it may have something to do with getting all the victims' families together."

"And holding that Agent Morgan's feet to the fire," Bonnie said. "I like that idea."

"Figuratively speaking, you mean."

Bonnie just raised her eyebrows and cocked her head a little to one side without saying anything.

Tom gave her a quick hug and a kiss and then left the house with Rodgers. The Ranger captain's Ford Tahoe was parked in the driveway. "We'll go in my truck," he said.

"Who's this fella you're taking me to meet?" Tom asked as they drove away from Kelly's house. The few reporters still on hand watched them go.

"You'll see when we get there. He probably knows as

much or more about Los Lobos de la Noche than any-body else on this side of the border, though."

That was good enough for Tom. He was well aware of how important it was to know your enemy.

Rodgers headed out on the northeast side of Laredo, toward the lake and the state park that had been the desti-nation of the kidnapped girls. When Tom realized that, he asked, "Are we going to look at where it happened?"

Rodgers shook his head. "Nope, that wouldn't do any good. Forensics teams from both the Rangers and the FBI have been all over the crime scene and gathered all the evidence already. The place we're going just happens to be in sort of the same direction." Rodgers looked over at Tom. "Unless you'd just like to see the place . . ."

Tom shook his head. "I don't need to see it to know what happened there."

"That's sort of what I figured."

After a few moments, Tom asked, "Did the forensics teams turn up anything that hasn't made the news, any-thing that might give us an idea where exactly the girls have been taken?"

"If that's the case, then nobody's told me. They made casts of the tread patterns from the tires on the kidnappers' trucks and were able to tell us that they were standard pickup tires. There were no bits of mud that had to come from a certain place or a leaf from an exotic plant that only grows in one spot in the world. Anyway, we know who the kidnappers are; we just don't know where the bastards are."

Tom frowned in thought. "All we've got to go by is that e-mail claiming to be from the Night Wolves. What if it's a fake, an attempt to throw us off the right trail?"

"That's a possibility. And it's one of the things I want to ask about when we talk to the fella we're going to see."

"You say he's some sort of expert on the Night Wolves?"

"You could say that," Rodgers replied with a grim edge in his normally cheerful voice.

A few minutes later, Rodgers pulled into a concrete driveway that circled in front of a low, sprawling building surrounded by lawns and flower beds. The lawns were strikingly green, evidence of a lot of fertilizing and especially a lot of watering in this semiarid climate. Fat palm trees flanked the glass doors of the entrance.

Tom looked for a sign indicating what this place was, but didn't see one. "Looks like a hospital," he commented.

"It is," Rodgers said as he brought the Tahoe to a stop in the parking lot. "A private hospital."

The air was growing hot already, despite the fact that it was only mid-morning. Cool air washed over the two men as the glass doors slid aside automatically and they walked into the building. The air had a carefully neutral scent, but Tom still smelled disinfectant. That and the hushed atmosphere were enough to tell him that he was in a hospital.

Rodgers took off his hat and led the way through the lobby, past a receptionist's desk and several offices. The pretty receptionist smiled at Rodgers and lifted a hand in greeting, indicating that she knew the Ranger. Rodgers returned the smile and then motioned with the hand holding the Stetson for Tom to follow him down a hallway that ran toward the rear of the building.

They came to a nurses' station, and Rodgers paused to ask the middle-aged woman behind the counter, "Is he in his room or outside this morning, Doris?"

She pointed to another set of glass doors leading out to what appeared to be a small garden of some sort. "Outside."

"How's he doing?"

She shrugged. "About the same as usual, Roy."

He nodded and walked on. The doors slid aside like

the ones in the front had, and Rodgers and Tom stepped outside.

A roof of green plastic extended out from the building and overhung the garden. It allowed some sunlight through but still provided shade. The plants in the garden were mostly various kinds of cactus—prickly pear, cholla, barrel, organ pipe. They grew in beds filled with polished stones. It was a pretty place, in its own thorny, somewhat forbidding way.

A man in hospital pajamas and a lightweight robe sat by himself in a wheelchair beside one of the beds of cactus. He was turned at an angle so that Tom could see the left side of his face. He appeared to be in his thirties, ruggedly handsome, with brown hair.

"Hello, Brady," Rodgers called as he and Tom approached. Tom figured he didn't want to startle the man.

Tom was the one who was startled, though, when the man gripped the left-hand wheel of his chair and turned it so that the chair spun toward the visitors. That gave Tom a good look at the rest of his face, which was covered with puckered scar tissue. The right eye was milky and obviously blind. From the looks of the damage, fire had done this.

That wasn't the extent of the man's injuries. His right arm hung useless at his side, and the wrist that stuck out from the pajama sleeve was a lot thinner than the still-muscular left wrist, indicating that the right arm had been incapacitated for quite a while. Bulkiness under the legs of the pajamas told Tom that the man had heavy braces on both knees. Obviously, he had been through a lot.

"Roy," the man said as he nodded slowly at the Ranger. His left eye shifted toward Tom, squinting as if he couldn't quite make him out, and Tom realized that eye had been damaged by the fire, too, although not blinded. "Who's that with you?"

"Fella name of Tom Brannon. Tom, this is Brady Keller. Brady's an agent with the Drug Enforcement Agency."

"A retired agent, as you can see," Keller said with a not-surprising bitter inflection to his voice. "Full medical disability."

"I'm sorry, Mr. Keller," Tom said. "I wish we were meeting under better circumstances."

"You a Ranger, too, Brannon?"

"No, I'm strictly a civilian, down here in Texas from Arizona."

Rodgers said, "Tom's here because of a case, Brady."

"What sort of case?" Keller demanded. "Nobody's told me about anything big going on."

"Well, I guess your doctor and the other folks here at the hospital thought it might upset you unnecessarily, and since—"

Keller broke in. "And since I can't get up out of this damn chair and do anything about anything anyway, why tell me? Is that it? No point in telling the crip anything, since he's useless to start with!"

"Damn it, Brady, you know it's not like that! You and me have been friends for a long time. I've always played straight with you."

Keller glared up at the visitors, and with his scarred face, it was a fearsome sight. "Then tell me what's going on," he snapped.

"It's about Guerrero and the Night Wolves."

Keller's lips drew back from his teeth in a grimace, almost like an animal's snarl, Tom thought.

"What have they done now?"

"Kidnapped a whole busload of girls from that Catholic school, Saint Anne's, and taken them somewhere below the border."

Keller stared at the Ranger for a long moment and then finally said, "Son of a bitch."

"Yeah."

Keller shook his head. "You can kiss those girls good-bye, Roy. You'll never find them without the Mexicans' cooperation, and you know you won't get any help worth shit from them."

"Brady . . . one of the girls is Tom's niece."

"Oh." Keller sniffed. "Sorry to've been so blunt about it, Brannon."

"That's all right," Tom forced himself to say. "I want to know the truth about the situation, and Captain Rodgers says you know more about the Night Wolves than anybody else."

"I've gone up against them and lived to tell about it. I've even seen Guerrero in person. But it's pure dumb luck that I'm still alive. Guerrero and his men murdered everybody else, but spared me to deliver a warning for him. A warning not to mess with Los Lobos de la Noche."

"Let me get some chairs," Rodgers said. "We've got some talking to do."

There were several folding chairs against the wall next to the door into the hospital. Rodgers fetched a couple of them, and when he and Tom were sitting down next to the cactus bed with Brady Keller, Rodgers explained what had happened to the DEA agent on a dark night months earlier. Keller sat expressionless throughout the story.

When Rodgers was finished with the details, he said, "Once Brady was up and around again, he started studying everything he could about the Night Wolves. I gave him a hand when I got the chance."

"Did my legwork for me, you mean," Keller said, "since I obviously can't do my own anymore."

Tom leaned forward in his chair and clasped his hands

together between his knees. "Tell me about them," he said. "About Guerrero and his men. What are they capable of?"

Keller's one good eye looked straight at him. "Anything."

Tom took a deep breath and said, "I was afraid you'd say that."

"You know they're mercenaries," Keller said. Tom nodded. Keller went on. "They're pretty loyal to one of the cartels and most of their work is related to protecting the drug-smuggling routes. They've assassinated dozens, maybe hundreds, of law-enforcement and military personnel in Mexico. It's no wonder that the authorities down there have pretty much washed their hands of the whole deal. If they make any effort to crack down on Guerrero these days, it's a halfhearted one, and I wouldn't be surprised if he gets warnings well before any action that occurs. The Night Wolves have also staged commando raids of their own on the rivals of their employers. They've stolen drugs, blown up warehouses and convoys, and gone after the families of the rival cartels' leaders."

Tom nodded. "Captain Rodgers and I wondered if this kidnapping could have something to do with that."

"How so?"

Rodgers said, "What if one of the girls on the bus is related to one of Guerrero's enemies in Mexico?"

Without hesitation, Keller said, "I guess it's not impossible," he said, "but as far as I know, none of the other cartels' leaders have any close relatives on this side of the border. They keep their immediate families stashed away in heavily protected villas and compounds."

"But if Guerrero's gone after them down there," Tom argued, "maybe it would be smart to hide their loved ones over here for a change."

"Because Guerrero would be scared to come after them on American soil?" Keller gave a short bark of laughter.

"If that was the case, they sure figured wrong, didn't they? The bastard's invaded us twice and gotten away with it both times."

"Then why grab those girls?" Rodgers asked.

"Ransom?"

The Ranger shook his head. "That was everybody's first thought, especially when we got that e-mail from Guerrero claiming responsibility. But there haven't been any ransom demands."

Keller waved his left hand. "Forget about that e-mail. That's just Guerrero's arrogance coming out. He wanted everybody to know what *he* had done, what *he* had gotten away with. He's just about the most vainglorious son of a bitch you'll ever see." Keller paused. "And he's smart enough to know that you'd think about waiting for ransom demands, too. The natural caution that goes with that would slow down your response a little and increase his edge, and he was likely counting on that to help him get away."

"If he didn't take them for ransom," Tom said, "then why did he take them?"

"These are schoolgirls, you say?"

"That's right."

"How old?"

"Juniors and seniors," Rodgers said. "Sixteen, seventeen, and eighteen."

Keller's left shoulder rose and fell in a shrug. "There's your answer, then. He's going to auction them off."

"Prostitution," Tom said grimly.

"Yeah, some of 'em will probably go to brothels. But there are rich drug lords in Mexico who'd probably pay a high price for a white, sixteen-year-old virgin." Another bark of humorless laughter. "Don't let the PC police hear you say something like that, but it's true anyway. And it's not just the Mexicans. These days there are a lot of Asians and Arabs mixed up in the drug trade down there. How many girls are we talking about?"

"Forty," Rodgers said.

Keller snorted. "Hell, Guerrero can clear a couple million easy by auctioning them. Maybe twice that or even more, depending on how pretty the girls are."

Tom felt sick to his stomach. "Couldn't he get more by ransoming them back to their families?" He clung to that idea because it seemed to provide a little more hope that the girls wouldn't be mistreated.

"Collecting ransom is a lot more trouble, and you always take a chance that something could go wrong. Bigger payoff, but a bigger risk. Sell 'em to the highest bidder." Keller nodded. "That's what Guerrero will do." His attitude softened a little. "Sorry to have to tell you all this, Brannon, but you asked."

"Yeah." Tom took a deep breath. "And it tells me something else, too."

"What's that?" Rodgers asked.

Tom looked squarely at the Ranger. "That we don't have much time," he said.

Sixteen

Rodgers looked hard at Tom. "Just what is it you intend to do, Mr. Brannon?"

Tom didn't answer, just sat there with his mouth set in a grim, taut line. After a moment, Brady Keller said, "Give us a little time alone, would you, Roy?"

Rodgers's gaze turned toward the man in the wheelchair. "If you've got something to say to Mr. Brannon, you can say it in front of me."

"Just a minute," Keller said, "as a favor to an old crippled friend."

"Damn it, Brady, you're putting me in a mighty bad position here."

"You're the one who brought him," Keller said.

Rodgers sighed and pushed himself to his feet. He put his Stetson on. "Anything I can bring you next time I visit?" he asked.

"Not unless you come across a Target that sells knees, elbows, and eyes."

Rodgers grimaced and turned away. "I'll be in the lobby."

They waited until the automatic door had slid shut behind Rodgers, leaving the two of them alone in the cactus garden. Then Keller said, "Roy's a good Ranger. It's just hard for him to walk the line sometimes. He's too good a man. Wants to do the right thing, even when the system doesn't want him to."

"What's the right thing in this case?" Tom asked.

Keller grunted. "You know the only chance those girls have is if somebody goes down there and gets them. The Mexicans won't do it. Neither will the Rangers or anybody from our side without proper authorization, which they won't be able to get because everybody below the border is too damned scared of Guerrero to cross him. So that leaves it up to you."

"You think I can invade Mexico, find Guerrero and the Night Wolves, and get those girls away from them by myself?" Tom asked.

"You'll need help."

"The law won't give it to me. The federal government sure as hell won't."

Keller's lips pursed. "You're right about that. I was in the DEA long enough to know how all the red tape and PC bullshit have just about strangled our ability to get anything done. It'll have to be a civilian operation."

"An outlaw operation, you mean."

"You want those girls back or not?"

Tom forced down a surge of anger. Keller was a prickly son of a bitch, but he'd earned the right.

Since they were speaking bluntly, he asked, "Where can I get the help I need?"

"You look like you can take care of yourself," Keller said. "You a vet?"

"Couple of tours in Vietnam. And a while back, there was some trouble out where I lived. Got through that all right."

"If you go after Guerrero, it'll be more than just some trouble. It'll be a war."

Tom didn't mention that the clash with M-15 had turned out to be pretty much of a war, too. He said, "I can handle it."

"There are bound to be relatives of some of those other girls who feel the same way. Guys who were in 'Nam or Desert Storm or Iraq. Guys who know how to take names and kick ass, if they're just given the chance."

Tom nodded. "I was thinking along those same lines. That's the real reason I've been trying to force the hand of the FBI agent in charge of the case and get her to call a meeting of all the families. I want a chance to scout out some help."

The left side of Keller's mouth lifted. It took Tom a second to realize that he was smiling.

"We're on the same wavelength, Brannon. You go ahead with that. I might be able to find a few people who'd like to go along with you, too. I still have a lot of contacts in the law-enforcement community, and some of them are pretty fed up with the way things are going these days."

"They'd be risking their careers if they helped me," Tom pointed out.

"Some of 'em might find that an acceptable risk."

Tom turned his head to look toward the building. "What about Captain Rodgers?"

"Roy's too much of a straight arrow," Keller said with a shake of his head. "He knows what you're up to, and he wants to help. He'd love to go along on the mission. But he can't do any more than turn a blind eye to whatever we hatch up."

"Well, I appreciate him doing that much, anyway. It's good to have an ally in this."

Keller raised his left arm and held out his hand. "It's good for an old cripple to have something to do again. I'll get on the horn, start making some discreet calls."

Tom used his left hand to shake with Keller. "Thanks." He knew he was putting his trust in a man he had known for only an hour or so . . . but he had to trust somebody. He couldn't go it alone. And every instinct in his body told him that Keller was worthy of that trust.

"Give me your cell number," Keller said. "No need to write it down. I'll remember it."

Tom would bet that was true. There was still a sharp brain behind that scarred face, and now Keller had a worthy reason to use it.

After giving Keller the number, Tom walked back into the hospital and found Rodgers waiting for him in the lobby, as the Ranger had promised.

"You and Brady have a good visit?" Rodgers asked.

"Just fine," Tom replied.

"He seemed to perk up better today than I've seen him in quite a while," Rodgers said as the two men walked out through the hospital's front door. "I hope I did the right thing by bringing you to see him."

"You did," Tom said.

The TV uplink truck was gone when Tom and Rodgers reached Kelly's house, and only one newspaper reporter was still there. As they got out of the Tahoe, the man hurried over to them and asked, "Any comment on the meeting this afternoon, Mr. Brannon?"

"What meeting?" Tom asked, although he hoped he already knew the answer to that question.

"The one with all the families of the kidnapped girls."

That was what Tom had wanted to hear. He said, "I think it's a good idea. I'll be there."

"Where's this meeting going to be held?" Rodgers asked the reporter.

"City Hall. Two o'clock. You didn't know about it? Where have you and Mr. Brannon been this morning?"

"No comment," Rodgers said with a shake of his head. Tom followed the Ranger toward the front door of the house.

When they got inside, Bonnie met them, excitement in her eyes. "Have you heard?" she asked.

"We just did," Tom told her. "Where's Kelly?"

"Cleaning up and getting ready. She's excited that something will finally get done."

"She'd better not get her hopes up too much," Rodgers warned. "Who's going to be in charge of the meeting?"

"Agent Morgan, I suppose. She was the one who came by here and told us about it." Bonnie smiled. "She's not happy about it, either, but evidently the families put enough pressure on their senators and congressmen, not to mention talking to the media, that she had to give in."

Tom nodded in satisfaction. The seed he had planted earlier had sprouted quickly. It remained to be seen whether or not it would grow into anything, but at least this was a start. With his meeting with Brady Keller, the morning's developments were the most promising since he and Bonnie had arrived in Texas.

Rodgers said, "Agent Morgan will just tell you that we're already doing everything that can be done to locate and rescue the girls."

"She'll have to tell that to a lot of angry people. Other federal officials will be there, too, along with the sheriff and the Laredo chief of police. They can't *all* stonewall us."

Tom wouldn't have bet on that—but he had already given up any hope of the authorities accomplishing anything, so it didn't really matter. He just wanted a chance to talk to some of the men who would be at the meeting.

Rodgers gave Tom a nod and said, "I'll see you later."

"You'll be there? At the meeting?"

"Yes. The Rangers have a stake in this, too."

Tom knew that Rodgers would have liked nothing more than to take a whole company of Rangers and cross the border and raise hell until they got those girls back, but that wasn't going to happen. The conflict between wanting to do the right thing and feeling like he had to follow the rules was eating Rodgers up inside; his eyes had something of that look about them.

"We all have a stake in it," Tom said.

Rodgers just nodded and left.

"Where did the two of you go?" Bonnie asked.

"To see a man who knows a lot about Guerrero and the Night Wolves."

"And?"

"What he had to say wasn't good . . . but then, we already knew the situation was bad." Tom didn't say anything about the other matter he and Brady Keller had discussed. Soon enough, he would have to tell Bonnie what he was thinking about doing. She wouldn't like it. She loved her sister and niece, of course, and she wanted Laura returned home safe and sound. But if the only way to accomplish that was by Tom putting himself in danger, she would go ballistic, and might even try to stop him.

But it was too late for that. Laura and those other girls had only one chance. The American and Mexican governments were helpless—by choice, Tom thought angrily—and the only way to save those girls was for those who loved them to take action.

Like it or not, Tom Brannon was going back to war.

Seventeen

The Laredo City Council normally held its meetings in this room. Seldom, though, had the chamber ever been as packed as it was this afternoon, when it had been taken over by the FBI, the Webb County Sheriff's Department, the Laredo Police Department, the Border Patrol, and the Texas Rangers. Every chair in the spectators' area was occupied, as were all the seats on the platform where the city council members usually sat. It would have been even worse if the media had been allowed into the meeting, but Special Agent Morgan had closed the proceedings to the press, despite howls of protest from the assembled reporters. They crowded into the foyer outside the chamber, and local police had been forced to form a corridor through which the members of the kidnapped girls' families could reach the meeting room.

Not surprisingly, it was a grim-faced bunch who sat there. Features were drawn tight with strain, and most eyes were red-rimmed from crying. Fear and grief were evident in their expressions, but there was plenty of anger and frustration there, too.

That was good, Tom thought. Anger and frustration

would fuel the need to do something about an intolerable situation.

Morgan leaned forward to the microphone in front of her and said, "Let's call this meeting to order, please." As resentful silence settled over the crowd, she went on. "Most of you know me already. I'm Special Agent Sharon Morgan of the Federal Bureau of Investigation, and I'm in charge of the effort to locate the victims of the kidnapping that took place yesterday morning."

"It's been over twenty-four hours," shouted a man in the audience, "and you're not a damned bit closer to finding them."

On the platform, a tall man with close-cropped white hair and deeply tanned skin stood up and glared at the man who had shouted. Tom recognized him from newscasts as Sheriff Phil Garza.

"We're not going to let this meeting turn into a free-for-all," he warned in a hard voice. "Sheriff's deputies and police officers are standing by to enforce order if need be."

A man in the audience shot to his feet. "You want to gag us, that's all! But you can't shut us up! Our daughters are gone and you're not doing a thing to get them back!"

"That's not true," Morgan said as sheriff's deputies started forward from their positions along the wall of the meeting room toward the man. She waved them back and went on. "Sir, we're doing everything in our power to determine exactly what happened—"

This time it was one of the women in the audience who interrupted. "We know what happened! Our children have been taken away!"

Shouts of angry agreement rang out from the audience. Tom almost felt sorry for Morgan and the other officials up on the platform. Almost.

Morgan sat back, shook her head, and let the uproar

continue for a minute or two. Then, wearily, she motioned for the officers to step in.

All it would take was an impulsive swing or two at a cop's jaw to turn this into a full-fledged melee. Tom didn't want that. He stood up, ignoring Bonnie as she said, "Tom?" and strode forward to the podium with its attached microphone. During City Council meetings, audience members could come forward and use it to address the council. He ducked aside as one of the cops reached for him. When he reached the podium, he grabbed the microphone from its stand and bellowed into it, "Everyone be quiet!"

His voice boomed out. The microphone was not only turned on, but the PA system worked very well. A sudden silence fell as everyone in the room was shocked into being quiet. On all sides, eyes stared at Tom.

In a more normal tone of voice, he went on. "Starting a riot won't do any good. Let's just listen to what the officials have to say, and then we'll have our turn to speak."

A woman near him in the audience asked, "Have you lost your daughter, too, mister?"

"We don't know that any of the girls are lost," Tom said. "But my niece was one of those who were kidnapped. Her mother is sitting right there." He pointed out Kelly, who sat beside Bonnie, biting her lower lip, her face drained of color.

Morgan said, "Thank you, Mr. Brannon. I must admit, I didn't expect to hear the voice of reason from you."

"Most folks are full of surprises, Agent Morgan. Why don't you go ahead and say what you've got to say?"

"All right." Morgan squared up some notes in front of her. "As you know, the group called Los Lobos de la Noche have claimed responsibility for the kidnapping. At the moment, we believe this claim to be true and have no information leading us to think otherwise. The Texas Rangers and agents of the Border Patrol were able to follow the tracks left by the vehicles used by the kidnappers and established that they forded the Rio Grande and entered Mexico at a point known as the Old Spanish Crossing."

"Then the girls are definitely in Mexico?" a man asked.

"We believe that to be true, and again, we have no information indicating otherwise. Unfortunately, we've been unable to determine where they were taken once they crossed the border."

"Have you looked?"

"We have requested that the Mexican government—"

"No," said the man who had asked the question. "Have *you* looked? The FBI, or the Rangers, or anybody?"

"Neither federal agencies nor local authorities have any jurisdiction or right to operate in Mexican territory," Morgan said. "Mexico is a sovereign nation, and we have to respect its boundaries."

Another angry murmur began to rise from the audience.

"But we've contacted the authorities in Nuevo Laredo," Morgan hurried on, "and the State Department in Washington has been in touch with the government in Mexico City and requested aid in the strongest possible terms. Deputy Undersecretary of State John Holland is with us here today." She nodded toward the middle-aged black man with graying hair who sat next to her.

There was a microphone in front of Holland, too. He said into it, "Let me reinforce what Agent Morgan has just told you. The secretary of state has spoken with the Mexican ambassador in Washington, and I'm told that the president plans to speak with the president of Mexico later today. Everything possible is being done, but it's being done through proper channels that respect the rights of the nations involved."

A thickset man stood up. "My name is Joe Delgado," he said. "I grew up in Nuevo Laredo, and I've still got family over there. The Mexican cops aren't going to do anything. They can't keep a chief of police in Nuevo Laredo for more than a few months without him getting assassinated. The ones who aren't scared to death of the cartel and the Night Wolves are getting paid off by them!"

Another man stood up and said, "I'm Frank Ramirez. I don't know Mr. Delgado, but he's right. We can't count on the cops, and the military is just about as corrupt and powerless. Nuevo Laredo's run by the cartel now. The government don't mean nothin' over there."

"I think you're overstating the case, sir," Holland said. "However, that doesn't change the fact that the United States is bound by treaty and international law to respect the rights of other countries. What would you have us do, send tanks across the International Bridge to roll through downtown Nuevo Laredo?"

A tall, lean black man got to his feet and drawled, "I'd be glad to lead them. I was in the National Guard and rode a tank into Baghdad a few years back. Nuevo Laredo can't be any worse."

That brought shouts of approval from quite a few members of the audience. A Hispanic woman stood up and called, "I flew a helicopter gunship during Desert Storm. A few Blackhawks could take care of Guerrero and his Night Wolves!"

Morgan said into her microphone, "Please! Please, ladies and gentlemen, this isn't getting us anywhere. You know as well as I do that the United States is not going to launch an armed invasion of Mexico. It's unthinkable! The repercussions of such an international incident would have an effect on the entire world."

"You mean France and Germany and England might not be pleased with us?" the black former tank commander asked. "My response to that is—screw 'em."

That laconic comment brought cheers and applause from the desperate people in the audience.

The officials on the platform exchanged glances. Clearly, they knew that they were about to lose control of the meeting again. Morgan said into her microphone, "We've explained the situation as best we can. Rest assured that everyone involved will do everything in their power to return your loved ones to you as soon as possible. In the meantime, please return to your homes, and we'll be in touch immediately if there's any new information—"

The muttering turned into angry shouts again, but this time Morgan didn't threaten the crowd with the cops who were on hand. She and the other officials on the platform just got up and left hurriedly through a door in the front of the room.

Tom returned the microphone he was holding to its stand on the podium. He had a place to start now. As everyone in the audience stood up and began to mill around, talking angrily among themselves, he made his way toward the tall black man.

By the time Tom reached him, the man was comforting an attractive woman who was probably his wife. She tried to wipe away tears as he hugged her.

Tom hung back for a moment until the man noticed him. Then he stuck his hand out and introduced himself. "Tom Brannon."

The man kept his left arm around his wife's shoulders, but extended his right hand to clasp Tom's hand in a firm grip. "Wayne Van Sant," he said. "You said some good things."

Tom smiled. "Not as good as you."

Van Sant said, "I'm not in the habit of being so crude. I just get so frustrated with the way the government of the greatest nation on earth runs scared so much of the time."

"Wayne," the woman at his side said, "this isn't about the government. It's about Michelle . . . and the rest of those poor girls."

Tom said, "That's right, ma'am." His eyes met Van Sant's again. "If I could have a word with you in private, Mr. Van Sant . . ."

Frowning in consternation, Van Sant said, "Sure, I suppose." He added to his wife, "I'll be right back."

Tom drew him aside, into a corner of the meeting room, and said bluntly, "You know the government's given up, don't you?"

Van Sant's lean face tightened and twisted with emotion. "*I* haven't given up. I'll never give up hope."

"I plan to do more than hope. I'm going after those girls."

Van Sant's eyes widened with shock. "What are you talking about, Mr. Brannon?"

"Call me Tom. I've been in touch with a retired DEA agent who's the closest thing to an expert on the Night Wolves that we've got. He's convinced that they're not holding the girls for ransom. They plan to auction them off."

"My God!" Van Sant said through clenched teeth.

"The only way to save them in time is to put together a group to go into Mexico, find them, and bring them out again. That'll take men with experience, men who can fight."

Understanding began to dawn in Van Sant's tortured eyes. "I was in the National Guard for twelve years. Did eighteen months in Iraq."

"Yeah, I got the feeling you'd be interested in the idea," Tom said. "You probably know some of the parents of the other girls, since they all went to the same school. Can you think of some more guys who might be willing to take a chance like that?"

"Probably every man in this room would charge into hell

to save one of his children. But some of them are a lot more qualified for something like that than the others." Van Sant nodded slowly. "Yeah, I can think of some guys, all right."

"Go talk to them," Tom said. "Keep it quiet, though. We have to spread the word but still keep the FBI and the other authorities from finding out."

"Because they'd shut us down if they knew about it," Van Sant guessed. Tom nodded, glad that Van Sant was already talking about "us." His instinct about the man had obviously been right.

With curt nods to each other, Tom and Van Sant moved apart, each of them heading back into the crowd of angry, frightened relatives. Tom spotted the man who had introduced himself as Joe Delgado. He was talking to Frank Ramirez. The two men seemed to have gotten acquainted with each other already. When Tom stepped up to them, they stopped talking and turned to look at him.

"You want something, man?" Ramirez asked.

"Yes," Tom said. "I want to go get those girls back. I think with enough of the right kind of help, I can do it, too."

Both of the men stared at him for a long moment before Delgado said, "Keep talkin'."

Tom talked and they listened, and by the time he was finished, tight little smiles had appeared on the faces of both men. They nodded, split up, and spread out through the crowd.

It was a good beginning, Tom thought . . . a good beginning that might mean salvation for those kidnapped girls.

But not, he feared, without some blood along the way . . .

Eighteen

Colonel Alfonso Guerrero leaned back in the heavily upholstered swivel chair behind his desk and snapped the
silver lighter in his hand. He held the flame to the tip of the
long black cigar clenched between his teeth. If he'd had a
beard, he would have looked a little like Fidel Castro, he
thought. He felt some admiration for Castro and for the
way the man had been able to change the destiny of an
entire nation with nothing but a band of ragtag guerrillas
from the hills. That admiration was outweighed, though,
by the disdain Guerrero felt for Communists in general. A
real man was born to gather wealth and power unto himself, not to share it with those less deserving.

Across the desk, Major Eli Cortez smiled and said,
"You appear to be thinking deep thoughts, Alfonso." Since
they were alone in the big, luxurious room, there was no
need for ranks. They had been amigos for many years.

Guerrero took the cigar out of his mouth and waved
away the comment. "Just idle musings," he said. "Have
the men you sent messages to responded yet?"

"Some of them," Cortez said. "Of those who run houses,
Lopez, Almanzar, Escobar, and Gallegos seemed to be the

most interested. And of course there were responses from Yusuf Bin Hamid and Pedro Laurenco."

"Of course," Guerrero said with a faint grimace of distaste. "Damned perverts."

"Yes, but perverts with a great deal of money who are willing to pay quite well for their perverse pleasures." Cortez paused. "And then there is Willingham."

Guerrero raised his eyebrows. "Ah, yes. Willingham. The Englishman."

"He wishes proof before he leaves his villa in Acapulco. He says he will not make the trip to a fly-infested hellhole such as Nuevo Laredo unless the merchandise is of the absolute highest quality."

Guerrero felt a surge of anger at Willingham's arrogance. He brought it under control. The Englishman had almost inconceivable amounts of money, and he was willing to spend it for what he wanted.

"Set up a computer connection with Señor Willingham," Guerrero ordered. "We will show him what he could get for his money."

Cortez nodded in understanding. "Any particular girl?"

"Use your own judgment," Guerrero said. "Young and pretty and innocent, at least in appearance. That is all that matters."

"I will attend to it." Again Cortez paused, and when he spoke again, it was in a careful tone. "Is Angelina any less upset than she was last night?"

Guerrero's face hardened as he shook his head. "Unfortunately, no. She stays in her room and refuses to see me. She is angry with me. What can I do?"

Cortez sighed sympathetically. "It is very hard to have an ungrateful child. All you wish to do is to give her everything she desires, and yet she turns her back on you."

Impatiently, Guerrero sat forward and stubbed out the

cigar in a heavy glass ashtray. "She will come to understand that what I have done, I have done for her own
good. I can afford to wait for her to see the truth." He
leaned back and forced a smile. "After all, I am a rich,
powerful man. I have all the time in the world."

There was nothing to do in the cell but sit and worry
and argue over inconsequential matters. As the day went
on, the heat grew worse even though the thick adobe walls
kept it out to some extent. But the air was warm anyway,
and drowsiness stole over all the girls.

Lunch broke the monotony to a certain extent. Once
again, the meal consisted of peanut butter and jelly sandwiches and bottled water. When Shannon was finished
with hers, she sighed and said, "God, I'd *kill* for a frappa-
cino right now!"

"You think you've got it bad," Aubrey said. "I haven't
had a cigarette in, like, forever."

Billie Sue chimed in. "Yeah, I could really use a smoke."

"I wish I had a Coke," Carmen said. "A big Coke with
a lot of crushed ice in it."

"And a hamburger," Stacy added. "A nice, thick, juicy
hamburger."

"I think eating meat is icky," Billie Sue said. "How can
you eat something that once had a face?"

"How can you smoke a bunch of dried-up weeds and
deadly chemicals?" Stacy shot back.

"I don't smoke cigarettes," Shannon said. "Not tobacco
ones, anyway."

Laura closed her eyes as she leaned against the adobe,
trying to shut out their inane chatter. She wondered how
long they would be locked up like this, not seeing anyone
except each other and the occasional guard.

On the other hand, as long as they were stuck in this cell, something bad was less likely to happen. She was sure that sooner or later things were bound to get worse.

Later in the afternoon, that hunch was proven right.

Laura had dozed off with her head back against the wall. The sound of heavy footsteps in the corridor woke her and made her jerk upright. She saw several men standing just outside the cell. One of them was Ricardo, and another was the older man with the grizzled mustache who had warned them to cooperate after Rosa Delgado's death the night before. He studied the girls in the cell intently. All of them looked at the floor most of the time, even Shannon, glancing up only occasionally, afraid to meet the man's eyes squarely.

"That one," he said after a moment. "Bring her."

Laura couldn't help but look up when he said that. With a shock like a physical blow that took her breath away, she saw that he was pointing directly at her.

"Are you sure, Major?" Ricardo asked nervously.

The older man glared at him. "Of course I am sure! Do not question my orders, Benitez."

"I beg your pardon, Major," Ricardo said quickly. "Of course I am not questioning you." He slung his rifle over his shoulder, took a big heavy key from his pocket, and approached the cell door. He unlocked it and swung it open.

Even in her terror, Laura made a mental note of the pocket in which Ricardo kept the key. Knowledge like that might come in handy in the future.

Ricardo stepped into the cell while the other guards in the corridor leveled their rifles. The major drew a pistol from a holster on his belt and held it at his side, ready for use. As Ricardo came toward Laura, the other girls shied away from him, even Shannon. The redhead looked as pale and scared as the others, her usual bravado gone.

Laura cringed back against the wall as Ricardo came to a stop in front of her. "Get up," he said.

"Wh-what are you going to do to me?" she asked.

"Get up and go with Major Cortez." His voice was hard and inflexible, but as Laura stared up at him, she thought she saw something wavering in his eyes. He didn't like what he was being forced to do, but he had to follow orders.

"I . . . I don't want to go."

Ricardo bent over her and grabbed her arm, jerking roughly on it. "You must. Now get up!"

Suddenly, Shannon exploded across the cell. "Leave her alone!" she cried as she leaped at Ricardo. She landed on his back and wrapped her arms around his neck, squeezing tightly. "I thought you were nice, you . . . you monster!"

Ricardo came upright as he struggled with Shannon. Billie Sue and Aubrey began to scream. Carmen lunged, grabbed Ricardo's left leg, and heaved. Already off balance from having Shannon on his back, he fell, going over backward.

The rifle slipped off his shoulder and clattered on the concrete floor of the cell.

It slid to a stop right in front of Billie Sue. She stopped screaming and reached out for it.

The huge, deafening boom that came from Major Cortez's pistol shocked everyone into motionless silence. The bullet struck Billie Sue in the chest just as her fingers touched the stock of the rifle. The impact of the heavy slug threw her back hard against the wall. Her head bounced off the adobe and then sagged forward. She sat there like that, unmoving, as a crimson stain spread rapidly on the front of her shirt.

Beside her, Aubrey's screams got even louder and shriller. Cortez stepped into the cell and slammed his pistol against her head. She fell over, landing across her twin sister's legs. Blood dripped from the cut on her forehead where Cortez had hit her. She was out cold.

"Benitez!"

As Cortez barked his name, Ricardo scrambled to his feet. The sudden outbreak had caused Shannon and Carmen to let go of him. He snatched up his rifle and then grabbed Laura's arm with his other hand. He hauled her to her feet so roughly that her head rocked back and forth, and practically threw her out the cell door. Stumbling, Laura caught herself before she fell.

"You are a careless fool, Benitez," Cortez growled as he followed them out of the cell. "Colonel Guerrero will hear about this."

"I . . . I am sorry, Major," Ricardo said. He looked almost as shaken by what had happened as the girls were. But he took hold of Laura's arm again with a grip like steel and propelled her toward the door into the rest of the building. She caught one last glimpse of the horrible scene in the cell, but then it was cut off from her view.

She heard Major Cortez's curt order to the other guards, though.

"Get rid of the dead one."

Just like that, in one unbelievably horrific second, Billie Sue was gone, her young life ended in a single burst of violence. A few minutes earlier, she had been asking how anyone could eat something that once had a face—and now she was dead. That was further proof, as if any of the girls needed it, of just how fragile existence really was. . . .

"You should have cooperated," Ricardo grated in Laura's ear as she hustled her along a hallway. "You should have done as you were told."

He sounded like he wanted to cry.

"I . . . I'm sorry," Laura gasped. "I was just scared."

She was still scared. Terrified, in fact. She barely noticed the fine tile floor in the hallway and the paintings in their antique frames and the ornate tapestries that hung on the walls. She was hardly aware of the gold and silver candle holders or the crystal chandeliers. The old mission, once the humble abode of priests, now reeked of wealth and opulence, but none of that mattered to Laura. Her heart pounded so hard in her chest, it felt like it was going to explode, and her senses were reeling.

She glanced over her shoulder again, and saw that Major Cortez was striding along the hallway behind them. The major still had his pistol in his hand and looked angry. The expression on his face was enough to convince Laura that if she didn't cooperate, he would shoot her, too.

The corridor twisted and turned until Laura had no idea where she was and knew that she would never be able to find her way back to the cell where the others were being held. Although she had wanted desperately to get out of that confining little chamber, this wasn't the way. Now she wished she was back there with Shannon and Carmen and Stacy and Aubrey and—

A sob welled up in her throat as she couldn't finish that thought. When she got back to the cell—*if* she ever got back—Billie Sue wouldn't be there.

Billie Sue would be in a shallow, unmarked grave somewhere, just like poor Rosa Delgado.

Major Cortez caught up to them and stalked past. He paused at a pair of double doors and opened one of them. "In here," he said, and Ricardo marched Laura through the door into a large room that was even more opulent than the corridor. On the other side of the room was a massive desk, and behind the desk sat a man Laura recognized, even though she had seen him only briefly, under hectic, terrifying circumstances.

He was the man who claimed to be Angelina Salinas's father.

The man who had murdered Sister Katherine without blinking an eye.

And now he was smiling at her and saying, "Come in. Come in, little one, and do not be afraid. No one will hurt you."

Yeah, right. Tell that to Sister Katherine and to Rosa Delgado.

And to Billie Sue.

Nineteen

Guerrero studied the girl as Ricardo Benitez pushed her across the room toward the desk. She didn't actually fight him, but she was reluctant to approach. Her eyes were wide with horror and fear and something else. . . . Anger, that was it. This one had at least a little spirit left in her. She would fight, if given the slightest opportunity.

She had pale blond hair pulled behind her head in a ponytail. She wore a blue, short-sleeved T-shirt, jeans, and tennis shoes. Unlike many teenage girls, she was not skinny, but she was not fat, either. She had some meat on her bones without being overweight.

Benitez brought her all the way to the desk. When he let her go, Guerrero waved him back. Benitez withdrew a few steps and then waited there, behind the girl and to her left. Cortez was behind her and to her right. She couldn't get away, and the slump of her shoulders seemed to indicate that she realized that. Her eyes moved constantly as her gaze darted around the room, taking in the luxurious furnishings and lingering on the state-of-the-art computer setup. As she noticed the camera, her eyes narrowed in suspicion.

Smiling in as friendly a manner as he could manage, Guerrero asked, "What is your name?"

"Laura," she said. "Laura Simms."

"Hello, Laura. I am Colonel Guerrero."

She didn't say anything. He didn't hold it against her that she was not glad to meet him. The only one of the girls whose opinion mattered to him was Angelina, and she was in the comfortable bedroom he had had prepared for her, under guard.

"How old are you?"

"Seventeen."

She had a good voice, somewhat strained by the situation in which she found herself, of course, but still firm and determined.

"A senior at Saint Anne's?"

"I would have been," she said, "as soon as school started."

"It is unfortunate that you will be forced to miss the opening of school. My apologies for that, and for any other inconvenience you and your companions have suffered."

She didn't buy the apology for a second, he saw.

"Laura, some terrible things have happened since you and the others have been with us," he went on, "but they do not have to continue. If you and your friends will simply cooperate and do as you are told, none of you will be harmed."

"I don't believe you," she said boldly. "What about Rosa and Billie Sue?"

Guerrero frowned. "Billie Sue?"

"I was forced to shoot one of the others," Cortez said harshly. "She tried to get a guard's rifle."

Guerrero's breath hissed between his teeth. Every one of the girls who died meant that much less money he and the Night Wolves would make. And Billie Sue sounded like the name of a white girl. Guerrero expected that they would fetch the highest prices. Such carelessness would not go unpunished.

"We will discuss that later," he said coldly to Cortez. "Now we must deal with other matters." He turned his attention back to Laura Simms. "Señorita, I must now ask you to remove your clothes."

Her eyes widened even more with fear. "Wh-what?"

"You heard me." His tone was brisk now, all business, allowing for no nonsense. "Remove your clothes. Strip."

She shook her head. "I . . . I won't."

"If you refuse," he said matter-of-factly, "I will simply order Benitez there to remove them for you."

She turned her head and looked at the young man. His face was set in stony lines. He could not refuse an order from Colonel Guerrero, and everyone in the room knew it.

With trembling hands, Laura reached for the hem of her T-shirt. She pulled it up and over her shoulders, peeling it over her head and arms. She stood with the shirt in her hands for a second, as if she didn't know what to do with it, and then dropped it on the floor at her feet.

She wore a plain white bra, the sort that was greatly appealing to some men, although Guerrero himself was for the most part immune to the charms of this girl. She was old enough to have a woman's body, but her mind and her heart were still young and innocent. She put a hand on the desk to steady herself as she pulled off first one shoe and then the other. She wore short, ankle-length white socks underneath them.

Guerrero waited patiently. Laura unzipped her jeans and unfastened the button holding the waist closed. She pushed them down over her hips, revealing white cotton panties. The jeans fell around her ankles. She stepped out of them.

She paused as if hoping that he would tell her that was enough. When Guerrero just looked calmly and intently at her and didn't say anything, after a moment she sighed and reached behind her to unfasten the bra's clasp. It came loose. She shrugged the straps down from her shoulders and with a certain touch of defiance let the undergarment fall away from her breasts. Then she hooked her thumbs in her panties, pushed them down, and stepped out of them. That left her clad only in her socks. Guerrero said nothing about them.

He studied her with an experienced eye. Her breasts were fairly large and had the firmness of youth. The nipples were pale pink. They grew puckered and hard under Guerrero's gaze, not from arousal but rather from fear and probably the coolness in the air. This part of the old mission was air-conditioned, of course. Guerrero dropped his eyes over her belly to the swell of her hips, the fine lines of her thighs and calves, and the triangle of fair hair that covered her sex. His gaze was not the caressing one of a lover, but rather the calculated study of a man assessing potential value.

In the case of Laura Simms, that value was quite high, Guerrero decided. It might go even higher.

"Make your hair loose," he told her.

Hesitating a second, more confused than defiant, she finally reached behind her head, pulled the elastic holder from her ponytail, and let her hair fall around her shoulders and a short distance down her back.

"Shake your head," Guerrero ordered.

Laura shook her head, making the blond hair fall more naturally.

"Now, tell me, Laura," Guerrero said as he clasped his hands together on the desk in front of him, "have you ever been with a man?"

She shook her head again, this time in reply to his

question. Her face flamed with embarrassment at being forced to stand naked in front of these men and answer such a humiliating query.

"You have never had intercourse? You swear this?"

"Y-yes, sir," she answered in a tiny voice. "I've never . . . done it."

"Excellent. Now, if you would, please turn toward that camera . . . there, the one attached to the computer."

Laura took a deep breath as if steeling herself for what was to come and turned toward the camera. Guerrero swiveled his chair and rolled it over to the workstation, where he tapped a key and said, "Señor Willingham, are you there?"

A voice came back from the computer's speakers. "Yes, Colonel, I am."

Guerrero smiled and said, "Prepare yourself for a vision of heaven, my old friend."

He clicked the mouse and turned the camera on.

"Oh, my word," Willingham said. "Is that beautiful angel there in your office right now, Colonel?"

"Indeed she is, *mi amigo.*"

"I . . . I've never seen anything quite so lovely." Willingham's voice trembled slightly, as if in the grip of powerful emotions. "Have her turn around. I want to see her ass."

"Please, Señorita," Guerrero said to Laura. "You heard my friend."

Slowly, she turned and stopped so that her back was to the camera.

"Oh, my," Willingham said. "Oh, my."

"Should she turn around again?" Guerrero asked.

"That would be fine."

Guerrero said, "Face the camera again, Señorita."

As Laura turned, Willingham asked, "What's her name?"

"What name do you like, Señor? If you purchase her, you can call her anything that pleases you."

"I think . . . I think I'll call her . . . Roberta. Yes. Roberta. I've always liked that name."

Guerrero happened to know that Roberta was the name of Willingham's late mother. He made it a habit to find out as much as he could about the backgrounds of his customers, just in case he ever needed to make use of such information. In this case, it was totally irrelevant. Guerrero had no interest whatsoever in the depth of the Englishman's perversions, except as they impacted his bank account.

Willingham went on. "How much will she cost me, Colonel?"

"Well, that is hard to say, my friend. It all depends on how interested the other bidders are."

"The other bidders?" Willingham sounded surprised and angry. "I thought you were offering her to me!"

"I wished to give you an advance look at the merchandise because we have done business together before, Señor. But to be fair to my men, I must get as high a price as I can. Therefore, an auction."

"Listen, Colonel, we can't have that," Willingham insisted. "I simply can't take a chance on letting this one get away. I haven't seen a girl of this quality for . . . for the Devil only knows how long! I'll make you a firm offer of a million dollars right now."

Laura gasped. Obviously, she couldn't help it.

"You see, Señor Willingham, you have surprised her," Guerrero said. "In her *innocent* state, she had no idea she was worth such a great deal of money."

"Innocent?" Willingham said quickly, snapping up the bait Guerrero had dangled. "Are you saying that . . . do you mean that she's . . . a . . ."

"Indeed," Guerrero murmured, but still loudly enough for the computer microphone to pick it up. "A virgin. Completely untouched."

A moan, an actual moan of longing, came from the speakers. "I must have her, I simply must," Willingham said. "Five million. Five million dollars, Colonel, but only if she doesn't go to auction. Also, you'll have to provide medical proof of her, ah, unsullied state."

"Done," Guerrero said without hesitation. "She will be waiting here for you, along with the proof you require."

"You can't have her brought here to me? I would think for that price, you could arrange delivery."

"Of course I could, Señor Willingham," Guerrero said smoothly, "but I thought you would like to attend the auction anyway, and you can pick her up then. There are many other girls, and you might be interested in some of them, as well."

"After paying five million for this one? Not bloody likely." Willingham paused, then went on. "But I suppose it wouldn't hurt to take a look, eh? All right, I'll attend. You'll let me know the time and the place?"

"Of course. And you will take care of the deposit on this transaction, Señor?"

"Yes, yes, the standard twenty-five percent, one-point-two-five million. I should transfer it to the usual Cayman Islands account?"

"That would be splendid," Guerrero said.

"It'll be taken care of by the end of business today. We'll be in touch, eh?"

"Of course. As always, a pleasure doing business with you, Señor."

"The pleasure is all mine, Colonel." Guerrero could almost see Willingham rubbing his hands together in anticipation. "Yes, all mine."

Guerrero tapped a couple of keys, breaking the connection and killing the little red light on the camera that showed it was on. He smiled at Laura Simms and said, "You can get dressed again now, Señorita."

Hurriedly, she pulled her clothes on, clearly relieved not to have to stand there naked and humiliated any longer. But she was worried, too, and that was evident in her voice as she said, "You . . . you just *sold* me to that guy?"

"Yes, I did."

"Then . . . I won't be going home, will I?"

"Unfortunately, no. However, there is nothing for you to worry about. You will lead a pampered existence with Señor Willingham, and I am sure it will not take long for you to grow accustomed to his . . . eccentricities."

Laura shuddered.

She didn't know the worst of it, Guerrero thought. He had no personal knowledge of what happened to the girls Willingham purchased, but the fact that the Englishman periodically needed another one did not bode well for their longevity. Either he tired of them and passed them on to some of his associates—all those perverts seemed to know one another—or he disposed of them in some other fashion. Either way, the future looked none too good for Laura Simms.

But the Night Wolves would be five million dollars richer, so what did it matter?

Twenty

Ricardo took Laura out into the hall while Major Cortez remained with Colonel Guerrero for a minute, getting instructions of some sort. As she pulled her hair into a ponytail again under Ricardo's watchful eye, she said to him in a low voice, "How can you do things like this?"

Stiffly, he said, "Please do not talk to me, Señorita. I am here to follow the orders given by my superiors, that is all."

"But you hate it!" she persisted. "You know what they're doing is wrong. You know that Rosa and Billie Sue didn't deserve to die. And I think you want to help us."

He looked away from her and shook his head. "I cannot."

"Sure you can. You don't have to do what they say. I'll bet you could turn us loose without anybody knowing—"

The door to Guerrero's office swung open then, and Cortez stepped out. Laura fell silent and looked at the floor. She hoped that Cortez didn't realize she had been talking to Ricardo. Despite the younger man's refusal to help the captives, Laura thought he might come around eventually if she had a chance to work on him.

"Take the girl to the first room in the old granary," Cortez said to Ricardo.

"Wait a minute," Laura said. "I'm not going back with the others?"

Cortez shook his head. "Colonel Guerrero feels that it would be wise to separate you from them."

"So I won't tell them what you have in mind for us." Laura's voice rose. She knew she shouldn't allow herself to get angry, but she couldn't help it. The past half hour or so had been just too much for her to withstand without venting some emotion. First to be forced to strip and stand there naked in front of those men, while some pervert ogled her over the computer, and now to be separated from her friends . . . "You don't want them to know that you're going to auction them off like cattle and make whores out of them!"

"Take her and stay with her until someone comes to relieve you," Cortez went on to Ricardo. He smiled coldly at Laura. "But such pretty cattle."

Ricardo nodded. "Of course, Major."

"Be glad that I did not fully inform the colonel of your negligence earlier," Cortez added. "He does not know that it was your carelessness which cost that girl her life."

"I am grateful for your discretion, Major."

His rigid tone easing a bit, Cortez said, "I think you have the makings of a good soldier, Benitez. Do not force me to regret the decision I have made."

He turned away and went back into Guerrero's office, leaving Ricardo in the hallway with Laura. She thought fleetingly about trying to get away from him, but discarded the idea almost right away. He was a lot bigger and stronger than she was, and he had a gun. She told herself that she had to be patient. Maybe the time would come when Ricardo would *want* to help her. That had to be her goal right now, because it represented the best bet for her and her friends to escape.

She had already given up hope of any help coming from outside. Nobody knew where they were. Nobody was going to come get them.

If they were going to gain their freedom, they would have to do it themselves.

Ricardo took her outside the mission's main building. Even under the circumstances, it felt good to be out in the fresh air and sunshine. She looked around, hoping to be able to tell something about where the mission was located. Knowledge was power. But high adobe walls cut off her view.

He led her across a courtyard lined with flower beds to another adobe building. From what Major Cortez had said, Laura knew that once this had been the mission's granary. These old missions had been designed to be self-sufficient, with gardens for growing vegetables, a herd of cattle for milk and beef, and nearby fields worked by the Indians where grain was grown. That grain was ground into flour at the mill inside this granary.

Those days were long gone, though, and now the old building had been converted into bedrooms. Ricardo took her to one of them and motioned with his rifle for her to go through the arched doorway.

The room had only one window, and it looked out into the courtyard, rather than outside the mission. The floor was Spanish tile, but part of it was covered with a woven rug. A bed with a heavy wooden headboard and wooden posts at the foot sat on one side of the room; a hardwood table with a couple of uncomfortable-looking chairs sat on the other. A chest of drawers with a lamp on it was the only other piece of furniture. An open door in one corner led into a tiny bathroom. Laura glanced up and saw an air-conditioning vent on the rear wall near the ceiling. It was much too small to offer any hope of escape.

Ricardo nodded toward the table. "Sit down," he said.

"I think I'd rather sit on the bed. Those chairs must be some old Spanish torture devices, from the looks of them."

"Suit yourself, Señorita."

"My name is Laura," she said as she sat down on the edge of the bed. "Why don't you call me that?"

He looked away without replying.

Laura sighed. Flirting didn't come naturally to her like it did to Shannon and some of the other girls. She'd had a couple of boyfriends, but their romances had consisted of eating lunch together at school, going out to movies with friends, and a few clumsy hugs and kisses. By no stretch of the imagination did she consider herself a seductress.

Anyway, it was too early for that. Ricardo wasn't going to betray his friends just because she dangled sex at him. Not right away. She would have to work on him for a while.

She told herself that she had time. That guy Willingham had made it sound like he wasn't all that close to Nuevo Laredo. If he was coming to the auction that Guerrero had planned—the very thought of which made a shiver go through her—then it might be several days off, at the very least. Maybe Ricardo would be assigned to guard her all the time, and she would have a few days to convince him to help her.

So for now she would take it slow. She sat on the bed and managed to smile at him, although a large part of her was still in shock from everything that had happened. She had to force herself not to remember what Billie Sue had looked like, slumped there against the wall of the cell, the bloodstain spreading on her shirt. . . .

Ricardo sat down at the table with his rifle across his

knees. "Food will be brought to you," he said. "This is a better room than where you were."

"My friends are still there, though." An idea occurred to her. "Could they come here and stay with me? They could bring their sleeping bags and put them on the floor. It would be like a . . . a slumber party."

"The colonel wants you kept apart from them. That is the reason you are here."

"Yeah, he figures he'd have trouble on his hands if they knew what he's going to do with them. Most of them still think they're being held for ransom, and that their families will get them out of here."

Ricardo didn't say anything.

Deciding to change tack a little, Laura asked, "Is Angelina Salinas really Colonel Guerrero's daughter?"

The sharp breath that Ricardo took in told her it was true. "Do you know this girl?"

"Not all that well." Just as a boy-crazy, pop-culture-obsessed slut, which wasn't surprising considering that Angelina was Shannon's best friend. But Laura didn't think it would be a good idea to say that.

"Where is she?" she went on. "What's happened to her? I'll bet if she's really the colonel's daughter, she's getting the royal treatment. She's not stuck in an old cell somewhere, is she?"

"I cannot discuss these matters."

"You mean you won't. I don't remember ever hearing Angelina say anything about her dad. I guess she knew he was some sort of gangster and was ashamed of him. I couldn't believe that he just killed Sister Katherine like that—"

Colonel Guerrero had shot a nun. Ricardo remembered how he had felt and allowed his stoic façade to crack.

Solemnly, Laura nodded. "After they had taken us all

off the bus, Sister Katherine tried to stop Guerrero. He had an automatic rifle in his hand. He shot her down in cold blood, just like that."

Ricardo's jaw tightened.

"You weren't there?" Laura asked.

He shook his head. "I was not part of the group that carried out the assignment."

"They blew up a bunch of cars on the highway, too. Probably killed a lot of people. People are dying right and left because of your friends, Ricardo."

"I do as I am told. . . ."

"You know, in world history class, we read about the trials at Nuremberg after World War Two. A lot of those Nazi war criminals claimed they were just following orders, too."

His head came up sharply. "We have not killed millions of people."

"Murder is still murder," Laura said. "It's just a matter of degree."

He looked intently at her for a moment and then said, "You seem . . . older than your years."

"I don't date much, so I have a lot of time to read."

"You should go out and enjoy life," he mused. "A girl so young and pretty."

"Well, in the future it looks like I won't be dating much of anybody except that guy Willingham."

Ricardo looked away. Laura was sure he felt badly about his part in all this, and that was good. The more guilt, the better.

Before either of them could say anything else, though, the door opened and a woman walked into the room. She was Mexican and probably around forty years old, with a lot of dark hair and a hawklike face that showed a lot of Indian blood in her ancestry. She wore jeans and a red silk shirt and had an earthy sexuality about her. Laura pegged her right away as the sort of woman who would be the colonel's mistress.

"You can go now," she said curtly to Ricardo. "I will look after this little one."

"You are sure, Señora Garvas?" Ricardo asked. "You are not even armed."

"I need no weapons to take care of a little *gringa* bitch."

Laura felt a strong, instinctive dislike for the woman, mixed with a healthy dose of fear. This Señora Garvas had a cruel look about her. Her dark eyes flashed as she looked at the captive, and Laura suddenly had visions of being strung up to a post while the señora lashed her with a whip.

Ricardo got to his feet, and Laura wanted to cry out for him to stay and not abandon her to Señora Garvas's not-so-tender mercies. She knew it wouldn't do any good, though, so she kept quiet as he left the room, closing the door behind him.

Señora Garvas sauntered over to face her, standing there with her hands on her hips and an unfriendly smile on her face. "You know why I am here?" she asked.

"To . . . to stand guard and make sure I don't get away?"

"That, and to make sure you do not harm yourself. The colonel fears that, knowing what is in store for you, you might seek to end your own life."

So they had her on suicide watch. To be honest, the thought of killing herself hadn't even entered Laura's mind until now. She was too much of a fighter for that. She was too busy trying to think of some way to get herself and her friends out of this mess before any more of them could be hurt.

"You don't have to worry," she said to Señora Garvas. "I wouldn't do that."

"You had better not. My orders are to keep you unmarked

for Señor Willingham. He will not pay five million dollars for damaged goods. But if you give me trouble . . . I can make your life a screaming hell, *chica,* without ever leaving a mark on you."

Laura didn't doubt it for a second.

With a contemptuous snort, Señora Garvas added, "Although why any man would pay so much money for a pale little thing like you is beyond me. You are too young to know shit. A real woman requires years of seasoning to be truly worth anything to a man."

"And I guess you're well-seasoned."

The smile disappeared from the woman's face and was replaced by an angry snarl. Her hand started to come up in a slap aimed at Laura's face. She stopped the motion well before the blow could land.

"I will allow you that bit of disrespect," she said. "The next one, you will pay for."

Laura looked down at the floor and muttered, "I'm sorry."

"Are you, truly?" Señora Garvas laughed. "I think if you had the chance, you would cut my still-beating heart out of my body and laugh in my face as I died."

Laura didn't respond, but the scenario did sound pretty appealing to her. She had never considered herself a violent person at all, but after everything that had happened to her and her friends, maybe she was changing. Maybe she was coming to realize that some people were cold and empty and evil, and they had to be dealt with as ruthlessly as possible.

Maybe she was coming to understand that no matter how deeply it might be buried, there was something savage inside her, too.

Twenty-one

Tom's cell phone rang while he and Bonnie were having a tense supper with Kelly. Since returning to the house after the meeting at City Hall, nothing had happened—no contact by the kidnappers, no calls or visits from the FBI or any other authorities. The reporters had all left, as had the two Laredo police officers. The FBI tech with his electronic equipment was the only outsider still there.

"I don't understand it," Kelly had said earlier. "It hasn't even been forty-eight hours yet. It's like they've all given up and written those girls off."

Tom and Bonnie had done their best to assure her that wasn't the case, but deep down, Tom feared that it was, at least where the authorities were concerned. He was plenty old enough to remember an embassy full of hostages sitting in Tehran while the people in charge dithered around and wrung their hands, unwilling to take any risks that might actually accomplish something. This situation was similar, although on a smaller scale. To the politicians in Washington, covering their asses was more important than rescuing those girls. Doing the right thing mattered a whole hell of a lot less than not doing the wrong thing—which in their minds meant anything that might hurt their chances of getting reelected.

It was a mess, all right, and Tom hated to think that the country had gone so far down that path. But that was why he had decided to talk to the relatives of the missing girls. So when the phone in his pocket rang, Tom felt a surge of hope. He answered it and heard a familiar voice say, "Tom, this is Wayne Van Sant. I've been talking to some guys I know, sounding them out about that idea of yours."

"Glad to hear it, Wayne," Tom said as he got to his feet. "Hang on a minute." He took the phone away from his ear and said to Bonnie and Kelly, "I'll be right back."

Bonnie frowned a little. Tom knew that look of suspicion. He would deal with it later.

He left the dining room, went through the kitchen, and stepped out into the backyard. He said into the phone, "Okay, Wayne, go ahead. We can talk freely now."

"What's the matter, there still a bunch of cops at your sister-in-law's house?"

"Worse, a suspicious wife."

Van Sant chuckled, but Tom could tell his heart wasn't in it. "I've spoken to a dozen of the other dads, and they're all interested in helping out any way they can. And I mean *any* way."

Tom's pulse quickened. He said, "That's good to hear. The first thing we need to do is get together and hammer out a plan."

"That's what I thought, too. You know anything about Laredo?"

"Not much," Tom admitted. "I can sort of find my way around, but that's all."

"There's a local gun club with a shooting range on the north side of town. Several of us are members. Why don't we all meet there, say around eight o'clock?"

"Sounds good to me."

Van Sant gave him directions for finding the shooting range, then said, "You know, Tom, some people would say we're crazy to even be thinking about this."

"Yeah, maybe, but I'd rather be crazy and have those girls back home safe and sound."

"That's the truth," Van Sant said with a catch in his voice. Tom was reminded that while he loved Laura and Kelly and wanted to do whatever he could for Laura, the men he would be meeting tonight had all lost daughters to the Night Wolves. All the fear and anger he was feeling would be even stronger in them.

"We'll get 'em back," Tom said. It was a promise that he intended to keep—or die trying.

Bonnie's suspicions grew even stronger when Tom announced that he had to go out for a while that evening. He could tell that by looking at her, but thankfully she didn't ask him any questions, and Kelly was too worried and upset to hardly notice that he was leaving. Tom had a feeling, though, that Bonnie would have a few things to say when he got back.

He followed Wayne Van Sant's directions and found the gun club without any trouble. It was a sprawling building that looked like it might have been a bowling alley at one time. About a dozen cars were parked in the lot. Tom added the rental car to them and walked inside. He heard the sound of firing from the shooting range.

Van Sant met him. "Come on back," the lanky black man said. "Everybody's anxious to talk to you."

There were a dozen targets ranged against the far wall, but only half of the stations had shooters at them, banging away with an assortment of handguns. Other people were standing back, watching and talking among themselves, although the shooting made conversation difficult. Tom made a quick head count and saw that there were fourteen men here—and to his surprise, two women.

He hadn't counted on any of the moms being involved in this. While he respected the right of women to be in the military, and knew quite well that many of them had performed admirably in combat in far-flung corners of the globe, men of his generation were still just a little uneasy about the whole idea. He could adapt to it, though, if necessary.

Tom's arrival changed the atmosphere in the room. The shooters gradually became aware of that and stopped firing. As the shots died away, everyone in the big room turned to look at Tom and Van Sant.

"This is Tom Brannon," Van Sant said, raising his voice into the silence that seemed to echo slightly after the racket caused by the target practice. "He's the one I told you about."

"The man behind the Patriot Project, out in Arizona," said one of the men. He was medium-sized and mostly bald, with thick glasses perched on his nose. "I looked him up on the Internet and read all about him. That whole thing struck me as vaguely racist."

Another man gave a curt laugh and said, "Don't mind Craig, Mr. Brannon. He's our token liberal. Don't ask me why he's a member of a gun club."

"Blast it, Wally, don't stereotype me," Craig snapped. "I just happen to have somewhat different views than you do."

"Yeah, *I* think gun control means hitting what I aim at," Wally drawled.

One of the women said, "Will you two clowns shut up? This is serious business here." Tom recognized her as the one who had mentioned piloting a chopper during Desert Storm. She turned to him and went on. "We're here to listen to what you have to say, Mr. Brannon. We're desperate enough we'll consider just about anything if it means a chance of getting our girls back."

"That's what it means," Tom said. "A chance. And by the way, everyone, don't bother with that Mr. Brannon business. My name is Tom."

The woman stuck her hand out. "Sonia Alvarez," she said as she shook hands with Tom. "This is my husband Ignacio."

"Nacho," the man said with a faint smile as he shook hands, too.

"Craig Lambert," the bald-headed "token liberal" said.

"Wally Chambers."

"Ed and Nora Gilman."

"Bert Hermosilla."

One by one, the people in the room introduced themselves to Tom and shook his hand. He tried to keep all the names straight, even though that wasn't really his strong suit. He didn't see Joe Delgado or Frank Ramirez, but he wasn't surprised by that. He expected they would be in touch with him later, once they'd had a chance to get together with their acquaintances who might want to take part in this effort.

When the introductions were over, Wayne Van Sant said, "Why don't you tell us just what it is you have in mind, Tom?"

"Of course," Tom nodded. "Simply put, the United States authorities won't go into Mexico to recover those kidnapped girls. The Mexican authorities won't do anything about it, either." He looked around at the group, his face growing grim. "That leaves it up to us to rescue them."

"Become vigilantes, you mean?" Craig Lambert said. "Take the law into our own hands?"

"What I mean is that it's time to take the lives of those girls we love in our hands and save them."

That brought mutters of agreement from the group. But one of the men spoke up in a pragmatic voice, saying, "There are only a few of us, and we're just common folks. How can we fight a group like the Night Wolves? They've all had military training."

"So have we," Sonia Alvarez said as she turned to face the man who had asked the question. "Nacho and I were both in Desert Storm. Wayne was there in Baghdad when Saddam's statue came down."

"I was in Grenada," Wally Chambers said. He shrugged and added, "I know it didn't amount to much, but I've been under fire before." His round face, which seemed much more suited to a cheerful expression, hardened into a stony mask. "I don't mind being under fire again, either, if it means getting my daughter Lindy back safe and sound."

"More likely, it'll mean getting yourselves killed, along with the girls," Craig Lambert said. Several men muttered angrily. Lambert looked around with a defiant jut to his chin and went on. "We're not a military force. No matter how much we want our daughters back, we're not equipped to . . . to go to war with Mexico to rescue them!"

Everybody started talking at once, trying for the most part to override Lambert's objections. Tom raised his hands and said sharply, "Settle down, folks! We won't accomplish anything by arguing about it." When quiet had descended again on the shooting range, he continued. "We wouldn't be going to war against Mexico, just against Los Lobos de la Noche."

"Which amounts to a small army in itself," Lambert pointed out.

"I'm told they only number about a hundred men."

"A hundred well-armed, well-trained, cold-blooded killers, against a dozen or so middle-aged parents who find it a challenge just putting on a school carnival," Lambert said.

"There's more to us than that," Sonia objected. "We can fight!"

"With what?" Lambert wanted to know.

"We all own guns," one of the men said.

"Target pistols and hunting rifles and shotguns," Lambert said. "That's hardly a match for the armament the Night Wolves can muster. My God, I've heard they even have rockets!"

"It's true we'd probably be outgunned," Tom said quickly before another uproar could build. "But we'd be fighting for our families. That's got to give us some sort of advantage."

"Nine times out of ten, a noble cause is no match for superior firepower."

"You're right," Tom told Lambert, "but what about that tenth time?"

Lambert just frowned and didn't answer. He had made a good point, though, as much as Tom hated to admit it. If they went down into Mexico both outnumbered and outgunned, they stood a good chance of not coming back.

"We have to figure out a way to put our hands on some better armament, that's true, but if we can do that—"

"Even if we do that, how do we know where to look for the girls?" Lambert asked. "As far as I can tell, the authorities have no idea where they are right now. They could be anywhere south of the border. We can't just wander around looking for them. We might never find them."

That was another good point. Tom didn't know how to respond to it.

He didn't have to, because at that moment, the door of the gun club opened and Texas Ranger Captain Roy Rodgers walked in.

They were busted.

Twenty-two

Tom stood there looking steadily at Rodgers as Wayne Van Sant stepped toward the Ranger and said, "This is a private club, Captain—"

Rodgers held up a hand to stop him. "I'm aware of that, Mr. Van Sant."

"You can't come in here without a warrant."

"If I have reason to believe that a crime is being committed, I can."

Van Sant shook his head. "There's no crime going on here. Just a peaceful get-together of club members."

"What about Mr. Brannon there? He doesn't belong to your club."

"He's a guest," Van Sant said stiffly.

Tom had already figured out that Rodgers must have followed him here. That was the only way the Ranger could have known about the meeting. After Tom had talked to Brady Keller, Rodgers had been suspicious. Now, after what had happened at City Hall, the Ranger had even more reason to think that Tom was up to something; otherwise he wouldn't be here with the parents of the missing girls.

"I think there's a reasonable chance under the law that

you folks are committing the crime of conspiracy at the very least," Rodgers said, raising his voice so that he could address the whole group. "There may be other violations you could be charged with. If you all go back to your homes, though, I suppose there won't be any need to bring the law into this."

"It's not home as long as my daughter isn't there," one of the men said hollowly. Others muttered agreement.

"All the law enforcement agencies involved are continuing to investigate—"

"What good does it do to investigate when the government won't do anything about it?" tall, balding, bearded Ed Gilman demanded. Beside him, his pretty blond wife Nora nodded.

Wally Chambers said, "Ed's right. Even if you knew where the girls were, you couldn't go after them. The Feds won't let you."

Rodgers's jaw tightened. "If the Rangers are able to obtain that information—"

"The FBI will step in and prevent you from acting," Tom said. "As long as the Mexican government doesn't want anything done about this, our politicians will go along with them."

"That's crazy!" Rodgers burst out. "America won't stand for it!"

"Think about the president and the party she belongs to," Tom said slowly. "They've done nothing for the past fifty years but tell us that America is to blame for everything that's wrong in the world. Every chance they've gotten, they've gutted the military with cutbacks. They've given a pulpit to every fringe nutcase who comes along, and carried political correctness to such an extent that you can't say Merry Christmas to your neighbor anymore. If somebody sneezes and you say 'God bless,' you've got to worry about being arrested for violating the civil rights of one of those nutcases."

"Oh, please," Craig Lambert said. "It's not *that* bad."

"It's getting there, Craig," Wayne Van Sant snapped. "It's sure getting there."

Tom went on. "With all that going on in Washington, and with the politicians on the other side getting elected more often than not because they're the lesser of the two evils, do you really think anybody's going to risk a war with Mexico over a few teenage girls?"

Rodgers flushed in anger and frustration, but he said, "There's all sorts of diplomatic pressure that can be put on—"

"Diplomatic pressure hardly ever works, and when it does, it takes forever. Those girls don't have time to wait."

"How do you know that?"

"Whatever the Night Wolves do," Tom said, "they won't waste any time doing it. We probably don't have more than a few days. That's what my gut tells me anyway."

"So in less than a week you're going to take a bunch of average citizens, arm them, find out where the captives are being held, and go down there to get them back?"

Tom said, "There's an old saying about how fortune favors the bold."

Rodgers stared at him for a second and then said, "Here's an old saying for you . . . you go down south of the border, you're liable to get your ass shot off."

"If we do that . . . and I'm not saying we are . . . it'll be *our* asses that we're risking, won't it?"

Rodgers stared for a moment longer, then shook his head. "I can't argue with a crazy man," he said. He added to the others, "But you folks don't have to let him lead you into more craziness, either."

With that, the Ranger turned on his heel and stalked out

of the building. Van Sant watched him go and asked worriedly, "Is he going to blow the whistle on us?"

"I don't think so," Tom said. "I think that deep down he wants to go with us. His devotion to duty just won't let him. But he won't try to stop us, either."

"We'll be wagering a lot that your instinct about him is right, Tom."

Tom said, "I know. We're betting the lives of all those girls."

The meeting broke up shortly after that, after everyone agreed to get together at the gun club again the following night. There was plenty to be done between now and then, and Tom was going to do most of it. For one thing, they needed to recruit more members to their cause. Tom hoped to talk to Joe Delgado and Frank Ramirez again and see if they had had any luck in rounding up more men who would be interested in such a highly illegal, dangerous effort. Being outnumbered two to one would be bad enough, and they still had a way to go before they reached even those odds.

Then there was the matter of weapons. Craig Lambert was right about a few things, one of them being the level of armament they would be facing. If they were going south of the border, they would need to go packing deadlier heat than what they had now.

Tom hoped that Brady Keller might be able to give them a hand with that angle. The crippled DEA agent had mentioned the contacts he still had in the law enforcement community. Maybe one of those contacts would be willing to take a chance on helping them. . . .

In the meantime, Tom still had to deal with Bonnie.

Just as he expected, she was waiting for him when he

came into the house. She sat in the living room, flipping idly through a magazine. Back in the den, Tom could see a bored-looking FBI technician, the third one who had taken a shift at the Simms house.

Bonnie put the magazine aside and stood up. Tom moved to take her in his arms. He kissed her on the forehead and asked, "Where's Kelly?"

"She's gone to bed. She took one of the sedatives the doctor gave her. She couldn't stand the waiting."

"I know how she feels," Tom murmured.

"Do you, Tom? Do you, really?"

He frowned. "Well, it's not our daughter who's missing, of course, so I reckon I don't. Not exactly, anyway. But I want Laura back here safely, you know that."

"Yes, I know," Bonnie said. "I also know you don't have a lot of patience with the proper authorities."

"If they really did their job properly—"

She cut in, "You're more of a do-it-yourself troublemaker, aren't you, Tom?"

A little angrily, he said, "I seem to remember you being right there with the rest of us when it came time to defend Little Tucson from M-15."

"I had no choice. We were left hanging out there to either defend ourselves or die."

"We've been left hanging here, too," Tom said. "Only this time it'll be Laura and the rest of those girls who die if somebody doesn't get them out of whatever hellhole they're stashed in."

"Somebody . . . meaning you?"

"Not alone," he said.

She slipped out of his arms and stepped back. "You're doing it again, aren't you?"

"Doing what?"

"Putting together an army to fight for what's right."

A smile touched his lips. "At least you didn't make some veiled crack about what I *think* is right."

"Oh, I know you're right," Bonnie said. "I've seen the government in action . . . or I should say, *in*action. As long as the Mexicans stonewall, the authorities won't do anything."

"That's right. It's up to the people."

"Just like in 1776."

"Wait a minute," Tom said. "Don't go comparing me to the Founding Fathers. This isn't a revolution. I love my country."

"You just want it to do the right thing, and when it won't, you do it yourself."

"I just want to get those girls back," he said. "It's really that simple."

"Yes," Bonnie said softly, "I guess it is. And you'll risk your life to do it, too, won't you?"

"If that's the only choice I have."

She turned away, her back stiff and straight as a ramrod. "I have a pretty good idea where you went tonight. Not the exact place, but I know you went somewhere to get together with people who feel the same way."

"Yeah," Tom admitted quietly with a glance toward the den. He didn't want the FBI agent eavesdropping on this conversation.

"Do you know what really bothers me, Tom?"

"Why don't you tell me?"

She looked at him again. "I'm upset that you didn't take me with you."

He gazed at her intently for a second and fought the urge to laugh. That was just like Bonnie, he thought. Here he had figured she would be mad at him for even being mixed up in such a wild-ass scheme, and in reality she was upset because she wasn't part of it, too.

Nor would she be, if he had anything to say about it. "Kelly needs you here with her," he said.

"Damn it, Tom—"

He held up a hand to stop her. "Listen to me, Bonnie. It's hard enough on Kelly having Laura in danger. She doesn't need to face the possibility of losing her sister, as well."

"What about the possibility of me losing my husband?"

"Women have to send their husbands—and their fathers and brothers and sons—off to war all the time, knowing that they might not come back. It's a hard thing, but it's part of life and probably always will be."

"This isn't a war," Bonnie said.

Tom disagreed with her. "That's exactly what it is. Sure, it's on a smaller scale than a war between countries, but it's still a war. The outlaws are on one side, and the decent folks are on the other."

"You're telling me you're doing it for Randolph Scott."

Again he almost laughed. Quoting Mel Brooks wasn't a tactic he had expected from her.

But actually, she was right, and he said so. "The country's changed since the days when Randolph Scott and John Wayne made movies. There's no real justice anymore. People don't stand up for what's right. They wait for the government to do it for them. They'd rather talk about how they can't do this and they can't do that, instead of figuring out what they *can* do. And when evil wins, they just shrug their shoulders and say that's how the world is. Well, that's not the way I'm built, Bonnie. I can't just roll over because the rest of the world does."

She reached up to brush her fingertips against his cheek. "I know," she said in a half whisper. "I know, Tom. If you ever gave up when you knew you were right, you wouldn't be the man I married." She kissed him quickly, and her voice broke a little as she went on. "But if anything happened to you, I . . . I don't know if I could bear it."

"Then believe that nothing will happen to me and keep on believing it," he told her. "Believe that I'll bring Laura home."

reading, sorting, and scanning... DEA confidential
informant book... *** *** *** *** *** *** ***
I have nothing to do with... *** *** *** ... fucking
complicated.

Twenty-three

When Tom's cell phone rang the next morning, he wasn't surprised to hear Brady Keller's voice on the other end.

"Can you come see me this morning?" Keller asked. "Better not bring Rodgers with you, though. I've got a feeling he won't want to be involved from here on out."

"Yeah, I've got the same feeling," Tom agreed. "I'll be there."

They settled on a time and broke the connection. Tom was in the kitchen, leaning a hip against the counter, while Bonnie mixed pancake batter in a bowl a few steps away. Without looking at him, she asked, "More commando stuff?"

"You sure you really want to know?"

She glanced angrily at him. "Don't shut me out, Tom Brannon. I want to know what you're up to, even if you are going to be stubborn about letting me be part of it."

Tom lowered his voice so the FBI agent in the den couldn't overhear and said, "Yeah, I have to go see Brady Keller this morning. He's that former DEA agent I told you about."

"The one who was hurt so badly in that ambush?"

"Yeah. He's sort of the resident expert on the Night Wolves."

A little shudder ran through Bonnie's body. "What a horrible name."

"A horrible bunch."

The phone that Tom had slipped back into his pocket rang again. He answered it and heard a man's voice say, "This is Joe Delgado, Brannon."

"Hello, Joe." Tom kept his own voice noncommittal and waited to hear what Delgado had to say.

"You still interested in what you talked about at City Hall with me and Frank Ramirez?"

"More than ever," Tom said.

"Yeah, well, so are we. And so are some of the guys we talked to later. We need to get together."

"How many men are we talking about?"

"Fifteen, I'd say."

That news buoyed Tom's spirits. The odds, though still high, were getting smaller. It was time now to bring the two groups together. Tom told Delgado to bring the men he and Ramirez had contacted to the gun club that night.

Once Bonnie had the pancakes ready, she went to wake up Kelly, who was still sleeping off the sedative. Tom was looking in the cabinet for syrup when he heard Bonnie scream.

He charged down the hall, not thinking about anything except getting to his wife. Bonnie wouldn't have screamed like that unless something was wrong. Tom's heart pounded heavily at the thought she might be in danger.

He skidded to a stop in the doorway of Kelly's bedroom. Bonnie leaned over the bed and clutched her sister's shoulders. She shook Kelly hard and shouted, "Wake up! You've got to wake up!"

Tom's eyes went to the bedside table and saw the

prescription bottle lying there on its side, empty with its cap off. He had no idea how many sleeping pills had been in it, but Kelly had taken them all. He lunged to the bed and reached past Bonnie to put his hand on Kelly's neck and search for a pulse.

He found one, but it was slow and irregular. Slipping his arms under Kelly's arms, he lifted her out of the bed and balanced her on her feet. "Call nine-one-one!" he told Bonnie. "We need an ambulance and paramedics here right away to pump her stomach."

Bonnie snatched up the phone beside the empty pill bottle and punched in the emergency numbers. While she was talking to the 911 dispatcher, Tom walked Kelly back and forth across the room. She was so limp that he was dragging her more than forcing her to walk, but he hoped that his actions would get her blood moving. Her head lolled on his shoulder. She muttered something, but he couldn't make out anything except Laura's name.

Even as he tried desperately to keep his sister-in-law from slipping away, Tom knew what had brought on this tragic attempt on her own life. Kelly had given up any hope of seeing her daughter again, and she didn't think she could go on without Laura.

If Kelly died, that would be one more score to settle with Los Lobos de la Noche. . . .

Tom wouldn't let himself consider that possibility. Allowing Kelly to die was not an option. As soon as Bonnie was off the phone, he said, "Go in the bathroom and turn on the shower. Cold water."

Bonnie hurried to do so. Tom followed her, hauling Kelly's seemingly boneless form with him. When Bonnie had the cold water blasting in the shower, Tom stepped under the frigid stream fully clothed and dragged Kelly with him. She jerked and gasped as the icy barrage struck her. Tom turned so that the water hit her in the face. She shook her head, trying to escape it. He moved back a little so she could breathe. He didn't want to save her from the suicide attempt only to turn around and drown her.

"The paramedics are on their way!" Bonnie called over the rushing noise of the shower. Tom saw the FBI agent standing in the bathroom doorway, drawn by the commotion. He looked confused and uncertain about what to do.

Tom stayed in the shower with Kelly, holding her up because she was still only semiconscious. After long minutes that seemed even longer, a team of paramedics rushed into the room and took over, lifting Kelly out of Tom's arms and placing her carefully on the rug. One of the EMTs told Tom and Bonnie and the FBI agent to step out of the bathroom and give them space to work.

Tom grabbed a towel on his way out and used it to dry his face and hair. Then he put it down on the kitchen floor and stood on it so that it would catch the water dripping from his soaked clothing.

Bonnie threw her arms around him and hugged him hard, ignoring the fact that she was getting wet, too. "Oh, Tom," she said, her voice breaking, "When I saw that pill bottle and she wouldn't wake up, I just knew she was dead."

"I think we got to her in time. She was trying to come out of it. She must not have taken the other pills until later in the night, or even sometime this morning."

"If you hadn't done what you did . . ."

"And if you hadn't found her," Tom said. "If she pulls through, she's got you to thank as much as me."

The FBI tech came into the kitchen and asked, "Is there, uh, anything I can do for you folks?"

Tom shook his head. "Does Agent Morgan know what happened here this morning?"

"Yeah, I thought she should know, so I just called her."

"Good. She needs to know what can happen when people give up hope."

The agent didn't know what to say to that, so he just shrugged and moved back into the den.

Bonnie said, "Lord, we both need some dry clothes. Why don't you go to the spare bedroom and change, Tom?"

"All right, but come and get me if the paramedics have any news."

Every bedroom in the house had its own bathroom. Tom peeled off his sodden clothes and dropped them in the shower, then dried off some more and pulled on clean underwear and socks, along with jeans and a khaki shirt. As he started back toward the kitchen, the paramedics emerged from Kelly's room. They had her strapped onto a stretcher now. She was pale and disheveled, but she was conscious. Bonnie hurried from the kitchen and caught hold of Kelly's hand, holding it as the men carried the stretcher through the house toward the front door.

The paramedic who wasn't carrying the stretcher said to Tom, "Her vital signs are stable." He shook his head. "Good thing you folks didn't wait another hour or two before checking on her this morning, though."

"You're taking her to the hospital?" Tom asked.

"Yeah, she'll need to stay there at least one night for observation. That's pretty much standard procedure in a case like this."

Standard procedure for an attempted suicide, that was what he meant, Tom thought.

He followed the third paramedic out of the house and watched the others load Kelly into the ambulance. Bonnie hovered nearby anxiously, and when the EMTs were ready to go, she asked, "Can I ride along with her?"

"Yes, ma'am," one of the men told her.

"Tom, get some dry clothes for me and follow us to the hospital."

He nodded, more than willing to do as Bonnie said in this instance. He still had some time before he was supposed to go to the private hospital on the outskirts of Laredo and meet with Brady Keller. As the ambulance pulled away, its lights flashing, Tom went back in the house to gather up a fresh outfit for Bonnie.

By the time he got to the hospital, Kelly was already in a bed in the emergency room, and Bonnie was waiting just outside in the lobby. Tom handed her the overnight bag he had brought with him. She said, "Thanks," and headed for the bathroom to change.

When she came back, Tom asked her, "Did Kelly make the trip over here all right?"

Bonnie nodded. "The paramedics all seemed to think she would be all right. They pumped her stomach and she's awake enough to be crying and apologizing." She sank wearily onto one of the plastic chairs, and Tom sat in the one beside her. "I just can't believe that she would do such a thing. It . . . it's just not like Kelly at all. She's always been strong. She's been able to raise Laura by herself for the past few years, and she's carried on with her career. . . ."

"You never know what's going to push somebody over the edge," Tom said. "Maybe Kelly just couldn't stand the thought of losing anybody else." Which was another good reason for Bonnie to stay right here in Laredo, he thought, instead of trying to come along when he and the others made their rescue attempt. Although he experienced a guilty twinge for feeling that way, he knew that in a way Kelly's suicide attempt was a good thing. Looking after her would keep Bonnie busy.

He kept those musings to himself and sat there quietly with his wife. About twenty minutes later, a

Hispanic woman in scrubs came out of the ER and said, "Mr. and Mrs. Brannon? I'm Dr. DeZavala. Mrs. Simms is doing fine."

Bonnie and Tom had both come to their feet as the doctor introduced herself. Now Bonnie sagged slightly against Tom and said, "Oh, thank God."

"She'll be groggy and a little nauseous for the rest of the day, and we'll keep her overnight just to make sure she's all right." Dr. DeZavala hesitated. "Of course, in cases such as these, it's often wise to extend that hospital stay for a short time."

"Because it was a suicide attempt?"

"Frankly, yes," DeZavala said. "We have an excellent psychiatric ward here, and it might pay to have a full evaluation of your sister's mental state done, so that there's no recurrence of this incident."

Bonnie looked over at Tom. "What do you think?"

"You have to do whatever you think is best," he said with a shrug.

"You don't have to decide right now," the doctor told them. "Like I said, Mrs. Simms will have to remain here overnight, at least, so you've got some time to think about it."

"Thank you, Doctor," Tom said. DeZavala nodded and went back through the door into the emergency room.

Tom didn't say anything about it, but he knew what Kelly needed even more than a psychiatric evaluation. The only real cure for what ailed her would be the safe return of her daughter.

And from the looks of the situation, Tom and his new-found friends were the only ones who could supply that particular medicine.

Twenty-four

Tom found Brady Keller sitting in the cactus garden again. The man in the wheelchair frowned when he saw Tom approaching.

"I thought you'd backed out on me," Keller said.

Tom shook his head. "I got delayed a little." He explained what had happened and concluded by saying, "It took me a little longer to get away from the hospital than I thought it would. The other hospital, I mean. There was a hell of a lot of paperwork to fill out, and my wife wanted me to help her with it."

Keller grunted. "Yeah, if there's one thing they've got more of in hospitals than sick people, it's paperwork. But you're here now, and that's all that matters. Were you able to talk to some of your people?"

"Yes, I had a meeting last night with more than a dozen who are interested. And there are more coming tonight."

"Do they know what they're letting themselves in for?" Keller asked with a frown. "There's a damned good chance a lot of them won't be coming back."

"They know that. They're willing to risk it rather than do nothing while God knows what happens to their children."

"Most people, when they get upset about something, they go whining to the government or somebody else and want them to fix the problem. They're not willing to put their own lives on the line to do what's right."

"This is a special situation," Tom pointed out.

"Yeah, but you want to keep a close eye on them anyway. When things get tough, some of them are liable to bug out. That can get the rest of you killed if you're not careful."

Tom said, "I've been in combat before. I won't trust my back to anybody unless I know they'll come through."

"Just remember that." Keller pointed to a low rock wall around part of the garden. "Sit down. My neck gets tired when I have to keep looking up at you."

"Sorry," Tom said as he sat on the rock wall. "Were you able to talk to some of those contacts you mentioned?"

A grotesque expression pulled at Keller's scarred face. After a second, Tom recognized it as a grin. "Damn right I did. I've got eight guys who are interested in going with you."

Now it was Tom's turn to frown. "Lawmen, you mean?"

"Yeah. Border Patrol agents and DEA guys."

"And they want to go into Mexico with us?" Worry surged up inside Tom. What if this was a trap? "They're willing to go against their superiors, knowing it might cost them their careers if anybody finds out?"

Keller hunched forward in his wheelchair. "Listen, Brannon. I know these men. They all lost good friends in the ambush that did this to me. In a couple of cases, they lost brothers. Trust me, they want to strike back at Guerrero and the Night Wolves as much as you do."

"Enough to turn outlaw?"

Keller snorted. "You don't really believe you're an outlaw, and you know it. You're just doing what a bloated, impotent government refuses to do. You've been there before, when you started the Patriot Project."

"That didn't involve crossing the border. We were on our own land, defending our homes."

"Guerrero crossed the border, didn't he? He attacked and killed American citizens on American soil. That makes him fair game as far as I'm concerned."

Tom couldn't argue with that. Guerrero and the Night Wolves had started this ball rolling, there was no mistake about that.

Slowly, he said, "If you say we can trust these men, Keller, then I believe you. With the addition of them, that will give us around forty people . . . assuming that none of the others back out."

"Guerrero's got a hundred men, maybe more. That's not even two-to-one odds. They'll be armed to the teeth, too."

Tom clasped his hands together and leaned forward. "That's something else I wanted to ask you about."

"Guns?" That ugly grin stretched across Keller's face again. "Yeah, I figured you might be a little light on fire-power. My guys can help you with that, too."

"Sounds like they'll be risking a lot."

"It'll be worth it to them if they can blast those sons o' bitches off the face of the earth."

Tom knew he was still taking a chance, but he was willing to put his faith in Keller's judgment. He told the former DEA agent about the gun club and the meeting scheduled there for that night.

"We should have the whole group together," Tom said. "We'll know then if what we've been talking about has any chance of succeeding . . . or if we've just been fooling ourselves."

"You can do it," Keller said. "I'm convinced enough that I wish like hell I could go along with you." He laughed bitterly. "I figure I'd just slow you down, though."

Tom said fervently, "Without your help, we wouldn't

stand a chance. As far as I'm concerned, you're contributing just as much as if you were going across the border with us."

"Yeah, well, that's not as good as the feel of a gun in my hand, but I guess it'll have to do." Keller looked away for a moment, and Tom wondered if he saw the faint gleam of a tear in the man's good eye. After a moment, Keller went on. "It's time to find out where those girls are being held."

"I know. That may be the one roadblock we can't get around. I have no idea where to look, and as far as I know, neither does the FBI or any other law enforcement agency on this side of the border."

"Maybe nobody on this side of the border knows, but I guarantee you that somebody on the other side does. The cartel pays off the Mexican police and military to look the other way, so those greedy bastards have to know what to look away *from*."

Tom felt his pulse quicken. That idea hadn't occurred to him, but now that he thought it over, he knew Keller was right. The Mexican authorities had to be aware of places to avoid because they might run into Los Lobos de la Noche.

"The DEA has deep-cover agents south of the border, too," Keller went on. "Some of them are so deep they can't risk getting in touch with their handlers unless they have something big enough to bring down not only the Night Wolves but also the whole cartel. But maybe, just maybe, one of them might pass something along that could help us. Together with the network of informants that we have in Nuevo Laredo, there's a chance somebody will give us a lead to the location."

"Have you already talked to anybody about that?"

Keller nodded. "Yeah, I put the word out, very discreetly. If I hear anything, I'll let you know right away."

"Back when you were in the DEA, you didn't know where Guerrero's headquarters were?"

"No, we never could pin it down. To tell you the truth, we never really tried all that hard to find out. We knew that if we did locate their HQ, the Mexican law wouldn't do shit. And since we couldn't cross the border . . ." Keller's left shoulder lifted in that half shrug. He didn't have to say anything else. Tom could just imagine that the rank-and-file agents were as frustrated as anyone else at the seeming inability to do anything about the problems plaguing La Frontera.

And in the big picture, nothing *would* be accomplished as long as the borders stayed open. It would take thousands of miles of barbed-wire fence, as well as troops, tanks, jeeps, and helicopters, to truly close the borders, and the liberals would never stand for that. The media, the politicians, and the ACLU would be screaming their heads off about police states and comparing the American military and police forces to the Gestapo—an assertion so wrongheaded that it sickened anybody who hadn't been brainwashed by the decades of bias that the media so self-righteously claimed didn't exist.

Nor were they the only ones to blame, Tom mused. If the borders were closed, the inexhaustible supply of cheap, easily exploited labor that so many businesses depended on would be shut off. The owners of those businesses weren't going to stand for that. The people who had whined so much about the Patriot Project and called them a bunch of racists had never understood that Tom and those who stood with him had nothing against *legal* immigrants. America had started out as a melting pot, the most open society in the history of the world, and that was how it still ought to be, as long as everything was done legally.

Keller heaved a sigh and said, "Well, I'll make some

more calls. Might be able to round up a few more men and a little more information before tonight. Good luck to you, Brannon."

"Thanks." Tom shook hands with the man again and turned to walk back through the private hospital to the parking lot.

He pretended not to hear when Keller said softly, "You're going to need all the luck you can get, you big, stubborn son of a bitch."

The parking lot at the gun club was more crowded when Tom drove into it that evening. He added his rental car to the others and walked inside. The first people he saw were Joe Delgado and Frank Ramirez.

The two men greeted him and shook his hand. Tom looked past them at the large group milling around. Ramirez said, "Everybody's getting acquainted. Most of them sort of know each other anyway, from school functions."

"Come on, Brannon," Delgado added. "We'll introduce you to the guys we brought."

Again there was a flurry of names that Tom knew he probably wouldn't remember all that well. All told, counting himself, there were thirty-three people at the meeting— thirty men and three women. Remembering how Bonnie and Louly and Deputy Sheriff Lauren Henderson had acquitted themselves during the Battle of Little Tucson, Tom told himself not to worry too much about these women. They wouldn't be here if they didn't know what they were getting into.

He didn't see any of the men Brady Keller had promised, though. These people were all parents of the missing girls.

"Some of the other guys wanted to come," Delgado said, "but Frank and I talked them out of it. Their hearts are in the right place, but they just don't have the training to take part in a mission like you're talking about."

"They've promised to do whatever they can to help, though," Ramirez said, "like furnishing money for equipment or things like that."

Tom nodded. "Good. We have to move fast, so cash will help to grease the wheels."

"Yeah," said one of the men, "you can't accomplish anything in Mexico without some *mordida*." He was talking about the ever-present bribery that was a part of everyday life south of the border.

Tom raised his voice a little to make sure that everyone heard him as he went on. "All of you have to understand that what we're going to do will be dangerous. We'll be going up against a force that's larger, better armed, and more ruthless than we are. I can almost guarantee you that not all of us will be coming back."

"Men have fought and died for their families since the beginning of time, Brannon," Wayne Van Sant said. "This is no different. We know the risks."

Nods and words of agreement came from the assembled group.

"All right, just so we're clear on that," Tom said. "I've put some things in motion that I hope will help us even the odds, including some better armament, but I don't know how long it will be until—"

The doors of the gun club opened behind Tom, and as if they had been waiting for their cue, several men strode into the building. Tom turned to look and saw to his surprise that one of the men was pushing Brady Keller's wheelchair.

Keller's scarred face contorted in his usual grotesque grin as he said, "Starting without us, Brannon?"

Twenty-five

"I didn't expect to see you here," Tom said.

"I decided I needed to get out of that damned hospital. Anyway, just because I can't go on this mission with you doesn't mean I can't be in on the planning of it." Keller lifted his good hand and waved at the men with him. "Especially since I'm providing part of your firepower."

The man who had been pushing the wheelchair stepped around it and extended his hand to Tom. "Charles Long," he introduced himself. He was a tall, muscular man with crew-cut brown hair.

Tom shook hands with him and guessed, "Border Patrol?"

"I'd rather not get into specifics, Brannon. Let's just say that I've got a stake in seeing that Guerrero and his Night Wolves are brought to justice." Long gestured with a big hand at the other men who had come in with him. "And so do these fellows."

Tom shook hands with them, as well. Like Long, they were all big and competent-looking, with an air of quiet strength and authority about them. He had seen that same air in a lot of law-enforcement officers and military personnel.

"Brady has explained what you're planning to do," Long said. "You know it's going to be deadly."

Tom nodded. "We know there are risks, and we're willing to accept them."

"As long as you go into this with your eyes open."

"They're open," Sonia Alvarez said. "We want our girls back, and we're willing to risk anything for that."

A frown creased Long's forehead. "I'm not sure it's a good idea to take women along. . . ."

"Tell that to all the members of the Iraqi Republican Guard who got their asses shot off by my chopper during Desert Storm," Sonia snapped.

"No offense, ma'am, but that was a long time ago. Since then, you've been doing what? Driving kids to soccer practice?"

Sonia's eyes widened. "You want to shoot against me, amigo? Come on, let's go back to the range. We'll settle this pronto!"

Long smiled. "No, that's all right. I'll take your word for it, ma'am . . . for now. I'll want to see all of you shoot before we go on a mission together, though."

"No offense, mister," Wally Chambers said, "but who died and made you boss?"

Craig Lambert spoke up, saying, "Yeah, we've sort of assumed that Brannon here is the leader. This is his idea, after all."

Long glanced at Brady Keller, who gave his customary half shrug. "You'll have to work that out among yourselves," Keller said.

Long looked intently at Tom. "Brady's told me quite a bit about you, Brannon. I know you're a good man, but you're not really qualified to take command of a mission of this sort."

"I've done all right so far, I think," Tom said. "I don't

want to butt heads with you over this, though. And you probably *are* more qualified than I am to be in charge."

"Wait a minute, Brannon," Van Sant said. "We don't know these men—"

"You didn't know me before yesterday, either," Tom said.

"That's true, but you're like the rest of us. You've got a personal stake in this. Your niece is a prisoner just like my daughter."

Long stepped forward. "You think I don't have a personal stake in this?" he asked. "My brother was a member of the task force that Guerrero ambushed a few months ago. He was burned down with a flamethrower. I had to identify his body because I didn't want his wife to have to see the charred husk of a man that didn't even look human anymore, let alone like the man she loved. But I saw my brother and what Guerrero did to him, and I swore then and there that the bastard would pay." Long's voice trembled from the emotion he felt. "These men with me have all lost loved ones to Guerrero and the Night Wolves. I promise you, mister, the hate we got for those shitbirds is every bit as personal as what you're going through. We wouldn't be here otherwise."

Silence hung over the group. After a moment, Tom said, "All right, Long. You're in command, if that's what you want."

Long nodded curtly. "Thanks. Now, you'll need better weapons than what you've got, more than likely. We brought some rifles with us—"

"I've been working on that," Tom cut in. "By tomorrow night we should have a truckload of the best rifles, pistols, Kevlar vests, and ammunition that money can buy."

Keller frowned up at him and asked, "How did you arrange that?"

"I called a friend of mine—Hiram Stackhouse."

"Who's that?"

Tom said, "He owns SavMart."

That brought looks of surprise from everyone. People started asking questions. Tom raised his hands to quiet them down and went on. "Stackhouse gave me a hand with that other trouble I had out in Arizona. He hates scum like Guerrero worse than we do, and he was glad to help out when I told him what we needed. He has his own private security force, and he's promised that we'll be as well equipped as they are. I wouldn't be surprised if Stackhouse asks some of them to come along with us into Mexico. He can help out if we run into any diplomatic or political problems, too."

"How can he do that?" Craig Lambert asked. "He just owns a chain of discount stores."

"That contribute more money to the country's economy than any other single business," Tom said. "If it was its own country, SavMart's gross national product would put it in the top ten in the world."

A smile pulled at the left half of Brady Keller's mouth. "Well, this is starting to look feasible," he said. "Maybe you can pull this off after all, Brannon."

"We have to pull it off," Tom said. "Those girls don't know it, but we're their only hope."

The rest of the night was spent by the three groups getting to know each other. Tom huddled for a long time with Keller, Long, Van Sant, and the Alvarezes, putting together a rudimentary plan. Once the girls were located, the rescue team would have to cross into Nuevo Laredo by ones and twos and rendezvous somewhere on the other side of the border. Their weapons would be smuggled across, reversing the usual pattern in which contraband was smuggled from Mexico into the United States. Once the force was together and armed, it would strike at the stronghold of Los Lobos de la Noche and free the girls.

Getting out of Mexico would be tougher than getting in. Sonia Alvarez came up with a suggestion. If they could put their hands on three or four helicopters, she and some other pilots could be waiting north of the border for a signal from the rescuers. When they got it, they could lift off, home in directly on the spot, and airlift the girls and their rescuers the hell out of there.

Tom thought that was a good idea and said, "I'll talk to Hiram Stackhouse again. If he doesn't already own some helicopters, he's bound to be able to put his hands on some."

"Not little traffic copters," Sonia said. "They've got to be big enough to carry quite a few people. And it would be better if they were armed with machine guns and a few missiles, but I suppose that might be a little too much to ask."

"Yeah, maybe," Tom said with a smile. "You never know with Stackhouse, though. When you have enough money, almost anything is possible."

By the time he left the gun club, he was more optimistic about the proposed operation than he had been since he'd come up with the idea. What had seemed crazy and impossible at first glance might just be possible after all. Still a little crazy maybe . . . but possible.

He headed for the hospital where he had left Bonnie earlier. When he got there, he found her in one of the small waiting areas on the floor where Kelly's room was located.

"How is she?" Tom asked after they had hugged a greeting to each other.

"Not too bad," Bonnie said. "Still a little sick to her stomach, and of course she's still terribly worried about Laura. And she keeps telling me that she's sorry for causing so much trouble." Bonnie looked intently at Tom. "I don't suppose you have any good news that might cheer her up."

Without hesitating, he replied, "No, not yet. We're still just talking about things. It would be better not to get Kelly's hopes up."

He didn't like lying to his wife, even when he was just stretching the truth a little. The day had seen plenty of positive developments, but the whole plan could still fall through. Also, he didn't want Bonnie to worry, and he knew she would if she was aware of how close to going into action he and the makeshift rescue force really were.

"Are you going to stay here tonight?"

Bonnie shook her head. "There's really no need for me to. Kelly's asleep and probably will be all night. The nurses are keeping a close eye on her, I thought we'd go back to her house and try to get some rest ourselves."

"That sounds like a really good idea to me," Tom said.

When they got back to the house, yet another FBI man was there, in case the phone rang and it was the kidnappers. Tom knew now that wasn't going to happen. Too much time had passed. If there was going to be a ransom demand, it would have come by now. He was more convinced than ever that Keller was right about Guerrero's plans for the prisoners.

How long did they have? Tom asked himself. How long before it would be too late?

He couldn't answer that. All he could do was pray that they would be in time to save the girls.

After they had both showered and gotten into bed, Bonnie surprised him by snuggling next to him and letting her hand play over his bare chest. Tom turned toward her, and her mouth met his in a passionate kiss.

When she pulled back after a moment, he chuckled and

said, "Have you forgotten that there's a federal agent in the house?"

"I haven't forgotten anything," Bonnie said as her caresses continued and became more bold. "I don't care. I want you to make love to me, Tom."

They had always had a good sex life. Of course, the ardor had tapered off some from when they were younger, but their desire for each other was still strong—and there was definitely something to the idea that some things got better with practice. Slowly, they stripped each other's nightclothes off, and Bonnie lay back and opened herself to her husband. Tom moved into position and entered her slowly. Her arms and legs folded around him, squeezing and drawing him in deeper.

"I love having you inside me," she whispered into his ear as he launched into the timeless rhythm of their coupling. They made love at a steady, deliberate pace, but as their passion built Tom sensed an added urgency growing within Bonnie. Her movements became more fervent than usual, and the words she gasped out to urge him on held a deeper degree of emotion.

She was afraid, he realized suddenly. The stresses and strains of the past few days had built up inside her until they were almost unbearable. She was afraid for Laura and now, after what had happened this morning, she was afraid for Kelly, too.

And she knew, even though they hadn't discussed it in detail, that he was going to be doing something highly dangerous, so she faced losing him, too. No wonder she was desperate for even a fleeting moment of reassurance and sought it in the affirmation of life represented by a husband and wife joining together in the most intimate way possible.

She cried out as they climaxed almost simultaneously. Tom didn't care if the FBI tech overheard, either.

When it was over and both of them had crested the peak and started the long, slow slide down the other side, Tom cradled her face in his hands and showered kisses on it. She took hold of his wrists and held his hands there as the last spasms died away. It hadn't been the galloping, earthshaking sex they had shared as newlyweds. It had been slower and much, much sweeter, and Tom knew he would never forget this moment as long as he lived.

"You come back to me, Tom Brannon," Bonnie whispered. "I hope and pray that you bring Laura with you, but whatever else happens, you come back to me."

"Bonnie, I—"

"No," she said, "don't promise. I know you can't promise me what's going to happen. Just do what I told you. Come back to me, because I love you."

"I love you, too," he said, and he bent his head to give her a long, lingering kiss.

It might have lasted even longer if the cell phone he had left on the bedside table hadn't rung at that moment. He lifted his head and grated, "Damn it—"

"Answer it," Bonnie said without hesitation. "It might be something important, something about Laura."

Tom rolled off her and reached out to snag the phone. He opened it and brought it to his ear. "Yeah?"

"Brady Keller, Brannon," said the voice on the other end. "You'd better come see me. I may have a line on where those girls are."

Twenty-six

"I'm sorry, sir, it's after visiting hours," the nurse at the desk said as Tom stalked quickly into the lobby of the private hospital.

He paused. "I know, but it's very important that I speak to Brady Keller. He called me and asked me to come."

"I'm sorry," the nurse said firmly. "We can't make any exceptions. Our patients need their rest—"

"What I need is for you to let him in," Keller said as he rolled his wheelchair around a corner and out of a hallway. The chair's electric motor whirred softly as he used his left hand to work the throttle switch. He handled the chair quite well, especially considering that he had only been in it for a few months.

"Mr. Keller, you know we have rules—" the nurse began.

"Rules are made to be broken. Besides, this is a matter of life and death."

The nurse looked like she doubted that, but after a moment she shrugged and said, "All right. You can visit with your friend in the TV room. But be quiet about it. You know you're not supposed to get all worked up about anything."

Keller nodded to Tom and said, "Push this damn chair. Batteries' charge is getting low. I'll tell you where to go."

Tom went behind the chair and took hold of the handles. Keller guided them down a hallway to a good-sized room with several sofas and armchairs scattered around it and a big-screen TV, now dark, on one wall. It was late enough so that most of the hospital's patients had turned in for the night.

After parking Keller's wheelchair so that it faced one of the armchairs, Tom sat down, too, and leaned forward eagerly. "What's happened?" he asked.

"I got a call from one of those contacts I told you about," Keller replied, keeping his voice down as the nurse had requested. "A guy in Nuevo Laredo. He said he could put me in touch with somebody who knows where the Night Wolves' headquarters is, but whoever it is will only pass along the information in person. He doesn't trust the phone." Keller grimaced in disgust as he nodded toward his crippled body. "Unfortunately, I'm in no shape to go gallivanting across the border."

"I'll go," Tom said without hesitation. "If you think the informant will talk to me, that is."

"I asked him about that, and whether or not he thought his source would go for it. He was agreeable to setting up a meeting, but it would mean going over there by yourself. That's a damned dangerous thing to do these days."

"You think this might be a trap of some kind?"

"Not likely, but that doesn't really matter. There are plenty of people in Nuevo Laredo who will cut your throat for whatever's in your pockets. They don't have to have anything to do with the Night Wolves to be dangerous."

Tom understood that, but he didn't see that he had any choice in the matter. "Is your informant reliable? Can he be trusted?"

"As much as anybody over there, I suppose. He's never lied to me or tried to double-cross me before, as far as I know."

"Then that's good enough for me," Tom said. "Just tell me where to find him and what to say when I get there."

"You know anything about Nuevo Laredo?"

Tom shook his head. "Nothing except how to get to the international bridge."

"All right. The place you're looking for is called the Flamingo Bar. It's on Calle de Hidalgo near the *mercado*. In the old days, it was kind of a rough part of town, but still a little touristy. Not anymore. Now there's not anywhere in Nuevo Laredo that's safe for tourists after dark, and mostly you wouldn't want to go there during the day, either. Park on this side of the bridge and walk across. There'll be cabs waiting at the other end."

"Even this late?"

"Twenty-four hours a day. You see, no matter how bad it gets, there are still gringo college kids who think a night on the town in Nuevo Laredo is a rite of passage or some such shit. Hit a few bars and whorehouses, get drunk and get laid, and come back across the river to brag to all your friends about it. That's the lucky ones. The unlucky ones wind up lying in an alley, knifed and robbed, or blindfolded and kidnapped, or locked up in the Nuevo Laredo jail. It's a toss-up which of those things is worse."

"You're really making me look forward to it," Tom said dryly.

"I want to make sure you know what you're getting yourself into," Keller snapped. "If you go over there, you might not come back."

Tom was well aware of that, and yet he didn't see that he had any choice. Keller's contact might be the only trail to the girls that they would ever uncover.

"I'll be careful," he said. "What do I do when I get to the Flamingo Bar?"

"Go inside, order a beer, and ask for Pepe."

"Sounds like something out of an old movie."

"Yeah, well, they watch TV in Mexico, too. You see all sorts of shit in real life now that got started because somebody thought it would look cool in a movie, like holding a gun sideways while you shoot it." Keller snorted in disgust. "That's a good way to get hot brass right in your face, but try telling that to all the young punks who shoot that way now."

"So Pepe's your informant?"

"That's right. If he decides to trust you, he'll let you talk to his source. Either that or just pass along the information himself. I don't really know how it'll go once you're there."

"So I'll wing it," Tom said. "It won't be the first time."

"Yeah." Keller slipped his left hand into the pocket of the robe he wore over his pajamas and looked around, carefully checking to make sure that he and Tom were alone. Then he pulled a gun from his pocket and held it out. "Take this. You may need it."

Tom reached out and took the gun, a flat little .25 automatic with a short barrel. Accurate only at close range and not very powerful, it could still be an effective weapon in the hands of a man who knew how to use it. Tom made sure the safety was set, then tucked it into the back of his jeans so that the tail of his shirt hung over it.

"I don't have a concealed-carry permit for Texas," he said.

"That's all right, the gun's not registered anyway. You'll already be in trouble if the cops pick you up on this side of the border. But if you need it over there in Nuevo Laredo, you'll be glad you took the risk."

Tom didn't doubt that. Just the hard reality of the gun

against the small of his back made him feel a little better about the prospect of venturing south of the border.

He put his hands on his knees. "Anything else you need to tell me?"

"Keep an eye on your cabdriver. The Flamingo is four blocks south of the bridge and then two blocks east. If your driver starts taking you some other way and tells you it's a shortcut, odds are he plans to deliver you to kidnappers. Put the gun against his head and tell him you'll blow his brains out if he doesn't take you where he's supposed to. Watch what the fare is, too. They overcharge like sons of bitches over there."

Tom smiled grimly as he pushed himself to his feet. Somehow the prospect of being overcharged didn't seem as daunting as being kidnapped.

"Thanks," he said to Keller. "And I mean thanks for everything. Without your help we wouldn't stand a chance of pulling this off."

"Yeah, well, you only stand a slim chance of it anyway. Sometimes, though, you've just got to roll the dice." Tom started behind the chair, but Keller waved him away. "Go on, Pepe's waiting for you. I can get back to my room."

Tom nodded and left him there, sitting in front of the TV with its big, blank screen. He thought he saw a look of longing in Keller's good eye, as if the man wanted to get up out of that chair and follow him, even though it would mean going into danger.

Once he got in the car, Tom debated with himself whether or not to call Bonnie and tell her what was going on. She knew that Keller had some sort of lead to the girls' whereabouts, but since Tom hadn't known beforehand that he would have to cross the border to get it, neither did she.

She wouldn't like the fact that he had kept her in the dark, but it might be better that way, he decided. If he called her now and told her where he was going, she would worry like crazy until he got back. If he didn't tell her about it until it was over and done with, he would save her some anxiety.

But if he never came back, he would have missed his chance to say good-bye to her. . . .

He shoved that thought out of his brain. It was the sort of negative thinking he didn't need right now. He was going to come back, and when he did, he would know where the kidnapped girls were being held.

With that decision made, he drove toward downtown Laredo and International Bridge #1, the main pedestrian bridge and point of entry to Nuevo Laredo.

There were several parking lots at the northern end of the bridge. They were mostly empty, and that told Tom just how much the current state of near-lawlessness in Nuevo Laredo had affected the tourist industry. In better times, Nuevo Laredo would have had a booming nightlife fueled primarily by visitors from north of the border. He parked the rental car and locked it, then started across the long, dimly lit span. A small Mexican customs office and guard station waited at the far end, but the bored-looking officer on duty just collected the twenty-five-cent toll and waved Tom on.

It was about ten-thirty by now. Some of the restaurants and bars were still open along the main drag just south of the bridge, but the little stores and shops along the street were closed. A street sign told Tom that he was on Avenida Guerrero, and his mouth quirked in a humorless smile at the irony. He was confident that the street hadn't been named after Colonel Alfonso Guerrero—but these days the leader of Los Lobos de la Noche was probably the most important man in Nuevo Laredo. Certainly the most feared.

Just as Brady Keller had predicted, several taxicabs sat parked at the curb, with their drivers leaning against their fenders. The men straightened as Tom approached, and one of them called in heavily accented English, "Hey, buddy, you need a ride?"

"Don' go with him," another cabbie said quickly. "His cab stinks like goat shit. I got your cab right here, amigo." He slapped a hand against the fender of a thirty-year-old Dodge.

The other cabbies called to Tom, as well, trying to attract his business. He didn't figure any of them were more trustworthy than the others, so he settled for the first one who had accosted him, prompting the others to mutter insults in Spanish. Tom ignored them as he got in the back and the grinning driver slid behind the wheel. He was a stocky man about thirty with a toothpick clenched between his teeth.

"Where you wanna go, buddy? You wanna drink or some pussy? I know plenty of good places, get you anything you want, anything at all."

"The Flamingo Bar," Tom said.

The driver turned halfway around in his seat and shook his head. "Oh, no, you don' wanna go there! Tha's a bad place, they'll rip you off really bad, man. You jus' let me take you to a place I know, you'll get your rocks off really good—"

"The Flamingo Bar," Tom said again. "How much?"

"Oh, man, the Flamingo's a long way an' nobody goes there. I couldn't get a fare back here, you know? And the people who run it, they're a bunch o' friggin' *bandidos*—"

"How much?" Tom knew perfectly well that the reason the cabbie didn't want to take him to the Flamingo Bar was because he didn't get paid off by the proprietor for steering suckers there. He didn't care about that, though. He would take one of the other cabs if he had to.

"Well, if you're sure, man, it'll cost you twenty-five bucks, American."

"It's six blocks from here. I'll give you a dollar a block."

"Oh, man!" The driver sounded like he was in great pain. "You know how much gas costs, man? I can't afford to start this sucker for six bucks." He paused. "Make it twenty."

"Ten," Tom said.

"Fifteen."

"Twelve."

The cabbie considered and then nodded. "Okay, you got a deal. Twelve bucks."

"And twenty more if you wait for me and bring me back here."

"Shit, no! How long you gonna be there? I can't sit around all night for no twenty bucks!"

"I thought you said you couldn't get a fare back here from there," Tom reminded him.

The cabbie grinned sheepishly. "Oh, yeah, I did say that, didn' I?" He shrugged. "Make it twenty-five bucks, and I wait half an hour. Tha's all."

Tom didn't know if half an hour would be long enough, but he supposed it would do for a start. "All right," he said. "Let's go."

The driver cranked the engine. It started with a rumble, and with a clash of gears and a squeal of rubber he pulled out and floored it, as if determined to break the land speed record for the four blocks between here and the place where he would have to turn. The acceleration pressed Tom back against the rattily upholstered seat.

His hand slipped behind him and touched the reassuring

hardness of the little pistol. He was ready to draw it if the driver deviated from the route that Tom knew he was supposed to take to reach the Flamingo Bar.

The cabbie didn't try any funny business, though, other than driving like a madman, and a couple of minutes later the old car rocked to a stop on worn-out shock absorbers. Garish pink light from a large neon sign in the shape of a flamingo filled the cab and spilled over the sidewalk. The cabbie turned around and said, "Here you go, man. Where's my money?"

Tom held out a ten and a couple of ones. The driver snatched them and said, "What about the twenty-five for waiting?"

"You get that when I come out."

"Your lack of trust wounds me, amigo."

Despite everything, Tom found himself almost liking the guy. He was a walking, talking stereotype, but he played his role with enthusiasm.

"If you're still here when I come out, you'll get your money," Tom said as he climbed out of the cab.

"If you come out, I'll be here," the cabbie said meaningfully. "Sometimes guys go in the Flamingo, and they're never seen again, you know what I mean?"

Tom knew, all right, but there was nothing he could do about it. He crossed the sidewalk, pushed open the heavy door, and stepped into the Flamingo Bar.

Twenty-seven

If the cabdriver was a stereotype, the Flamingo Bar was a cliché—dim, smoky, loud, and filled with all sorts of unsavory characters. The driving beat of Tejano music made the soles of Tom's feet vibrate and put his teeth on edge.

No one seemed to be paying any attention to him as he walked in, but he would have been willing to bet that wasn't really the case. In fact, he could feel eyes on him. He just couldn't pin down who they belonged to.

As he walked toward the bar, he studied the crowd. It was predominantly male and predominantly Hispanic, but there were quite a few white males mixed in, those dumb college kids Keller had mentioned. There were no white females; all the women were Latinas.

Neon beer signs behind the bar provided a mixture of light. Tom stepped up to an open space at the hardwood and caught the eye of a bartender. He gave the man a nod and said, *"Cerveza."*

The bartender took a bottle of beer from a cooler. Water and bits of ice dripped from the brown glass as he set it on the bar in front of Tom. With a practiced twist, he removed the cap.

"Five dollars."

That was an expensive beer, but Tom supposed the bartender charged whatever he thought the market would bear. He didn't argue, just dropped a bill on the bar and then took a swig of the beer. It was extremely cold and surprisingly good.

As Tom set the bottle on the bar, he asked in Spanish, "Is Pepe around tonight?" He felt like a character in a movie saying it, as he had told Keller.

In decent English, the bartender said, "There might be a dozen guys in here named Pepe, Señor. You can call the one you're looking for . . . like a dog."

He snickered.

Anger boiled up inside Tom. He wanted to reach over the bar, grab the smart-ass's dirty shirt, and smack his face down into the bar a couple of times. That might teach him a little respect and get a straight answer out of him.

But it would also cause half the men in the bar to come after him, Tom reflected, and then at the very least he'd get the shit beaten out of him for no good reason. He forced himself to smile instead and drawled in his best B-movie hero voice, "I think you know the Pepe I'm looking for, amigo."

The bartender sneered and started to turn away. "Drink your beer and go back where you came from, gringo. You ain't welcome here."

"You want to do this the hard way, eh?" The words were out of Tom's mouth before he could stop them.

The bartender stopped turning and glared at him. "What you sayin' to me, man? You loco or something?"

A small man stepped up to the bar beside Tom and said tentatively, *"Tequila, por favor?"*

The bartender ignored him and continued glowering at Tom. "You're too old to come in here and act like a tough hombre, gringo. Get out."

Tom shook his head. "Sorry. Not until you tell me where I can find Pepe."

That was when something hard dug into Tom's side. His head jerked in surprise to the mousy little man beside him, who smiled and said, "I'm Pepe, Señor Brannon. Don't make a scene, just come with me, please."

Tom knew the thing digging into his side was the snout of a gun. It seemed he didn't have any choice in the matter. He nodded and said, "All right. Lead the way."

"Walk with me," Pepe said. "Don't try anything."

Tom didn't. With Pepe close beside him, indicating which way he should go with prods of the unseen gun, Tom walked toward the rear of the big, smoke-filled room. Pepe steered him toward a beaded curtain that closed off an arched doorway. They moved through it, the beads rattling around them, and went down a narrow, dim hallway. A door at the end led into a cluttered office dominated by a large desk. Pepe closed the door behind them and told Tom, "Sit down."

Tom sank into a chair with torn upholstery in front of the desk. Pepe went behind it and lowered himself into a large swivel chair that seemed to swallow up his slight form. He put a short-barreled revolver on the desk in front of him and sighed.

"The hard way?" he said. "You really told my bartender you were going to have to do this the hard way?"

"You're a fine one to talk. A beaded curtain? A sign in the shape of a flamingo? It's not 1957 anymore."

Pepe's narrow shoulders rose and fell in a shrug. "Tourists expect a certain . . . ambience, I suppose you could say."

"I didn't think the tourist trade amounted to much in Nuevo Laredo anymore."

"It doesn't. All because of that damned Guerrero!" Pepe's

hand slapped down on the desk next to the gun. "As you've probably guessed, this is my place. It used to be a gold mine, Brannon, a damn gold mine. Now the gringos are too scared to come over here, most of them, and even the Mexicanos don't come like they used to. This is not a good time to be a crooked night club owner, let me tell you."

"You have my sympathy," Tom said dryly. "Right now, though, I just want to know about—"

Pepe held up a hand to stop him. "I know what you want to know. But I can't tell you."

Tom frowned and hunched forward in his seat. "Brady Keller said—"

"Again, I know. I can't tell you because I don't have the information. But I know someone who does. Will you come with me to the place where that person waits?"

Without hesitation, Tom got to his feet. "Let's go."

"I warn you, it is not a pleasant place."

"There's nothing pleasant about this business. Let's just go."

Tom tried to curb his impatience as Pepe stood up and sauntered out from behind the desk. The little man led him out of the office, through another door, and into an alley behind the Flamingo Bar. It was almost completely dark back here, with just enough light so that Tom could follow Pepe's slight figure. The possibility that this could all be an elaborate trap of some kind still lurked in the back of his mind, but he had come this far. He wouldn't have turned back, anyway, not so long as there was any chance that he could find a lead to the place Laura and the other girls were being held.

As the two men made their way through a maze of alleys and narrow, dark streets, Tom realized that he had no idea how to get back to the bar. He was utterly lost. They went around another corner, and wheels rattled on

the rough, poorly repaired concrete sidewalk. In the light
that spilled faintly through a dirty window, Tom saw a
grotesque figure coming toward them. The man had no
legs. His torso was strapped onto some kind of wheeled
platform. He pushed himself along with his arms. His hair
was a wild black tangle and a scraggly beard adorned his
jutting jaw. He came to a stop in front of Tom and Pepe.

"*Hola,* Ramón," Pepe said. "I have brought the gringo."

Ramón looked up at Tom. A tin cup dangled from a
string around his neck, and Tom realized that the man was
a beggar. Ramón said, "You seek Alfonso Guerrero and
Los Lobos de la Noche?"

Tom glanced around. They were on the sidewalk, in the
open, with dark buildings looming nearby. Anyone could
have been hidden in the shadows, eavesdropping.

"Are you sure it's safe to talk about these things?" he
asked.

Ramón laughed. It was an ugly sound. "What more can
Guerrero do to me than he has already done? But fear
not. Pepe and I have many friends here. They keep us
safe. The Night Wolves and their friends cannot venture
near here without me knowing."

"All right," Tom said. "I'll take your word for it. I don't
have a whole lot of choice."

"No, Señor. You don't." Ramón tapped the tin cup. "One
hundred dollars."

Tom hadn't expected that the information he wanted
would be free. In fact, he had figured that the amount
would be higher. He took out the money and put the bills
in the cup.

"I do this because I hate Guerrero, you understand,"
Ramón said. "The payment is . . . a token, you could say.
All information must have its price."

"Of course. You know about the girls Guerrero and his men kidnapped several days ago?"

"Yes."

"I need to know where he's holding them. Where his headquarters are, because I suppose that's the most likely place for the girls to be."

"One of these girls . . . your daughter?"

"My niece."

"I see," Ramón said. He looked at the club owner. "Pepe, step back. There is no need for you to hear this. Some knowledge is dangerous to possess."

Pepe murmured agreement and moved away along the sidewalk. Somehow, that made Tom feel a little more nervous, although he had no reason to trust Pepe more than he did Ramón.

Ramón motioned for Tom to kneel in front of him, bringing Tom down to his level. Tom remembered that Brady Keller had wanted to meet his eyes squarely, too. He couldn't blame either of the men for feeling that way.

"I was once one of Los Lobos de la Noche," Ramón said quietly. "You would not think it to look at me now, would you?"

"No," Tom said, figuring that Ramón wanted an honest answer.

"I was not always as I am now. Once I was a commando in the Army, and I deserted and went to work for the cartel when my colonel did. You know the story of the Night Wolves?"

"I do," Tom said.

"Then you know there was a great deal of devotion among us. We would have died for each other. But when there is that much devotion, there can also be great anger, in the case of a betrayal."

"Guerrero betrayed you?"

"No. I betrayed him. And he caught me."

Tom didn't particularly care about Ramón's sordid history. The man had already admitted to being one of the Night Wolves, and that made him the scum of the earth as far as Tom was concerned. Even scum could be valuable, though, and if Ramón could tell him where to find Laura, the beggar was priceless. Tom reined in his impatience and allowed Ramón to tell the story his own way.

"The colonel wanted to know the details of my betrayal, but I would not tell him. So he took a saw and cut my toes off, one by one, and then he cut off part of my feet, and then cut the rest off at the ankle. By then I was talking. But after I had told him everything he wanted to know, he took the saw and cut the rest of my legs off . . . three or four inches at a time. Then he did the cruelest thing of all. The best doctors in Nuevo Laredo work for him. He had them save my life, so that I could live out the rest of my years . . . like this."

It was a horrible story, and hearing it made Tom even more determined to get Laura and the other girls out of the hands of that mad butcher. He said, "Even though he wanted to continue your torture, I'm surprised he left you alive. He has to know that you'd want revenge."

Ramón spread his hands. "But that is the arrogance of the man, Señor. He believes that I cannot touch him, that I am so insignificant he had no need to fear me. And until now, it has been true."

"If you know where his headquarters are, you could have passed along that information to the authorities at any time," Tom pointed out.

"And what good would that do? The Mexican police and military avoid Guerrero like, as you Americans say, the plague. They want nothing to do with him. They certainly do not want to be placed in the position of having to try to arrest him. Anyone who even made the attempt would be assassinated immediately, along with his family. And as for the Americans . . ." Ramón waved a hand dismissively. "The Americans believe too strongly in rules and borders. They refuse to recognize that evil follows no rules and acknowledges no borders. No, Señor, I have been waiting for a man such as you . . . a man who will do what is right, and to hell with the rules."

"So tell me," Tom breathed. "Where is Guerrero? Where are those girls?"

"There is an old mission, five miles or so south of town. Several years ago, Guerrero took it over and had it remade to his own satisfaction. Now it is his home and the headquarters of the Night Wolves. The girls are there."

Tom closed his eyes for a second and mentally gave thanks. It was like a weight had lifted from him. Freeing the girls still remained a huge, dangerous task, but locating them had been the first step. Without that, he and his allies could accomplish nothing.

Ramón reached out and wrapped skeletal fingers around Tom's arm. "You must hurry, though, Señor. Two nights from now, men will come to the mission and bid on those girls. Some of them will be taken away and forced to work in houses of ill repute. Their lives will be short, brutal, and degrading. And they will be the fortunate ones. The less fortunate will be bought by . . . other men."

A shiver went through Tom. "We'll get them out. Thank you, Ramón. I owe you a debt I can never repay, as do the families of those other girls."

"You know, of course, that Guerrero will not allow you to just take the girls. You will have to fight for them."

Tom nodded. "I know. And the odds will be against us. But we *will* fight."

"Then you can repay your debt to me, Señor." A smile lit up the hollow features of Ramón's face. "Just be sure that before you leave there, that bastard Guerrero is dead."

Twenty-eight

When the conversation with Ramón was finished and the crippled beggar rolled himself away into the shadows, Pepe approached Tom again and said, "Now I will take you back to the bar, Señor Brannon."

"I'm much obliged for your help," Tom said. "Whatever I owe you—"

Pepe dismissed the offer with a wave of his hand. "Unlike Ramón, I require no payment, Señor. Brady Keller is an old friend of mine, and I am happy to do a favor for a friend of a friend. Besides, there is a chance you will break Guerrero's power and lift his foot from the throat of Nuevo Laredo, so that men such as myself can get back to making a dishonest living."

Tom chuckled. "Well, you have my gratitude, anyway."

"That I will accept, Señor."

Pepe led the way back to the Flamingo Bar—whether retracing their steps from earlier or taking a different route, Tom never knew. They entered the night club through the rear door and went through the main room. *"Vaya con Dios,* Señor Brannon," Pepe said as they reached the front door. "I hope your mission will be successful."

Tom nodded his thanks and stepped out onto the sidewalk. Pepe pulled the door closed, which muted the sound of the Tejano music without silencing it completely.

The cabbie who had brought him here was standing at the curb, leaning on the fender of his old car. Tom was a little surprised to see that the man had actually waited for him. It had been longer than the half hour the cabbie had promised to wait.

"Hey, buddy, you ready to go?"

Tom took a step toward the cab, nodding as he said, "Yes, let's head back to the bridge."

The cabbie rolled the toothpick to the other side of his mouth, grinned in the garish neon light of the flamingo-shaped sign, and said, "Sorry, buddy, that ain't where you're goin'."

Tom tensed at the menacing tone of the cabbie's voice. He heard the scuff of shoe leather on concrete and looked quickly over his shoulder. Two men had emerged from the shadows along the street, one to his right and one to his left. They moved in quickly, cutting him off so that he couldn't spin around and duck back into the night club. All he could do was move forward, and that took him toward the cabbie, who stepped away from the car and brought a switchblade out of the hip pocket of his jeans. The blade snapped open and glittered in the light from the neon sign.

"You should've let me take you where I wanted to earlier, amigo," the cabbie said. "We could have saved all this trouble."

"You mean I should've let you turn me over to thieves or kidnappers, whatever it is you and your friends have in mind?"

"You come down here, you got to expect somethin' bad to happen, hombre. Now come with us, and if you don' fight, maybe you won't get hurt too bad. You might even live to go back home."

"I'm not going anywhere with you," Tom said, "not without a fight. And if there's a commotion out here, they're liable to hear inside the club."

The cabbie laughed harshly. "You think they care in there?" He weaved the point of the switchblade back and forth in the air in front of him. "Come on, you bastard, or I'll cut you up."

The man suddenly darted the blade at Tom's face. Tom stepped to the side instinctively to avoid the thrust. The cabbie laughed again, showing that he was just playing a cruel game with Tom, like a cat with a trapped mouse.

The problem was that this mouse could fight back. Tom used his avoidance of the knife as concealment for the way he swung his right hand behind him. His fingers closed around the butt of the pistol Brady Keller had given him. He brought it out and around in a smooth, efficient move that left it pointing at the cabbie's startled face as he stood frozen a few feet away on the sidewalk.

Tom heard quick movements from the men behind him, but the cabbie called out in Spanish for them to stop. Tom smiled tightly and said, "That's smart. Even if your amigos jump me, I'll be able to pull the trigger before I go down. And if that happens, you'll be a dead man."

"Stay back," the cabbie said to the other men. "This hombre is loco!" To Tom, he went on. "Don' you know you can't do this, man? It . . . it just isn't done!"

"What, fighting back when someone tries to do you wrong?" Tom's lips drew back from his teeth in an expression that was half grin, half snarl. "Get in the cab. You're taking me back to the bridge, just as we agreed." He chuckled grimly. "I'll even give you the twenty-five bucks. That's how much of a generous guy I am."

The cabbie closed the switchblade. "You gonna be sorry about this, man," he said darkly.

"Drop that knife," Tom ordered. "I'm not getting in the cab as long as you've got it."

The cabbie sighed and said, "All right."

But instead of dropping the knife, he suddenly threw it hard, right at Tom's face. Tom ducked to avoid it, and as he did, the cabbie flung himself to the side, out of the line of fire in case Tom pulled the trigger.

Tom didn't fire, though, because he heard rushing footsteps closing in on him from both sides. Now that the cabbie was momentarily out of danger, the other men figured it was safe to attack.

Spinning to his left, he chopped at the head of the man coming at him from that direction. The blow landed with a solid thud. The man grunted in pain and stumbled. Tom tried to turn back to meet the threat of the other one, but he was too late. The second man crashed into him, knocking him off his feet.

Tom managed to hang onto the gun as he rolled across the dirty sidewalk. A figure loomed above him, shouting vile obscenities. It was the cabbie, and he swung his foot at Tom's head in a vicious kick.

Tom kept rolling to avoid the kick. He reached up with his left hand and grabbed the cabbie's ankle as the kick missed him. He heaved as hard as he could. With a startled yell, the cabbie went over backward and crashed to the sidewalk.

The other two men were still on their feet. They came after Tom, and he couldn't stay out of the way of both of them. A foot slammed into his ribs, sending shards of white-hot pain through him, and a second later another kick connected with the wrist of his gun hand. The little pistol slipped out of his fingers and slid spinning into the dark street.

Hands grabbed Tom and hauled him roughly to his feet. A few feet away, the cabbie was just getting up. He reached out and snagged the switchblade he had thrown at Tom. It had fallen to the sidewalk, and now it was back in the cabbie's hand. With a flick of his wrist, he opened it.

"You damn gringo," he snarled at Tom as he advanced toward him. The other two men tightened their grip on Tom's arms so that he had no chance of getting away. "Now you gonna pay for what you did, man. You can't threaten me an' get away with it, you son of a bitch."

Tom's heart pounded furiously in his chest. He was more angry than afraid, and as soon as the cabbie came close enough, he was going to try to kick the bastard in the balls. It might not change anything in the end, but he wanted to deal out as much punishment as he could while he still had the chance.

But as the cabbie approached, again weaving the point of the blade through the air in front of him, Tom felt his heart sink. If they killed him, he would never get back to Laredo with the knowledge of where the kidnapped girls were being held. He cursed the fate that had sent him crossing the path of these thugs. Just as Brady Keller had warned him, not all the dangers in Nuevo Laredo had anything to do with Los Lobos de la Noche.

The cabbie was almost close enough. Tom tensed himself, ready to lash out at the man and then try to tear himself free from the two who held him. He didn't have much chance, but he couldn't give up.

Then suddenly there was movement in the shadows behind the cabbie. With a dull gleam of metal, the barrel of a heavy revolver crashed down on the man's head. He let go of the switchblade as his knees unhinged. The knife rattled to the sidewalk. The cabbie was right behind it, pitching face-first to the concrete.

Texas Ranger Captain Roy Rodgers stepped into the light, leveled the gun in his hand at Tom's captors, and said in a quiet, dangerous voice, "Let him go."

Instead of following orders, the men practically threw Tom at Rodgers, making it impossible for the Ranger to fire. Rodgers darted aside as the two men grabbed for their own guns, tucked behind their belts.

"Drop 'em!" Rodgers shouted, but the men paid him no heed. Their guns came up and spouted flame.

Tom threw himself into the street as shots roared. He wasn't trying to escape. He reached out in the direction his pistol had gone when it was kicked out of his hand earlier. His fingers touched metal, and he grabbed it up and rolled over onto his stomach, facing back toward the sidewalk.

He saw Rodgers fire and saw one of the gunmen spin off his feet. But then Rodgers staggered as he was hit by a shot from the other man. The Ranger tried to bring his gun around, but he was moving too slowly.

The little pistol in Tom's hand cracked wickedly as it bucked twice against his palm. Knowing the gun wasn't all that accurate, he aimed for the largest possible target, the middle of the man's body. The man jerked back a step, grunted, and doubled over as his gun slipped from his fingers and thudded to the sidewalk. He crumpled, clutching his belly where the .25-caliber slugs had ripped into it.

Tom scrambled to his feet and ran to Rodgers's side. He gripped the Ranger's arm with his left hand, steadying him. "How bad are you hit?" he asked.

"Not bad," Rodgers grated. "Just grazed me on the side, maybe broke a rib. I'll be all right, though, if we can get out of here."

Tom didn't waste any time asking the Ranger what he

was doing there. He just steered Rodgers toward the cab, which was still parked at the curb. Along the way he stepped on the outstretched hand of the unconscious cabbie and heard bones snap. It hadn't been intentional—but he couldn't bring himself to feel sorry for the son of a bitch, either.

He pulled open the passenger door and helped Rodgers into the car. Then he slammed the door and hurried around to get behind the wheel. The keys were in the ignition. Tom started the car and put it in gear. He drove toward the international bridge, but not at the breakneck pace the cabbie had achieved on the earlier trip.

"Wait a minute," Rodgers said, his voice stretched taut by pain. "I can't walk across the bridge and through U.S. customs with this bloodstain on my shirt. Take the next right and then the next left after that. That'll take us to Bridge #2. You can drive across that one." Rodgers took off his Stetson and handed it to Tom. "Put that on and pull down the brim. You'll just be a Mexican cabbie taking a drunken gringo back to Laredo."

Tom nodded and put on the hat. He pulled over and helped Rodgers into the rear seat, where a passenger would normally ride. Then they resumed the trip and drove the few blocks to International Bridge #2. Straight across the river, just past the customs booths, was the southern tip of Interstate 35.

A few cars and trucks were crossing the bridge, even at this time of night. Tom got in line and waited his turn. When he pulled up to the customs booth, he muttered something in Spanish about having a fare for one of the hotels in downtown Laredo. The U.S. customs agent asked him a few perfunctory questions, collected the dollar toll, and waved him through after glancing into the backseat at Rodgers, who was hunched over looking sick. It was certainly a convincing imitation of being drunk.

A feeling of relief washed through Tom as he drove away from the bridge. Just being on American soil again meant a lot. He took the first exit from the interstate highway, made a few turns, drove a few blocks, and wound up back at the parking lot where he had left his car earlier in the evening. That seemed like a long time ago now, and it seemed even longer since he had left Kelly's house to meet with Brady Keller. The get-together at the gun club was ancient history, even though it had taken place only five hours earlier.

The two men transferred from the cab to Tom's rental car. Rodgers said, "I'll try not to get blood on the seat. The rental company wouldn't be happy about that."

"You saved my life," Tom pointed out. "I'm not too worried what the rental company thinks."

"Well, you saved mine, too. That second hombre would've dropped me if you hadn't gotten him first."

"And you wouldn't have been there if it wasn't for me." Tom drove steadily through downtown Laredo. "You've been following me, haven't you?"

"Yeah."

"So you know what we're doing?" Tom's voice was grim as he asked the question.

"I know enough to make a good guess."

"The question now is, what are you going to do about it?"

"We can talk about that while your wife is patching up this bullet crease in my side."

Tom glanced over at the Ranger in surprise. "I figured I ought to take you to the emergency room."

Rodgers shook his head. "That'd mean the gunshot wound would have to be reported, and we'd have to put this whole thing on an official basis. I'd rather not do that just yet, until we've had a chance to talk."

"What makes you think my wife can take care of that wound?"

"She's married to you." Rodgers laughed. "I figure she's bound to have some experience patching up gunshot wounds."

"I'm not the Lone Ranger, you know, going around getting into gunfights all the time."

"Just drive," Rodgers said.

Twenty-nine

Tom went into the house first, moving quietly. The FBI technician in the den was sound asleep, stretched out on one of the sofas. The guy would undoubtedly get his ass chewed out if Agent Morgan ever got wind of his dereliction of duty, but Tom sure as hell wasn't going to tell her. He was glad the agent was sleeping on the job. It made getting Rodgers in the house that much easier.

He took the Ranger into the bathroom just off the master bedroom and got his first good look at the extent of the bloodstain on Rodgers's shirt. It was pretty large, and Tom wasn't surprised that Rodgers was pale and unsteady, after losing that much blood.

Rodgers sat down on the toilet while Tom said, "I'll go get Bonnie." Rodgers nodded weakly.

Tom found Bonnie sitting in a rocking chair in the guest bedroom, wearing her robe, a paperback book lying in her lap where she had obviously dropped it when she dozed off. She had tried to wait up for him to return from his meeting with Brady Keller, but the hour had gotten too late and weariness had overtaken her.

He put a hand on her shoulder and said her name softly.

She gasped as she came awake. Her eyes flew open and she stared up at Tom for a second as if she didn't recognize him. Then her brain cleared and she threw her arms around his neck, coming up out of the chair as she hugged him hard.

"Oh my God!" she said. "When it got so late, I was afraid something had happened to you, Tom." She drew back a little and looked him over, and she must have noticed his disheveled state because she went on. "Goodness, it looks like you've been rolling around in the street!"

"That's a pretty good guess," Tom told her dryly.

"And what's that on your hand? Is it . . . it's blood! Are you all right?"

Tom looked down at his hand and saw the crimson smear on it. He must have gotten the blood on him while he was helping Rodgers.

"It's not my blood," he said. "It belongs to Roy Rodgers."

She blinked and frowned in confusion, then her expression cleared. "The Texas Ranger?"

"That's right. He's sitting in Kelly's bathroom right now with a bullet crease in his side. I thought maybe you could help me with him."

Bonnie's eyes widened. "You stay out half the night and then bring home a Texas Ranger with a gunshot wound? Tom, what in the world have you been doing?"

He didn't think it would hurt to tell her. "Finding out where Guerrero and his men are holding Laura and the other girls."

That news made Bonnie's eyes widen even more. She brought a hand to her mouth. "Really?" she asked, as if she couldn't quite bring herself to hope that it was true.

"Really," Tom told her. "Come on and help me with Rodgers, and I'll tell you all about it."

They made their way quietly down the hall to the master bedroom as Tom whispered to her that he didn't want to wake the FBI agent in the den. When they reached the bathroom, they found Rodgers with his head leaned back against the wall, his eyes closed. He didn't stir when they came in, and Tom knew he had passed out. He felt a moment of doubt about this; Rodgers might need more medical attention than he and Bonnie could provide. But the Ranger had been right about the dangers of an emergency room visit. Once his injury was on record, his superiors would want to know how he had gotten shot, and he would have to tell them.

Bonnie took a deep breath and her jaw set stubbornly. "Let's get that shirt off of him," she said as she picked up a small pair of scissors from the vanity and went to work cutting the bloody garment away.

Rodgers stirred and his eyelids fluttered, but he didn't quite regain consciousness until they had the shirt off and began using wet paper towels to wipe away the blood around the wound. The bullet had left an ugly gash about four inches long in his side. It had knocked out a small chunk of meat and resulted in a lot of blood, but Tom could tell by looking that the injury wasn't all that serious, just messy and probably quite painful. He clapped a hand over Rodgers's mouth to keep the Ranger from yelling as Bonnie doused the wound with alcohol. Rodgers's eyes opened wide at the touch of the fiery liquid.

Tom squeezed the Ranger's shoulder with his other hand. "Hang on," he said. "We're almost done. The worst is over."

Bonnie found some gauze and adhesive tape in a cabinet and fashioned a thick bandage that she taped in place over the wound. The blood had started flowing again and the bandage would probably have to be soaked off when it was changed, but Bonnie made it tight enough that it ought to staunch the bleeding.

"Thanks," Rodgers choked out. "Feels like you did . . . a good job."

"You ought to be in a hospital," Bonnie said. "I'm not a doctor."

"No, but you're a mother, and this is just like a really bad scraped knee," Tom said.

"I'm serious," Bonnie insisted. "Captain Rodgers may need stitches, and he might have a broken rib."

Rodgers lifted a hand and waved off that suggestion. "No hospital," he said. "No stitches. I can tell now . . . no ribs broken. Don't want to . . . report this."

"Because of the girls?"

Rodgers nodded.

Bonnie turned to Tom. "You said you'd tell me what happened."

He sat down on the edge of the tub and motioned for Bonnie to sit beside him. When she was perched there, he said, "Brady Keller got a lead on somebody who knows where the Night Wolves have their headquarters."

"Not sure I . . . need to hear this," Rodgers murmured.

"You're hip-deep in it already," Tom told him bluntly. "I'd say you've already made your choice which side you're on, Captain."

Rodgers looked intently at him for a moment and then nodded slowly. "I figured it had to be something like that when you went over to Nuevo Laredo. Go on, Brannon."

Bonnie said in surprise, "You went to Nuevo Laredo?"

"Keller's contact wanted a personal meeting," Tom explained. "I didn't have any choice. I thought about calling you to tell you, but I decided it would be better to wait until after it was done, so you wouldn't worry."

She frowned. "You should have thought that through a little more . . . but we'll let it go for now. What happened?"

Tom explained what Brady Keller had told him and then

sketched in the highlights of his visit to Nuevo Laredo. Bonnie paled when he reached the part about being accosted by the cabbie and the man's two accomplices.

"You could have been killed," she exclaimed.

Tom nodded solemnly. "I could have been," he agreed, "if Captain Rodgers hadn't come along." He turned to the Ranger and asked, "How long have you been following me?"

"Ever since I took you to see Brady Keller the first time," Rodgers admitted.

"I never spotted you."

Rodgers smiled tiredly. "It's nice to know I'm good at *something*. I don't seem to be doing the rest of my job very well. If I was doing my duty, I'd put a stop to this crazy rescue plan you're cooking up, Brannon."

"You know you've got a higher duty than that. You've got a duty to see that those girls get home safely."

"That doesn't give you or me the right to break the law."

"What law? The law that says Guerrero and his killers can invade our country and go on a rampage of murder and kidnapping, and we can't do a thing about it because they go back on the other side of a piddling little river?" Tom shook his head. "That doesn't sound like much of a law to me, Captain. It sounds like madness."

Rodgers sighed. "I don't want to argue with you. I just wish you'd give up the idea."

Tom shook his head. "I wasn't born with much backup in me, I guess. And now that I know where to find those girls, I'm sure as hell not going to abandon them. Especially when I know what's going to happen to them in a couple more days."

"What?" Bonnie asked quickly. "What is it, Tom?"

"Guerrero plans to auction them off to the highest bidders."

"Good Lord," Rodgers muttered. "Are you sure about that, Brannon?"

Tom nodded. "The man who told me about it used to be one of Guerrero's Night Wolves. Obviously, he's still got connections inside the gang."

"Can you trust what he told you?"

"After what Guerrero did to him, I believe him when he says he wants revenge. One way of getting it is to ruin Guerrero's plans. And I sort of promised him that if I got a chance to kill Guerrero . . ."

"Oh, Tom, no," Bonnie said.

"I'm not a murderer," Tom declared. "I won't kill Guerrero in cold blood. But it won't ever come to that, because Guerrero and his men will fight when we come to take the girls."

Rodgers said, "You and a bunch of middle-aged civilians."

"They're all Americans," Tom said. "Don't ever underestimate them. Hitler and Hirohito had professional armies, some of the best in the world, and we took them on with farmers and hardware store clerks and teachers and bowling alley managers. A bunch of men with something worth fighting for can do just about anything they set their minds and hearts to do." He shrugged. "Besides, we've got some professional help, too."

"Charles Long and his friends? I saw them go into that gun club tonight. They're risking their careers, as well as their lives."

"I guess they think the risk is worth it," Tom said quietly.

The three of them sat silently for a few moments. Finally, Rodgers asked, "Where are the girls?"

Tom didn't answer right away.

"Blast it, like you said, I'm already hip-deep in this. I've concealed evidence, I've ignored a criminal conspiracy, and I shot a man in Nuevo Laredo tonight when I wasn't even supposed to be there. It's a little late to stop trusting me now."

"Are you sure about that?"

Rodgers glared at Tom. "You've got my word on it."

"That's what I've been waiting to hear," Tom said. "The Night Wolves are using an old mission five miles south of Nuevo Laredo as their headquarters."

Rodgers nodded. "I know of the place. It's a fairly large compound, with the mission itself and several outbuildings. It's been abandoned for years, though."

"Not according to my source. He says Guerrero took it over several years ago and had it redone to suit himself. He probably fortified the place, too."

"If he's there, I'm sure he did," Rodgers agreed. "And that's where he has the girls?"

"According to the man I talked to."

"Well, that's a lot more solid information than we had before. Maybe we ought to get in touch with the Mexican government—"

"I trusted you, Ranger," Tom broke in, his voice hardening. "Don't give me cause to regret that."

"You're right," Rodgers said with a sigh. "Old habits, I guess. The Mexican authorities wouldn't do anything about it. They steer clear of Guerrero as much as they possibly can."

"Exactly. That's why it's up to us."

"I still don't see how you can do it. You'll be outnumbered, outgunned . . . you'll just get yourselves killed, along with all those girls."

"No," Bonnie said unexpectedly. "No, they won't, Captain."

"How do you know that?"

"I don't have any choice but to believe it, now do I?" she asked quietly.

Rodgers just sighed again. "You're right, Mrs. Brannon." His head came up, and Tom saw a resolute something in his eyes that hadn't been there before. "Might as well go whole hog, I guess. What can I do to help?"

Thirty

The loneliness was the worst part of Laura's captivity. Except for the cruel and surly Señora Garvas, she was alone all the time. Guards brought meals three times a day for both of them, but Señora Garvas met them at the door and took the trays of food, so Laura didn't even get to see the gun-toting men. She hoped for a glimpse of Ricardo Benitez, because that would mean that he could see her, too, and the sight of her might increase his feelings of guilt.

But reluctantly, she admitted to herself that she couldn't count on any help from Ricardo. That was too much of a long shot to be realistic.

She couldn't help but wonder what was happening with the rest of the prisoners. The thought that some of them might have been raped or even killed by now tormented her. Even though her current existence was far from pleasant, at least it was better than being locked up in a cell, never knowing what was going to happen next.

Thoughts of the future ate at her mind, as well. She was destined to be sold to that English pervert Willingham, and there was no telling what he might do to her. It wouldn't be anything good, though, she was sure of that.

She tried to keep her spirits up by telling herself that there would be people looking for her and the other girls, people who wanted to help them. But in her darker moments she had to admit that their predicament seemed almost hopeless. They were locked up in this fortresslike old mission, guarded by dozens of hardened criminals, and there was no way anybody could even reach them, let alone free them from the Night Wolves.

And all because Colonel Guerrero had wanted to reclaim his daughter. His desire to take Angelina away from her mother was behind the invasion of the United States and the kidnapping, Laura knew. She had thought about it a lot. Guerrero wanted Angelina back, and he had decided to combine that goal with a chance to make millions of dollars by kidnapping a bunch of schoolgirls and selling them off to the highest bidders.

What a scumbag.

Another bad part of being locked up was that it was hard to keep track of time. Laura wasn't sure how much of it had passed since she was taken from the cell, forced to strip in Guerrero's office, and then brought to this room in the old granary. She thought she had been here a couple of days, but she couldn't be certain of that.

She learned more about what had been going on when, unexpectedly, a fist pounded on the door. Señora Garvas shot a warning glance in Laura's direction. "It is not time for a meal," she muttered. "Stay back, you."

She strode to the door and jerked it open. Major Cortez stood there, a pistol holstered on his hip. Behind him were two guards with rifles. Laura craned her neck to get a look at them and saw that one of the men was Ricardo. He turned his head so that he wouldn't have to meet her gaze.

"We have come for the girl," Cortez said.

"It is not time yet," Señora Garvas said with an angry frown. "Not until tomorrow night."

Cortez shrugged. "There is no need to keep her separated from the others anymore. These are the colonel's orders." He crooked a finger at Laura. "Come with me, girl."

Laura stood up tentatively from the chair where she had been sitting. As she started toward the door, Señora Garvas said angrily, "He promised me time with her."

"You've had your time," Cortez replied curtly. "If you did not take advantage of it, that is no fault of mine."

Señora Garvas hissed a curse at him, then turned sharply toward Laura, who stopped short in fear and uncertainty.

"You would have come to understand soon enough," the woman said, and then to Laura's shock, Señora Garvas reached out, grabbed her arms, jerked her close, and planted a kiss on her mouth.

"Enough, woman!" Cortez exclaimed. He drew the pistol. "Let go of her."

Señora Garvas broke the kiss and shoved Laura away. "You never had anything to fear from me, little one," she said. "Not really. I would not have hurt you."

She could have fooled Laura. She *had* fooled Laura. During the time they had spent together, Laura had been convinced that Señora Garvas hated her and would have gladly tortured her. Now it was clear that had been an act.

Laura was pretty sure that she would have preferred not knowing that.

Major Cortez took hold of her arm and pulled her out of the room. He slammed the door, cutting off the sight of Señora Garvas. He muttered something under his breath about perversions and steered Laura toward the big mission building again.

She scrubbed the back of her free hand across her mouth as they crossed the courtyard.

Although she couldn't see outside the walls of the compound, she could see the sky overhead, and from the looks of it the time was late afternoon. As before, the fresh air and being in the open felt good. Laura didn't expect it to last very long, though, and she was right. It didn't. Major Cortez, Ricardo, and the other guard took her back through the mission. The hallway began to look familiar, and sure enough, a moment later they went through a door and found themselves in the long wing of the building where the cells were located.

Ricardo unlocked the cell where Laura had been held before, and Major Cortez pushed her inside. The barred door clanged shut behind her. Shannon and Aubrey were gone, but Carmen and Stacy were still there, along with three other girls from the school. Laura knew them, but not well.

Being returned to the cell like this was surprising. Laura wasn't sure if she liked it or not. It was good to see her friends and not to be alone anymore, but she knew she wouldn't have been brought back here unless their time at the mission was drawing short.

Cortez, Ricardo, and the other man left. Laura clung to the bars and tried to catch Ricardo's eye as he walked out, but he looked resolutely elsewhere, determined not to meet her gaze. When they were gone, Laura sighed and slumped against the door.

Carmen and Stacy came to her and each of them put a hand on one of her shoulders. "Thank God you're all right," Carmen said. "We didn't think we would ever see you again, Laura. We didn't know what had happened to you. Nobody would tell us anything."

"Where are Shannon and Aubrey?" Laura asked dully.

"They came and took them away yesterday," Stacy said. "After the . . . examinations."

Laura frowned and turned to look at her. "Examinations?" A dark inkling of what the other girl might be talking about stirred in her mind.

"They took us out, one by one," Carmen said in a stony voice. "There was a doctor and a nurse. They . . . they examined us to see if we were . . . you know . . . intact."

"Virgins," Stacy whispered.

Laura nodded, not that surprised by what the girls were telling her. The incident with Willingham had proven to Colonel Guerrero just how much more valuable the virgins among the captives were, so he had taken steps to make sure that none of them lost that added value before the auction took place. To that end he had separated them, the virgins from the nonvirgins, and no doubt had given strict orders that the untouched girls were to remain that way.

But as for the girls who were sexually experienced . . . as she stood there at the barred door, Laura listened hard and heard sobbing and whimpering coming from some of the other cells. She said, "Shannon and Aubrey and the others . . . ?"

"The guards have been taking turns with them," Carmen said, her voice still as hard as flint as she tried to control her emotions. "We can hear the screaming and the crying, but there's nothing we can do to help them."

Laura closed her eyes for a moment and leaned her forehead against the cool iron bars of the cell door. Shannon and the other girls like her were destined for short, brutal lives in some brothel, so being gang-raped now wouldn't really have any effect on their value to Guerrero and the Night Wolves. Laura had never gotten along very well with Shannon, but the thought of what the girl was going through was enough to make a horrified shudder go through Laura's body.

She was lucky, she supposed. The colonel had accepted

her word for it that she was a virgin, so she hadn't been forced to undergo the humiliation of a medical examination like the others. Things were so bad, that was what passed for good luck these days.

"Where have you been, Laura?" Stacy asked. "Do you know what they're going to do with us? Are they still trying to get ransom from our families?"

Laura turned away from the door and looked at her friends. They deserved to hear the truth, as bad as it might be.

"They never planned on ransoming us," she said. "They're going to *sell* us."

Carmen frowned. "Sell us? What the hell do you mean? Like an auction?"

"Exactly like an auction," Laura said. "I've already been promised to some guy named Willingham. He . . . he's paying Colonel Guerrero five million dollars for me."

The other girls gawked at her. "Five million?" Stacy finally said.

"Yes. I had to . . . take my clothes off and stand in front of a camera while this perv Willingham looked at me over a computer linkup. When he found out I was, you know, a virgin, he said he'd pay five million for me."

"Holy Mother of God," Carmen breathed.

"That's what they're going to do with the rest of us?" Stacy asked, an edge of hysteria creeping into her voice. "They're going to sell us to a bunch of horny old guys so they can . . . can . . ."

"Yeah, deflower us," Laura said wryly. "So to speak."

Carmen began cursing bitterly in Spanish. Stacy said, "What about the others, the ones like Shannon?"

"They'll be sold to guys who own whorehouses and put to work," Laura explained. "They'll probably bring pretty good money, since they're young. But that's just a guess; I don't really know much about things like that."

"When is this auction supposed to be?" Carmen asked.

"It's got to be soon. After I found out what was going on, Guerrero had me locked up by myself so I wouldn't tell the rest of you. That's where I've been, in another building. But I guess the auction is coming up so fast now, he figures it doesn't matter anymore if you know."

"Isn't there anything we can do?" Stacy asked shakily.

"We can hope and pray that somebody comes to get us out of this place," Laura said. "That's about all."

"No, that's not all," Carmen said.

The others all looked at her.

"We've got our clothes," she went on. "We can rig up ropes from them and hang ourselves from the bars on the door. It's a bad way to go, but maybe not as bad as what we've got facing us."

Stacy gaped at her for a second and then made the sign of the cross. "Carmen, no!" she said. "We can't do that! It would be a mortal sin. We just can't."

"You want to be turned over to some guy who'll rape you every day until he's tired of you and then probably pass you along to his friends, or even kill you? You'd rather be murdered?"

"It's not a sin to be murdered," Stacy insisted. "A tragedy, but not a sin."

"Well, I say if we just sit back and let them do whatever they want to with us, we're committing suicide in slow motion. Better to get it over with in a hurry."

Laura figured she had better put a stop to this talk. "Nobody's committing suicide, slow or fast," she said firmly. "We can't give up hope. There could be help on the way. And I've talked to that guard, Ricardo. He doesn't like what they've got planned for us. I'm sure he wants to stop it. . . . He just hasn't figured out how yet."

"What can one man do?" Stacy asked.

"Everything has to start with one person," Laura said. "One person who wants to do what's right. Sometimes that's all it takes."

She prayed that this was one of those times . . . and that that one special person was really out there somewhere.

Thirty-one

Tom brought the rental car to a stop in front of the large barn on the ranch outside of Laredo. Quite a few other cars were parked there already, and a group of people stood in the barn's open doorway. A stocky figure broke away from them and came toward Tom.

"Glad to see you found the place all right, Brannon," Joe Delgado said. "This was my parents' spread, where I was raised. Nobody's been working it since they passed away, so I thought it would be the perfect spot for us to get together and figure out our plan, and maybe get in some target practice."

Tom nodded. "That was good thinking, Joe. Folks were liable to get suspicious with so many people showing up at the gun club all the time."

Delgado grinned. "Come on in the barn and look at the guns Long and his bunch brought with them."

Tom nodded a greeting to the people he recognized as he and Delgado walked into the barn. Charles Long and the other law-enforcement personnel who were joining the mission were inside, standing around a large tarp spread out on the ground. Tom saw numerous high-powered pistols and assault rifles lying on the tarp.

Long nodded to Tom and said, "With the stuff your guy Stackhouse is sending to us, Brannon, we ought to be well armed, anyway."

"Those guns will be here before the day is over," Tom said. "I talked to Stackhouse this morning and passed along the directions to this place that Joe gave me."

It was the next day after Tom's foray across the border into Nuevo Laredo. He was stiff and sore from the kick that had landed on his side the night before, but like Rodgers, he didn't have any broken ribs. He could get around all right.

He didn't have much choice in the matter. In less than thirty-six hours, the degenerate monsters who planned to bid on those kidnapped girls would be arriving at the old mission. Tom and his allies had to rescue the captives before then, or tomorrow night at the latest.

Tom hadn't seen or heard from Rodgers since dropping the wounded Ranger off at his apartment early that morning, before dawn. Injured as he was, Rodgers was in no shape to take part in the rescue mission, but he had promised to keep quiet about it, and said that he would call Tom's cell phone if he heard any important news or thought of anything that might help. Tom knew that once Rodgers had made up his mind to go along with the plan, he had wanted to join in wholeheartedly, but that just wasn't possible.

Besides, he had already done his part by helping Tom get back safely from Laredo with the vital information about the location of the prisoners.

Long motioned Tom over to a table and took some papers from a briefcase sitting there. As he spread them out, he said, "These are satellite surveillance photos I was able to pull off the government's satnet. A guy who owed me a favor enlarged and enhanced them."

Tom leaned over the table to study the photos, and knew without being told that he was looking at pictures of the Night Wolves' headquarters compound. He could identify the old mission itself, as well as the various outbuildings.

Long moved his finger around one of the photos and said, "As you can see, there's a wall around the entire place. It looks like adobe, but I'd be willing to bet that it's been reinforced somehow. The area outside it may be mined. But the road into the place isn't, because vehicles come and go on it." He tapped the picture. "We'll have to breach the gate to get in."

"Do you have any idea where the girls are being held?" Tom asked.

"Well, we can't be certain," Long said as he shuffled through the satellite photographs, "but there are always well-armed people around this wing here, attached to the rear of the mission itself. We're pretty sure they're guards, and the only reason to have guards posted is if there's something valuable inside there."

"Like the prisoners."

"Exactly."

Tom studied the photographs intently. He agreed with Long's assessment. That rear wing was the most likely place for the girls to be. It was probably where the priests had lived when the mission was still being used for its original purpose, and those small, spartan chambers could be converted to cells for the prisoners without much trouble.

"If we go in the front gate," he mused, "we'll have to fight our way all through the mission to reach the wing at the back. That might take too much time."

"You're thinking that Guerrero would kill the girls rather than let us have them?" Long asked with a frown.

"He's just crazy enough, and ruthless enough, to do something like that." Tom rubbed a hand over his short-cropped hair as he thought. "We need a two-pronged attack. Is this courtyard back here big enough to set down a helicopter?" He touched one of the surveillance photos, pointing out the area he was talking about.

Long nodded slowly. "Maybe. Not one of those big choppers like Sonia Alvarez was talking about, though. It would have to be a smaller one, manned by four or five guys."

"That would be enough for a quick strike in the rear. Launch the attack on the front to draw Guerrero's men away from this wing, drop in fast with the chopper, take out the guards who are left back there, and secure the prisoners. Then while the main body of our force is keeping the Night Wolves occupied, the other choppers can land just outside this rear gate here"—again Tom's finger stabbed at the photo—"and we'll load the prisoners up and take off."

"There's what looks like a machine-gun emplacement on the wall back there," Long pointed out. "The gunners manning it will open up on a chopper as soon as it comes in range."

"Is there any way to take out the machine gun?"

Long rubbed his jaw. "We'd need a missile launcher of some sort. You think Hiram Stackhouse might have one in his back pocket?"

"He just might," Tom said with a smile. "You never know until you ask."

After the planning session, Tom gathered everyone and set up some target practice so that he and Long could see how the volunteers handled weapons. Long hadn't been able to get hold of enough guns for everybody, so they had to take turns. As soon as the armament being provided by Stackhouse arrived, there would be plenty of firepower to go around.

The makeshift firing range was behind the old barn. Tom and Long watched carefully as round after round was fired off. Some people were better with rifles than they were with handguns, and vice versa. Tom made notes and kept a list. He was pleasantly surprised to see that everyone shot fairly well, even the ones who hadn't even touched a gun in years. Wayne Van Sant, Craig Lambert, Wally Chambers, and the others who were regular members of the gun club were all excellent marksmen. Long and the other professionals would be the point men in the attack on Guerrero's compound, but Van Sant's people would back them up. The others would form the third wave.

Tom had already decided that he would be in the first helicopter, the one that would take out the machine gun and then land in the rear of the compound. By the time the afternoon was over, he had settled on Van Sant and Lambert as two of his companions. They were excellent shots, and he had a gut feeling that they would be cool under fire. He hadn't decided yet who the fourth man would be.

Sonia Alvarez insisted on piloting the craft. "I can fly any chopper ever built," she said. "You'll want a steady hand on the stick when you go in."

Tom agreed with that.

Late in the afternoon, while everyone was taking a break in the barn, a distinctive sound drew them outside. Tom looked up and saw three large helicopters approaching, along with one smaller chopper. He grinned at the sight. He had called Hiram Stackhouse and told the businessman that they needed a small, fast helicopter as well as the larger transport choppers, and Stackhouse had promised to get right on it. Obviously, he had been successful.

With a deafening egg-beater sound from the revolving blades and huge clouds of dust billowing into the air, the helicopters set down near the barn and the old ranch house. As the roar of their motors died away and the dust began to settle, Tom and Long ran forward to greet the men who hopped down from the cockpits. They all wore plain gray coveralls with no markings, but the military precision with which they moved told Tom that they belonged to Stackhouse's private security force. He had seen men like that in action back in Little Tucson and knew how competent they were.

The leader of the group, who introduced himself as Captain Jennings, shook hands with Tom and said, "We're at your disposal, Mr. Brannon. Mr. Stackhouse has placed us under your orders." Jennings jerked a thumb over his shoulder at the choppers. "We're loaded down with guns, ammunition, and body armor."

"Let's get those choppers unloaded," Tom said to the people who had gathered around. They moved forward eagerly, anxious to get their hands on the hardware that would help them free their daughters from Guerrero's unholy captivity.

"You'll be wanting us to fly these choppers over the border?" Jennings asked.

Tom shook his head. "No, I've got pilots lined up for them. You've done enough by bringing them here, along with those supplies."

Jennings frowned and said, "Mr. Stackhouse was under the impression that we would be taking an active part in the operation."

Tom considered the suggestion, but before he could say anything else, Sonia Alvarez stepped forward and said, "No way! I don't care about the transports, but I'm flying that little chopper." She looked at Tom. "Don't take that away from me, Mr. Brannon."

Tom gave her a reassuring smile and said to Jennings, "Thanks, Captain, but I think we can manage. This is sort of a personal mission for us."

"You're making a mistake," Jennings said with a frown. "I guess you don't want any help from those guys, either?" He nodded toward the choppers, where more men in coveralls were disembarking. Tom's eyes widened in surprise as he realized that more than forty of Stackhouse's security men had arrived along with the supplies.

Long put a hand on Tom's shoulder. "Listen, Brannon," he said. "This will even up the odds and give us a real chance of getting those girls back. Don't be stubborn. You need to take any help you can get."

Even as Long spoke, Tom knew the man was right. This operation had grown from a small, personal mission to a full-scale military assault. Tom was beginning to feel out of his depth, and he didn't like the feeling. But the most important thing, of course, was the safety of the kidnapped girls. He had to utilize whatever advantages he might have in trying to free them.

"All right," he said, "you can all come along. And thank you. You know you'll be risking your lives, as well as your freedom once you get back here. There may be federal charges waiting for all of us."

"Mr. Stackhouse explained that," Jennings said. "That's why we're all volunteers. We know the lives of those innocent girls are at stake, and that's good enough for us. We'll run the risk."

Sonia Alvarez said stubbornly, "I still want to fly that little chopper."

"I'll check you out on it, ma'am," Jennings offered. "Maybe we can arrange something."

"Then come on, flyboy. I'll show you what I can do with that bird."

Tom walked over to the area where the supplies were being unloaded. A tall, grizzled man had taken charge. His bearing was evidence of a long career in the military. The salt-and-pepper in his hair and mustache said he was probably retired. He greeted Tom with a salute and said, "Sergeant William Elliott, sir."

Tom grinned. "I'll bet they call you Wild Bill, don't they?"

Elliott returned the grin. "How'd you know, sir?"

"Well, I've already run into Roy Rodgers since I came here to Texas. I just figured it made sense they'd call you Wild Bill Elliott. And you don't have to call me sir. I'm a civilian."

"You're in charge of this operation, aren't you?"

Tom shrugged. "Most of it, I guess."

"That makes you an officer in my book, sir. After all, this business is pretty much back-channel, isn't it?"

Thinking about how the authorities on both sides of the border would likely react if they knew what was going on, Tom nodded and said, "Just about as far back-channel as you can get, Sergeant."

Thirty-two

The next twenty-four hours were a whirlwind of activity as the rescue force, which had now grown to eighty members with the addition of Stackhouse's men, was outfitted and a plan of attack was developed by Tom, Charles Long, Captain Terry Jennings, and Sergeant William "Wild Bill" Elliott. The two former military men, Jennings and Elliott, were in agreement with the basic plan hatched by Tom and Long. The main body of the force would attack the front of the mission compound while a smaller force would perform a quick, hard strike in the rear designed to free the girls. Destroying Guerrero and the Night Wolves would be a nice bonus if it proved to be possible, but the primary objective was the rescue of the prisoners.

That night, as the entire group gathered inside the barn, the leaders went over the plan. "When are we going in?" Ed Gilman wanted to know. "We don't have much time left. That bastard's having his filthy auction tomorrow night."

"We're well aware of that, Ed," Tom replied. "In fact, we've just been talking about the timing of the attack. Early tomorrow evening seems to be the best time."

"Wait just a minute," Nacho Alvarez said. "That's cutting

it too damned close. If it doesn't work, we'll only get one chance at the girls."

"You'll only get one chance anyway," a new voice said. Everyone turned to look and saw Brady Keller being wheeled into the barn by Roy Rodgers. Tom had talked to them both earlier in the day and given them the latest information about the impending raid. Keller went on. "If you don't get the girls out of there on your first try, whenever it is, Guerrero will move them, and by the time you could find them again, it'll be too late. They'll probably be scattered all over Mexico, maybe even beyond. So you just get the one shot, that's it."

"And who are you, sir?" Elliott asked.

"Brady Keller. The only one here who's crossed swords, so to speak, with Guerrero."

Tom said, "Brady knows what he's talking about. We never would have found the girls to start with if it hadn't been for his help."

"It still seems dangerous to wait," Wally Chambers put in. "We won't be able to see what we're doing."

"No," Long said, "the Night Wolves won't be able to see what we're doing. We'll try to get as close as we can before they spot us. The odds are a lot more even than they were, but we're still outnumbered. We need the element of surprise on our side."

"I agree," said Jennings. "We'll hit them before moonrise."

Craig Lambert protested, "That means the auction will already be going on, doesn't it? There'll be more men there, and some of them will probably have bodyguards with them. Plus the girls may not be in that rear wing anymore. They might have already been moved to wherever those bastards are going to be bidding on them."

"Guerrero likely won't bring them out until all the bidders are there," Tom said. "That's why we're going to hit them early in the evening, just before the auction is ready to start."

"How do you know when that will be?" Lambert asked insistently.

"Well, we don't, for sure," Tom admitted. "But wherever the girls are, we'll find them, and the idea of hitting the place from two directions at once is still good, regardless."

Lambert still looked a little doubtful, but he nodded. "I suppose in something like this, you have to rely on guesswork and luck to a certain extent."

"It ain't brain surgery, friend," the grizzled Sergeant Elliott said. "Comes down to it, you go in hard and fast, kill all the bad guys you can find, and hope for the best."

The rescue force was broken up into smaller squads, each civilian squad being under the command of one of Long's group of law-enforcement professionals, while Stackhouse's security men had their own cadres already established. While the squads were going over their particular roles in the mission, Tom went to Elliott and said, "Wild Bill, I need another man in that first chopper with me. How about taking the job?"

Elliott's leathery face creased in a grin. "Sounds good to me. Who else is gonna be with us?"

Tom waved Van Sant and Lambert over and introduced them. Elliott's eyes narrowed slightly as he shook hands with Van Sant. "Desert Storm?" he asked.

"That's right. My tank group was one of the first into Baghdad."

Elliott nodded. "Thought you looked familiar. I was there, too."

"Really? What unit?"

"Civilian contractor," Elliott said shortly.

"Oh." Van Sant knew quite well what that meant. In all likelihood, Elliott had been working for the CIA at the time. The man had black ops written all over him.

Elliott turned to Lambert. "You were the fella who seemed to have some doubts about this."

"I believe in asking questions when questions should be asked," Lambert said.

"Uh-huh."

The balding man bristled. "What does that mean?"

"Means I like goin' into battle with a fella who wants to be there, who's eager to do the job."

"Mister," Lambert said between gritted teeth, "my daughter is in the hands of those bastards and has been for days now. There's nobody here who's more eager to do the job than I am."

Elliott nodded slowly. "I reckon you'll do, then."

With those introductions out of the way, Tom sought out Keller and Rodgers. The Ranger was still moving stiffly. "How's that wound in your side doing?" Tom asked.

"It's healing fine," Rodgers said. "I've been changing the bandages and keeping a close eye on it. You and Mrs. Brannon did a good job of patching it up. I hope you'll pass along my gratitude to her."

"I'll do that," Tom promised. "I'll be talking to her later tonight."

"Are you going back to Mrs. Simms's house?"

Tom shook his head. "Now that we're all here, we're staying here until it's time to head for that old mission. We don't want to take a chance on the authorities finding out what's about to happen."

Rodgers made a wry face and said, "It wasn't so long ago that I was one of those authorities you're talking about. I suppose this is the end of my career as a Texas Ranger."

Keller snorted. "Why in the hell would you say that, Roy? None of your superiors know that you're mixed up in this."

"*I* know. And if I can close my eyes to something so illegal, I'm not really fit to be a lawman, am I?"

"That's the biggest load of bullshit I ever heard," Keller said hotly. "Every lawman who carries a badge knows that there are times you can't go by the book. At least the ones who really try to do their job the right way know that."

Rodgers shook his head. "The law's got to mean something, Brady. You can't just pick and choose how to apply it."

"There are laws against kidnapping and murder, aren't there?"

"Sure."

"Well, Guerrero sure broke those laws, and to my mind these people are just performing a citizen's arrest. That's perfectly legal."

"Not when you throw in crossing a border."

Keller waved his good hand dismissively. "Now you're not talking about *law*, Roy, you're talking about rules and regulations. And you know who makes those? I'll tell you. A bunch of candy-ass politicians and bureaucrats make those rules." Keller shook his head. "The *law* . . . the law I believe in and swore to uphold . . . says those girls should be freed and Guerrero and his goons deserve to have their asses shot off. I care more about that law than I do about a bunch of pissant rules."

Rodgers looked like Keller's argument had swayed him, but he just said, "We'll wait and see how it all turns out."

Tom left them there and walked outside. He found a quiet spot on the porch of the old ranch house and pulled out his cell phone. A push of a button sent a call through to Bonnie.

She answered on the second ring. "Tom?"

"Hi, darlin'. How are you holding up?"

"I'm fine. What about you?"

He smiled, even though she couldn't see him. "Ready to go." He didn't say any more than that, not wanting to go into detail over the phone. He was pretty sure the FBI wasn't trying to tap into his cell phone conversations, but on the other hand, he wouldn't put much of anything past Agent Morgan. "Where are you tonight?"

"I'm still at the hospital. I've been here all day. Kelly's going to undergo a psychiatric evaluation, and I want to be here for her, as much as the doctors will let me."

"Don't wear yourself out," Tom warned. "You'd better go back to her house pretty soon and get some rest."

"No, I thought I'd stay here until . . . until it's over."

He knew she wasn't talking about her sister's psychiatric evaluation now. She was referring to the raid on the old mission that would result either in freedom for those kidnapped girls . . . or more death and tragedy for everyone concerned.

"All right," he said quietly. "Do whatever you need to do, honey. And so will I."

"Yes. I know you will. Tom?"

"Yeah?"

"You know I love you more than life itself?"

He smiled again. "Of course I know. And I love you the same way."

There wasn't much to say after that. She told him to take care of himself, and he promised that he would. They said their good-byes with a slight awkwardness that was unusual in two people who had been married for so long. But each of them knew that they might be saying good-bye for the last time. That possibility loomed in the backs of their minds, and there was nothing they could do about it.

After Tom had folded up his phone and slipped it back into the pocket of his work shirt, he stood at the edge of the porch, leaned on the railing, and looked out at the barn. The rumble of the generator that provided light inside the rambling structure was the only noise he could hear.

But he could see the shadows of the people moving around inside, and as he watched them, he thought about how the plight of forty helpless girls had brought such a wide variety of individuals together in an attempt to help them.

Inside that barn were a lot of average, everyday men and women who had thought that their lives would go on peacefully for years to come. They had had their moments of facing danger, many of them, as they served in the military in various clashes around the globe, but those times were supposed to be past. And surely they had never dreamed that a new enemy would venture boldly onto American soil and threaten everything they held dear.

Then there were the men such as Charles Long and his fellow lawmen, men who, like Brady Keller, subscribed to a higher law than that laid down by timid politicians. Their frustration with the flaws of the system had led them to risk not only their careers but their very lives in defense of that higher law. Men such as them were prepared to live with the smaller injustices—the criminals who got away with their crimes because of some technicality, a procedural error or something like that. Such was the price that a civilization sometimes had to pay for its continued reliance on its legal system. But some wrongs were so huge, so evil, so monstrous, that they had to be addressed no matter what the technicalities and the procedures said. The invasion of their country, the wanton slaughter of innocents, the kidnapping and degradation of defenseless children . . . those were things that could not be tolerated, no matter what.

And finally there were the men like Terry Jennings and Wild Bill Elliott, men who could be called mercenaries because they were paid to fight. Tom knew there was more to them than that, however. He could see it when he looked in their eyes. Wild Bill had probably fought in countless brushfire wars around the world, but Tom would have been willing to bet that in each clash, he had taken the side of the underdog, the people who wanted to set things right and were willing to fight and die for their cause. Those were the sort of men who now worked for Hiram Stackhouse.

Tonight, they were all united with one goal: to free those prisoners, no matter what it took. Revenge was not uppermost in their minds, although Tom was sure that any of them would be more than happy to line up Colonel Alfonso Guerrero in their sights. That would have to come second, though, after the primary objective was achieved.

So, in approximately twenty-four hours, hellfire would descend on that old mission. Where once humble men of God had brought a message of love and peace, desperate warriors would deliver a different sort of message . . . a message of fire and death to the evildoers who now trespassed there. The eternal struggle, it was sometimes called.

Tom closed his eyes for a moment and pressed his fingertips to his temples. He didn't care about eternity right now. He just wanted those girls reunited with their families. He wanted to see the joyous embraces, to hear the sobs of happiness and relief as those who had been lost were brought home.

That was all the reward he wanted, and if in the end it cost him his life . . . then so be it.

Thirty-three

Colonel Alfonso Guerrero looked at the trembling, frightened, yet still defiant girl who stood in front of him and said to her, "Please, Angelina, you must understand."

The words came hard to him. He had never begged anyone for anything in his life. Every since he had been a child, he had realized quite clearly that if he wanted something, it was up to him to take it. No one was going to give it to him.

And yet now, the one thing he wanted the most had to be freely given. He couldn't wrench it away from the one who possessed it.

He wanted his daughter to love him and to admit that she belonged with him, rather than with her witch of a mother. He should have killed that slut a long time ago, he thought. When she first left him and ran off to Laredo, taking the child with her, he should have gone after her and taken the appropriate measures. Instead, out of some misguided vestiges of affection, he had allowed her to live and to keep him separated from his daughter. Even though it had been difficult, he might have been able to let that situation continue.

But then he had discovered that she was moving away and taking Angelina with her, and Alfonso Guerrero—not the colonel, not the commander of the fierce Night Wolves, but rather the father—had known that he could never allow that. Using his men, his Los Lobos de la Noche, for a personal mission was also difficult for him to do, even though he was attempting to justify it with this auction of the captive girls, but he'd had no choice. He had to get Angelina back while he still had the chance.

Now she was with him again, as it was meant to be, but she was being stubborn about recognizing the reality of the situation.

"I don't have to understand anything," she said with a pout on her pretty face. "You're just as bad as Mama said you were. I hate you and I don't want to have anything to do with you!"

No one dared to speak to him like that. He had had men killed for less.

But she knew that he could never harm her. Of all the people in the old mission compound, Angelina was the only one safe from his wrath.

His anger and frustration got the best of him for a moment. He slammed his open hand down on the polished top of the big desk. "You refuse to see that what I have done, I did for you!" he shouted. "I had to get you away from your mother, so that I could protect you!"

"Protect me?" she echoed. She gave a hollow laugh. "You could have killed me when you hijacked that bus!"

He shook his head. "My men were extremely careful. They had their orders."

"If it was so important to you, why didn't you just take me off the bus and leave the other girls there?" Her voice caught. "Why did you have to kill Sister Katherine?"

Guerrero grimaced and waved a hand. "The nun's life

meant nothing. Her death served as an example to the others, so that they would know to cooperate with me or risk the same fate. As to why I had to take them, that is none of your business."

"But they're my friends!"

"No!" Guerrero thundered. "They are *not* your friends! I have proof of their wicked ways. Sooner or later they would have led you down the same sinful paths. Did you know that fully half of them suffer the shame of no longer being virgins, even at their young age?"

Angelina stared at him for a long moment, then, surprisingly, she began to laugh.

Guerrero frowned. "What is wrong with you?" he demanded.

"Y-you!" she managed to say as laughter almost choked her. "You can't be serious. You murder nuns and kidnap people, and you talk about sin! And then you turn around and think it's horrible because some of the girls aren't virgins! Well, I've got news for you, Papa—"

"No!" Guerrero came to his feet and started around the desk. "Say no more!"

"I will say it!" she spit at him. "I'm not one of your precious virgins, either, Papa! Hell, I've been screwed by half the boys in school—"

His hand lashed out and cracked across her face in a vicious slap. She cried out in pain and staggered backward.

"You lie! You evil, lying girl!" He was shaking from the rage that gripped him.

Angelina lifted a hand to her face, which glowed bright red where he had struck her. "Oh, it's true, all right," she said. "Your precious little girl is nothing but a tramp!"

Guerrero wanted to grab her by the shoulders and shake her, as if he could shake all the evil out of her. But he knew that would do no good. She was what she was.

He could have the doctor examine her to determine the validity of her claim, but he knew in his heart there was no point in it. She had told him the truth.

It had all been for nothing, he thought despairingly. She was already ruined.

Then he thought of the auction that would take place that night and the ten to fifteen million dollars he expected to make for the Night Wolves before the night was over, and he felt a little better.

His daughter's innocence was gone. He had been too late to save it. But at least he would be richer.

Taking deep breaths in an attempt to calm the emotions raging inside him, he turned to the desk and pressed a button on it. A moment later the door opened and Major Cortez came into the room. "You summoned me, Colonel?"

"Yes, old friend," Guerrero said. He forced himself to keep his voice flat and hard as he went on. "Take this girl and put her with the others."

"Colonel?" Cortez couldn't contain the startled exclamation. At the same time, Angelina said in an anguished voice, "Papa, no!"

"You heard me, Major. Put her with the others. The ones who are . . . available to the men."

Cortez nodded. "As you wish, Colonel."

Angelina began to scream as Cortez grabbed her arm and began tugging her toward the door. A couple of guards had followed him into the room. At his command they took hold of Angelina, as well. She continued to struggle and cry out.

Guerrero almost weakened before they got her out of the room and the thick door swung shut, muffling her terrified screams. It would have been easy, so easy, to call them back and order them to let her go. But he couldn't allow himself to do that. She wasn't the girl he had gone after. That girl was gone forever. She had changed, and she no longer had a place in his life. Therefore, her fate was sealed.

If she wanted to be a whore, then a whore she would be.

Ricardo could hardly believe his eyes when he saw Major Cortez and two other men drag Angelina Salinas into the rear wing of the old mission where the prisoners' cells were located. She was screaming and fighting, but she was no match for the men who held her. Her long black hair whipped around her head as she jerked from side to side, to no avail. Ricardo was so startled that he couldn't hold back a question.

"Major, what is this?"

"This girl is to be put with the other prisoners," Cortez answered stonily. He pointed toward the far end of the corridor, where the cells were located that contained the girls who were fair game for the men. "Back there."

Ricardo was even more stunned by this. He recognized the girl and knew that she was Colonel Guerrero's daughter. She was the reason the Night Wolves had invaded the United States and hijacked that school bus and its passengers. And now Guerrero was, well, throwing her to the wolves, so to speak?

It made no sense, but it was obviously happening. The guards pulled the struggling Angelina past the first cells. A couple of other men unlocked one of the chambers and forced its occupants back at gunpoint. Roughly—but not *too* roughly, because none of these men could completely forget who the girl's father was—Angelina was thrust through the open door into the cell. Then one of the guards grabbed the door and slammed it shut.

Ricardo glanced at the nearest cell and instantly knew

he had made a mistake. The fair-haired girl, the one called Laura, stood there with her companions, gripping the bars, pressing their faces against them so that they could look on in horror as Angelina was dragged past. Ricardo wanted to pull his dark eyes away from Laura's blue ones, but he could not. Their gazes locked together, and he felt the powerful impact of the fear he saw there, along with the hope that for some reason she still clung to. Had she not figured out by now that he was unable to help them? He wished he could explain about all the time and effort he had put into infiltrating the Night Wolves, not to mention the blood that had been shed.

But even if he could, that wouldn't make any difference to her. Her life was at stake. She didn't care about deep-cover operations. Of course she wanted to live and to be free.

Her mouth moved, and he heard her say something over the noise Angelina was making as she began to shriek curses at the guards. "All for nothing." That was what it sounded like.

All for nothing.

And God help him, he knew exactly what she meant.

"What's going on?" Carmen said as she clutched at Laura's arm. "That was Angelina!"

"Why is she here?" Stacy wanted to know. "I thought you said she's the daughter of that guy Colonel Guerrero!"

Laura nodded. "She is. The fact that she's here now, with us, must mean that he's given up on her. He kidnapped her—and us—so that he could force her to live with him and love him again, like he thinks she should. But she wouldn't, and now she's paying the price for it."

"Yeah, Angelina was always one stubborn bitch," Carmen said.

Stacy added, "But I wouldn't wish this on her. I can't believe her own dad would . . . would throw her in with the ones who are being . . . raped."

Laura didn't say anything to that, but she figured that Angelina was relatively safe for the time being. Even though Guerrero's men apparently had permission to do whatever they wanted to Angelina, she thought most of them would be leery of actually attacking her, just in case the colonel changed his mind later.

But if he didn't change his mind—if Angelina was included in the auction that would be taking place in just a few hours—she would be sold off to the highest bidder and then there would be no saving her.

There would be no saving any of them. Time was rapidly running out, and once the auction got under way, it would be too late. Their dismal fates would overtake them like a runaway freight train.

It seemed now that their only hope was Ricardo Benitez. Laura had caught his eye as Angelina was being dragged past, and she thought her anguished expression and mental pleading had struck a nerve in him.

But she had thought that before, and still he hadn't done a damned thing to help them. He might sympathize with their plight, but he wasn't going to cross Colonel Guerrero and the rest of the Night Wolves.

Sympathy wasn't going to do Laura and the others a damned bit of good, not now. There wasn't time anymore to play on his guilt. Ricardo had to make up his mind, once and for all, about what he was going to do, and Laura had the sinking feeling that the decision had already been made.

She had pinned her hopes on him, and he had let her down. Now she and the others would pay the price.

Suddenly, Carmen's suicide idea didn't look so bad after all. There might still be time to cheat Colonel Guerrero out of his profit. That was the only blow they could strike against him.

But somehow, no matter how much she wanted to give up, a tiny flame of hope still flickered deep inside Laura. . . .

Thirty-four

Tom saw the cloud of dust first, spiraling up into the hot, dry, late-afternoon air several miles distant from the old ranch. Here in this mostly flat terrain, such things were visible for a long way. Frowning, he stepped over to the chopper where Terry Jennings was going over a last-minute checklist with Sonia Alvarez and asked, "Captain, do you happen to have a pair of binoculars handy?"

Jennings said, "Sure," and reached into a compartment inside the little helicopter's cockpit. He brought out a pair of military binoculars and handed them to Tom.

Walking quickly, Tom went back to the porch and up the steps. He turned toward the distant dust cloud and lifted the glasses to his eyes. After focusing in on the dust, he lowered his gaze along the column until he came to the base of it.

That was when he saw the dozens of flashing lights.

"Son of a bitch," he breathed. His worst fear had come true. Somehow the authorities had found out what was going on—and they were coming to put a stop to the rescue effort before it had a chance to really begin.

"Trouble coming!" he bellowed as he leaped down

from the porch and ran toward the barn. "The Feds are on the way!"

Instantly the place was a beehive of activity. The day had been spent in going over not only the main plan, but also several contingency plans. Premature discovery by local, state, and/or federal authorities was definitely one of the contingencies they had prepared for. Everyone knew the rendezvous point on the edge of Nuevo Laredo. Now they had to scatter and clear out before the badge-toting bureaucrats arrived to shut them down.

Jennings leaped out of the little chopper's cockpit and ran toward the larger helicopters, waving a hand over his head in the revolving motion that meant "Crank 'em up!" Sonia already had the smaller chopper's blade turning.

Tom saw Wayne Van Sant, Craig Lambert, and Wild Bill Elliott running toward the helicopter from different directions. Like him, they wore kevlar vests and carried assault rifles and had pistols holstered on their hips. They were ready to go, and unlike the others who would have to make the rendezvous and then launch the attack on the old mission, these four men would fly out of here. Sonia would head across the border, set the chopper down in some isolated location, and wait there for H-hour. The other helicopters would also be hidden in the desert, waiting for the signal to move in.

Tom, Van Sant, Lambert, and Elliott piled into the chopper. Tom took the seat beside Sonia while the other three men filled up the small area in the rear. The aircraft lifted off so abruptly that Tom felt his stomach bottoming out.

"What the hell happened?" Elliott shouted over the beating of the rotor. "Did somebody sell us out?"

"Don't know!" Tom replied with a shake of his head. "But I'll bet that was the FBI on the way to the ranch!"

As the chopper banked, he got a good look at the scene unfolding below. A dozen or more cars and SUVs with flashing lights on their roofs were approaching the ranch, but they were still more than a mile away. Meanwhile, the other three choppers were lifting off, and dozens of cars and pickups shot away from the ranch buildings at high speed, scattering in different directions across country. Tom bit back a curse. Not all the members of the rescue force would get away. The authorities would probably corral some of them. All he could do was hope that enough made it across and were able to form up again in Nuevo Laredo to make the attack on the old mission possible. If they lost half of their numbers, the odds against them would be well-nigh overwhelming.

But the strike would go ahead anyway, he thought. They had come too far to abandon their plan now, and any chance those girls had, no matter how slim, was better than none.

The ranch was deserted by the time the caravan of law-enforcement vehicles rolled in and stopped. Special Agent Sharon Morgan got out of the lead SUV and cursed as she looked around and saw that everyone was gone. A dozen or more columns of dust in the distance all around the place told her that the people she was after had scattered to the four winds. She turned and screamed, "Get after them!" at the U.S. marshal who was emerging from the second vehicle in the long line of cars and SUVs. "Spread out and catch as many of them as you can!"

Then she took a cell phone from the pocket of her blazer and thumbed in a number. When it was answered, she told the person on the other end, "Get on the horn to Kelly Air Force Base in San Antonio and have them scramble interceptors! Those bastards have helicopters! We've got to stop them from getting across the border!"

She snapped the phone closed and turned toward the vehicle from which she had emerged. She stalked over to it and jerked the rear door open.

"Damn you," she said to the man inside. "You didn't tell me they had helicopters!"

Texas Ranger Captain Roy Rodgers looked down at the handcuffs on his wrists and said, "I didn't tell you much of anything, Agent Morgan, except to go to hell. If you hadn't been able to trace some of those cell phone calls Brannon made to me, you wouldn't be here now."

Morgan leaned closer to him and snarled, "When I get through with you, Rodgers, you'll never work in law enforcement again. You won't even be able to get a job as dogcatcher!"

Rodgers smiled thinly. "It's been a long time since I heard that one. Everything comes back around sooner or later, I guess."

"Except your career," Morgan snapped. "That's over."

Rodgers shrugged. "Some things are worth the risk," he said. "A friend of mine told me that, and I understand now that he was right."

Tom had to give Sonia Alvarez credit for one thing—she could flat out fly a helicopter. The chopper rose high into the sky and took off like a shot toward the border. The larger, somewhat slower choppers followed as quickly as possible, but Sonia soon left them far behind.

Leaning over in his seat toward her, Tom asked, "Do you think they'll have aircraft try to stop us?"

"You know more about the Feds than I do," Sonia

replied. "I wouldn't put much of anything past that bitch of an FBI agent, though."

Tom wouldn't, either. He didn't know if Morgan's animosity was personal, or if she was just so caught up in doing everything in the politically correct, by-the-book way that any deviation from normal procedure made her furious. Morgan should have stayed a lawyer and not joined the Bureau. Her thinking had been molded too rigidly by her time in Washington.

He saw the Rio Grande ahead of them and far below as they approached the border. Another couple of minutes and they would be across it, safe for the moment.

That was when Elliott drawled, "Bogie at nine o'clock Alvarez."

Sonia muttered a curse. So did Tom as he looked past her and saw the jet fighter streaking toward them. The chopper's radio crackled as a voice said, "Unidentified helicopter, turn away from the border and land immediately. Repeat, turn away from the border and land immediately."

"Screw you, flyboy," Sonia said as she sent the chopper diving toward the ground. The jet roared past, a good distance overhead.

Tom felt a little sick by the time Sonia pulled out of the dive. As she leveled out, he saw that the helicopter was flying barely twenty feet off the ground. He said, "I didn't know a helicopter would do that."

"Yeah, well, if the rotor doesn't come off, it's usually fine."

"Okay," Tom said slowly.

The jet pilot said angrily over the radio, "Chopper, I don't want to fire on you—"

"Of course you don't want to fire on us," Sonia broke in as she keyed the mike on her headset. "We're Americans, just like you." The Rio Grande flashed past below. "And anyway, we're in Mexican airspace now, amigo."

The jet pilot didn't say anything else. He circled away, heading back to his base in San Antonio.

"I'm surprised he didn't hang around and try to stop the other choppers," Van Sant commented.

"Maybe what Sonia said got through to him," Tom said. "Maybe he realized that if he stayed, he might wind up having to shoot down his own countrymen."

Elliott rumbled, "It's a hell of a note when it comes to such a thing. Americans shootin' at Americans. It just ain't right."

"Yeah, well, we don't have to worry about that anymore," Sonia said with a taut smile on her face. "Now all we've got to worry about is the Mexicans shooting down our asses."

Colonel Guerrero sat in his plush, luxurious office, complete with all its high-tech gadgetry, and wondered just how things had gone so wrong. Why had Angelina not been able or even willing to understand? Everything he had done, he had done for her. Could she not see that?

And why, in a moment of anger, had he turned his back on her and given her to his men? Had he been insane?

It was not too late, of course. He could have her brought back to him at any time. But perhaps it would be better to wait a while. He was confident that his men would not touch her, no matter where she was held. Let her worry about her fate. Perhaps he would even let her be a part of the auction. He would stop things before anyone could bid on her, of course. But such an experience would open her eyes and make her realize that she would be better off to just accept everything he wanted to give her.

As for her whorish behavior . . . that was in the pa
From now on, things would be different. Very different

He had decided that his Angelina would become a nu

Major Cortez came into the room and said, "The vis
tors are beginning to arrive."

That shook Guerrero out of his reverie. He looked u
and said, "Make them comfortable in the old chapel."

Cortez nodded, but frowned a little and hesitate
before turning away.

"Something wrong, Eli?" Guerrero asked.

"Since you brought it up, Alfonso . . . it seems to m
that having the auction of those girls in what was once th
chapel is, well, sacrilegious."

Guerrero snorted contemptuously. "What should I fea
amigo? That El Señor Dios will smite me with a lightnin
bolt? Once this may have been a house of God, but th
old man has been driven out. Now it is the lair of th
Night Wolves!"

Cortez muttered something and started to lift a hand ɛ
if to cross himself, but he stopped the gesture before
could begin. "As you command, Colonel," he said.

The phone on the desk rang as Cortez started towar
the door. Guerrero scooped it up and said sharply, "Wha
is it? . . . Ah, General Montero, it is good to hear fror
you, as always." Even though the man he spoke to was
general in the Mexican Army, there was no hint of sub
servience in Guerrero's voice. Rank meant nothin
anymore. Both men knew which one was truly superie
to the other. That was why Montero had a habit of tippin
off Guerrero any time anything was going on that migl
have an effect on Los Lobos de la Noche.

As he listened, Guerrero's face hardened. "Are yo
sure?" he asked gutturally. When Montero answered i
the affirmative, Guerrero slammed the phone down.

Cortez had waited at the door. "What is it, Colonel?" he asked.

Guerrero looked up with a snarl on his face. "The Americans have alerted the Mexican authorities that a group of civilians and renegade law-enforcement personnel plan to raid this mission tonight and attempt to free the prisoners. In fact, some of them may already be on their way here now!"

"I will alert the guards," Cortez said crisply. "The foolish Americans will never make it past the wall."

"Excellent. And Eli . . ."

"Yes, Colonel?"

"Make sure that they all die," Guerrero said. "Every last one of them. No survivors. No quarter."

He wondered if anywhere in the old mission he might find a recording of "El Deguello." He had a sudden desire to listen to the old song that Santa Anna's musicians had played outside the Alamo. . . .

Thirty-five

From the air, Tom had no trouble seeing the Sierra Madre Oriental, the mountain range that lay to the west. East of the Sierra Madres, all the way to the Rio Grande, was nothing but flat, semiarid landscape that stopped just short of being a desert. That was going to make it difficult to find a place to hide for the next couple of hours until it was time to launch the raid on the old mission. If the Mexican authorities were looking for them—and it seemed likely that Morgan would have alerted her counterparts south of the border about what was going on—then an aerial search might come along at any time.

Sonia spotted a dry arroyo and banked the chopper toward it. "That wash is wide enough we can set down on its bed," she told Tom. "It won't keep us from being spotted from the air, but it ought to hide us pretty well from anybody on the ground. They'd have to be right on top of us to see us."

Tom nodded agreement, and Sonia took the bird down, setting it deftly and gently on the dry bed of the arroyo.

Everyone got out to stretch their legs. Tom wondered what had happened to the other helicopters and all the members of the rescue force who had been forced to flee from the ranch. The squad leaders were all carrying portable radios, but they had to maintain radio silence for now, since they couldn't afford to let anyone who was looking for them home in on their signal.

Sonia asked, "What do we do when the time for the attack comes if we haven't heard from any of the others?"

"We carry on as planned," Tom said. "That was the agreement. If everybody split up, anybody who made it to the mission at the right time would go ahead with the attack."

"But what if we're the only ones who are left?" Lambert asked. "We won't have a chance."

Elliott said, "You can be outnumbered a whole hell of a lot and still do considerable damage if you hit the enemy hard enough and fast enough. Maybe we won't be able to take those girls out of there, but even if we don't, we might raise enough hell so they can escape on their own. Not all of 'em would get away, more than likely, but at least they'd have a fightin' chance that way."

Tom looked at the flaming, reddish-orange ball of the sun as it touched the peaks of the Sierra Madres. "If a fighting chance is the best we can do," he said, "it's a lot better than the prospects they're facing now. We carry on, even if it's just the five of us."

He looked around at the others and got grim nods of agreement from every one.

All evening, as the sun set and the shadows of dusk gathered, Ricardo saw them arriving at the mission, these laughing, well-dressed, obviously wealthy men who thought nothing of buying an innocent young girl to use for their own filthy pleasures or to put more money in

their own pockets. As the slender, expensively dresse
Englishman called Willingham climbed out of a limo
sine, Ricardo had to fight down the urge to lift his rifl
and put a bullet through the bastard's diseased brain.

Ever since this situation had developed, the young ur
dercover agent had been at war with himself. He ha
argued that preserving his cover identity might sav
many, many more lives in the long run if he could help t
bring down Guerrero and the Night Wolves. But at th
same time, his inaction doomed those girls to short
brutal lives of degradation and terror. Could he live wit
that on his conscience?

He was coming to realize at last that the answer was n
He couldn't live with that.

Bare lightbulbs glowed in their fixtures on the ceilin
as Ricardo entered the long corridor lined with cell door
on both sides. He nodded to the guard at the near end,
man named Ortega. Two other guards were posted in th
hall, one halfway along it and the other at the far en
where the door led out into the rear courtyard.

"Major Cortez sent me to relieve you," he said to Ortega
"You're wanted in the barracks."

Ortega frowned. "What for?"

Ricardo just shrugged his shoulders eloquently, con
veying the information that not only did he not know, h
didn't care, either. Muttering curses, Ortega left to go t
the barracks, which was on the far side of the compound

When he got there, he wouldn't find Major Cortez. Th
major was in the chapel with Colonel Guerrero, greeting
the men who had come for the auction. The barracks wer
empty because all the Night Wolves were prowling
tonight, forming a strong perimeter around the old mis
sion. Ricardo had heard the rumors—the authorities
might try to attack the place tonight. He didn't believe fo

a second that such a thing would ever happen. The Mexican government made all the appropriate noises about curbing the drug traffic and the violence along the border, but the military and the police never actually did anything about it.

He was equally certain that the Americans weren't going to try a raid of some sort. If that were the case, he would have gotten a heads-up from his DEA handler, even though it was risky making contact. He was convinced that he was the last hope those girls had.

Finally, at long last, he had decided that he wasn't going to let them down.

He looked into the cell where the blond girl, Laura, waited with several of the others. She was on her feet, gazing back at him with those soulful, hopeful eyes. He smiled faintly.

For once, Laura wasn't going to be disappointed in him. That knowledge made him feel surprisingly good.

He took a sudden step toward the barred door and called out sharply to the other two guards. "Come quickly!" he told them. "*Dios mío!* I think one of these stupid girls has slit her wrists!"

The possibility of the merchandise damaging itself brought the others on the run. They had been warned by Major Cortez to be especially watchful for such things. And as they pounded along the corridor, Ricardo looked at Laura Simms and closed one eye in an encouraging wink.

He was going to do it, she thought with a sudden surge of hope. He was really going to help them at last.

None of the girls in the cell had slit her wrists, of course. That was just to lure the other guards into the trap.

Laura played it up, though, yelling, "Help! Oh, please, help her!"

She sure hoped she was guessing right about Ricardo.

The other two men rushed up to the cell door. One of them slung his rifle over his shoulder and began fumbling with his keys, trying to get the door unlocked. He hadn't really looked inside the cell yet, so he didn't know that Ricardo's yell of alarm was false.

While that guard tried to get the door unlocked, Ricardo suddenly struck at the other one.

He lifted his rifle and drove the butt of it into the side of the man's head. Standing only a couple of feet away, Laura saw the guard's eyes go wide with pain and shock and heard the crunch of bone as the rifle butt shattered his skull. His body stiffened but his knees unhinged. He dropped to the concrete floor.

Ricardo tried to lower his rifle so that he could cover the other guard, but the man realized too quickly that something was wrong. He whirled away from the lock, and instead of trying to unsling his rifle from his shoulder, he lunged at Ricardo instead, getting his hands on the other man's rifle and wrenching the barrel upward toward the vaulted ceiling of the corridor. His knee came up in a vicious blow aimed at Ricardo's groin.

Laura watched anxiously as Ricardo twisted aside so that the man's knee struck his thigh. They struggled desperately over the rifle, lurching back and forth in the corridor just outside the cell door. Laura knew that if the other guard won this fight, he would shoot Ricardo, and the last hope she and her friends had would be gone.

That looked to be the direction the fight was going, too. The other guard was bigger, older, and more experienced at this sort of struggle than Ricardo. A vicious grin appeared on his face as he felt Ricardo's grip on the rifle slipping. Frantically, Ricardo shoved him back against the bars of the cell door, but that failed to turn the tide of battle.

Suddenly, Laura acted on instinct. She had been saving the plastic rings off the water bottles for days now, and she had woven and twisted them together into a thick, stout plastic rope about a foot long. She'd had no plan, no real reason for doing this other than thinking that such a thing might come in handy sometime.

Tonight was the time.

She pulled the length of plastic from the pocket of her jeans and lunged forward, reaching through the bars with both hands. With one hand she slung the plastic around the guard's neck from behind, and grabbed the other end with her other hand. With a grunt of effort, she hung on for dear life and pulled back as hard as she could.

The makeshift garrote tightened across the guard's neck and brought his head back sharply. His skull thudded hard against the bars. Laura leaned against the bars on her side, twisting the plastic. She was so close to the guard that she could smell his sweat and the tonic he used on his hair. The frantic gurgling noises he made sounded almost in her ear.

She had never committed violence against anyone in her life, at least not beyond the level of a schoolyard scuffle. This was deadly serious. If it was within her power, she wanted to choke the bastard to death.

It didn't come to that. Ricardo ripped the rifle out of the man's hands and drove the butt of it into his face. Once, twice, three times he slammed the rifle butt home as the man hung there, pinned against the bars by Laura. After the third blow, the man's body sagged and Laura smelled an even worse stench as his bowels and bladder voided in death.

"You can let him go," Ricardo said breathlessly to her. "He's dead."

Laura released the plastic and stepped back. The guard's body pitched forward to sprawl on the floor of the corridor next to the other dead man.

Panting a little from the effort of the fight, Ricardo went to the lock, twisted the key in it, and pulled open the door. "Come on," he gasped. "All of you. You are free."

Free of the cell, maybe, but they were a long way from being free of the Night Wolves. Laura knew that. She shuddered as she stepped past the bodies of the dead guards—one of whom she had helped to kill, but she wasn't going to think about that right now—and looked back to motion to Carmen, Stacy, and the other girls in the cell. "Let's go," she said.

She didn't have to tell them twice.

Laura's heart pounded wildly as the other girls scrambled out of the cell. Ricardo pressed another set of keys into her hands and said, "Unlock the cells on the other side of the hall. I will get the ones on this side."

A part of her didn't want to get that far away from him. She wanted to stay close by his side. But she knew he was right. Time was of the essence. She ran from cell to cell, unlocking the doors and jerking them open. "Let's go, let's go," she said impatiently to the other prisoners. "Everybody out!"

When she came to the cell at the far end of the hall, where some of the girls were kept who were considered fair game for the guards, they cringed away from her, as if so terrified by their ordeal that they didn't really recognize her. Laura's breath caught in her throat as she recognized Shannon, whose haunted eyes looked up at her from a bruised face. Obviously the redhead had been treated roughly.

But then understanding dawned in Shannon's eyes. She croaked, "Laura?"

"Come on, Shannon," Laura said gently. "We're getting out of here."

Shannon got to her feet and walked unsteadily out of the cell. The other girls followed her. Angelina Salinas was one of them. She didn't look like she had been touched yet, but her eyes were big with fear.

"Are we getting out of here?" she asked Laura.

"We're sure going to try."

Angelina nodded. "Good. My father . . . he's a monster."

Laura couldn't argue with that. Nor did she have time to, because a scream ripped out and as she turned she saw that Shannon had gone along the corridor to the place where the dead guards lay. She picked up the rifle dropped by the first man Ricardo had struck down, and even as Ricardo lunged at her and called, "No!" Shannon fired, blasting a bullet into the already dead face of the guard. She kept firing, the shots booming and echoing deafeningly in the corridor, until Ricardo reached her and wrenched the weapon out of her hands. By then the faces of the two guards were nothing but bloody smears that no longer looked human after the almost point-blank blasts.

Laura's nerves drew even tighter. Those shots would draw the attention of Guerrero's men. She understood Shannon's rage and desire for vengeance on the men who had abused her. . . .

But her moment of bloody revenge might have just cost them all their lives.

Thirty-six

The chopper's rotors clawed at the shadow-thickened air as it flew toward the old mission. Its running lights were off, and only the faint glow from the instruments lit the cockpit. Behind it to the west, a narrow band of the faintest reddish gold over the mountains marked the last light of day, but ahead, darkness lay over the land and stars glittered like diamonds in the night sky.

The five people inside the helicopter were grimly silent as they leaned forward intently. A sprawl of lights on the northern horizon indicated the location of Nuevo Laredo and Laredo on the other side of the border. Down here, though, south of the border towns, the landscape was mostly dark, with only an occasional light showing at some isolated farm or ranch.

Not so the old mission that was their destination. The whole compound around it was brightly illuminated by floodlights, making it stand out starkly from the darkness around it. Tom spotted it as the chopper drew closer. He lifted the binoculars to his eyes and studied the mission as best he could through the Plexiglas that surrounded them.

"It all looks quiet," he said in a strained voice. "The attack was supposed to start five minutes ago."

Had none of the others gotten through? Was it just the five of them, against a hundred or more bloodthirsty killers? If that was the case, they wouldn't get very far, and they stood almost no chance of coming out alive.

But they couldn't turn back. Not now, not this close. His niece Laura was up there only a mile or two away, along with the daughters of Sonia and Van Sant and Lambert. None of them would ever be able to live with themselves if they came this close and then abandoned the operation, abandoned their loved ones.

As for Wild Bill Elliott, that mission was where the fight was waiting for him. He had never turned his back on a fight and wasn't about to start now.

"See anything?" Sonia asked anxiously.

"No, there's nothing going on around the mission," Tom replied.

Elliott drawled, "Looks like we go it alone, then. Won't be the first time."

Not for him, maybe, Tom thought. But the rest of them weren't professional warriors. They were strictly amateurs.

They would have to do their best anyway, regardless of that. As Elliott had said, if they went in hard and fast, they might be able to bust the girls out of wherever they were being held, and some of them would have a chance to get away.

Sonia veered to the south and circled so that they could come at the compound from the rear. As they drew nearer, she announced tightly, "There's that machine-gun emplacement on top of the wall. I can see it."

"Wild Bill, you'd better get that toy from behind the seat back there," Tom said. "You know how to handle it, I think."

"Damn right I do," Elliott grunted. He twisted around and brought out a bulky, shoulder-mounted missile launcher. It looked a little like an old-fashioned bazooka, but it was shorter.

Tom warned him, "You'll probably only get one shot."

"One's all I need," Elliott said confidently.

He lifted the launcher to his shoulder and settled it there comfortably. Coiled wires ran from the firing mechanism to the tail of the rocket that was nestled in the tube. Elliott leaned closer to the open door at the side of the cockpit and rested his face against the laser-guidance sight attached to the launcher.

"Angle just a little to the left, ma'am," he told Sonia.

She obliged, swinging the chopper slightly to the side so that Elliott could line up the shot, and as she did so, bright orange sparks suddenly spurted into the darkness from the position atop the adobe wall where the machine gun was located.

"They've opened fire," Tom said calmly. "They must have heard us coming. But they can't see us yet, so they're firing blind."

"Bad luck for them we ain't," Elliott breathed, and then he tripped the trigger and sent the missile screaming from the launcher on a tail of flame, its targeting system sending it straight toward the chattering, bullet-spewing machine gun.

The ordnance provided by Hiram Stackhouse's money and connections did its job. The missile flew true, slammed into the machine gun nest, and erupted in a ball of flame that not only destroyed the machine gun and the Night Wolves manning it, but also took a sizable chunk out of the wall.

"Well," Elliott said as he lowered the launcher from

his shoulder, "I reckon now they know for sure that we're comin'."

Guerrero tried to be polite to his guests, of course, since they would be in debt to him for millions of dollars before this night was over, but sometimes it was difficult. There was toadlike Oscar Zamora, who owned whorehouses in Monterrey, Saltillo, and Matamoros and sampled all his girls before he put them to work; Alejandro Rivas, gaunt with the disease that ravaged his body, the disease that would surely kill him in a year or less, but not before he had passed on its curse to as many girls as he could get his hands on, in an act of vicarious revenge on the prostitute who had given it to him; Yusuf bin Hamid, who had an extensive collection of whips that had caressed the soft flesh and tasted the warm blood of countless unfortunate young women; Jerry Dupre, who couldn't go back to his native Louisiana—or anywhere else in the States—because of the blood-drenched horrors he had perpetrated there; and a dozen more evil men whose monstrous natures were concealed by the wealth and sophistication in which they cloaked themselves.

And then there was Cedric Willingham. Sir Cedric, if the truth be known, a peer of the realm. That honor had come his way before the truth about him had been discovered by the British authorities. He had been forced to flee when his crimes were uncovered, first to Argentina and then eventually to Mexico. He was not only a sexual deviant and a sadist par excellence, he was also quite an accomplished criminal and had built up huge amounts of ill-gotten gains in Swiss banks and offshore accounts scattered around the world. It seemed unbelievable that one man would spend so much money on a mere girl, but

Laura Simms was worth it to Willingham. Besides, he would recoup the five million through his far-flung business interests in a matter of days.

It was Willingham who came toward Guerrero now as the buyers gathered in the chapel of the old mission, where once the priests had said Mass. The benches where the parishioners sat were long gone, of course. The place had been redecorated. Food and drink were available for the guests; nothing but the finest for men who were willing to shell out so much *dinero* to indulge their lusts.

Guerrero made himself nod and smile at Willingham. The Englishman's eyes glittered with excitement and anticipation. "Good evening, Colonel," he said. "I don't mean to rush you, but when will the lovely young ladies be here? I simply cannot wait to see that innocent blond beauty you showed me the other day in the, ah, flesh."

"Soon, my friend," Guerrero said heartily. "In fact, I was just about to send Major Cortez to fetch them." He looked around, saw Cortez standing near the wall along with several of the armed guards who were stationed around the room, and caught the major's eye. Cortez started toward him.

"Yes, Colonel?" Cortez asked as he walked up briskly.

"I believe it is time to bring our other . . . guests . . . to this gathering," Guerrero said.

It was obvious that Cortez wanted to salute, but he settled for nodding gravely and saying, "Of course, Colonel. I will be back shortly with them."

"*Muchas gracias,* Major."

Cortez left the room along with several of the guards. Guerrero could just imagine the reaction when they returned with the prisoners. Earlier, Guerrero had given orders that the girls be stripped before they were brought to the chapel. It would be a truly impressive moment when they were prodded nude into this once-holy place, to be paraded before the avid eyes of the men who would buy them.

"You seem to have an awfully large number of armed men on hand this evening, Colonel," Willingham went on. "You aren't expecting trouble, are you?"

"Of course not," Guerrero said. "The presence of my men is simply a precaution. There are many very important guests here tonight, yourself not least among them. In fact . . ." Guerrero lowered his voice. "I would venture to say, Señor, that no one here tonight is more important than you."

The sick bastard preened at that, visibly pleased. Guerrero didn't mind lying to him. And he didn't say anything about the rumored attack on the mission compound, either. For one thing, he didn't believe that it would actually come about, and for another, even if it did, he had every confidence that his men would massacre the raiders without difficulty. Such a thing might even be to his advantage. Once people saw how easily he crushed anyone who dared to defy him, his stranglehold on power in northern Mexico would be stronger than ever.

He chatted idly for a few more minutes with Willingham, but then began to grow impatient. The Englishman was getting impatient. "I say," Willingham finally exclaimed, "shouldn't Major Cortez be back with the young ladies by now?"

"Any minute, I'm sure—" Guerrero began.

The huge explosion that suddenly rocked the old mission overwhelmed anything Guerrero might have said.

And he knew in that instant that perhaps he should have been worried after all.

* * *

Ricardo had barely ripped the rifle out of Shannon's hands when a rush of footsteps sounded on the other side of the door leading into the main part of the old mission building. He said to Laura, "Unlock the rear door and lead the girls out. Hurry!"

She hesitated. "What about you?"

He had slung his rifle over his shoulder. He unslung it now and gripped it tightly. "I will stop whoever is coming," he said. "Now go!"

Laura didn't want to leave him, but he had risked his life to save them, and all the rest of the girls were depending on her. Reluctantly, she turned and ran toward the rear door, pushing her way through the crowd of girls that thronged the corridor.

Ricardo turned toward the other door. As he did so, it burst open and Major Cortez rushed through, trailed by three more armed men. Ricardo leveled an arm toward the girls and shouted, "The prisoners! They are getting away!"

Cortez growled a curse and ran past him, followed by the other men. Ricardo let them go. He looked along the hall, which stretched for about fifty feet. The terrified girls were crowding into the other end now, blocking his view of Laura. He hoped she was successful in unlocking the far door.

Major Cortez fired his pistol into the vaulted ceiling. The roar of the gun was deafening as it bounced back from the thick adobe walls. Several of the girls screamed.

"Stop!" Cortez shouted. "Stop, all of you! I do not want to hurt you, but I will kill the first one who tries to escape!"

"Too late, Major," Ricardo said from behind him. "They are all escaping."

Cortez started to turn toward him in confusion, and Ricardo pressed the rifle's trigger.

Bullets ripped out from the barrel in a lethal burst that

chewed through two of the men closest to Ricardo. They went down, their riddled bodies spouting blood. Ricardo swung the rifle and kept firing, and the third man staggered back, momentarily blocking Ricardo's line of fire at Cortez. The pistol in the major's hand jutted out past the jittering body of the third guard and spurted flame. Ricardo felt the slug slam into him.

The impact threw him back against the open door of the cell where Laura had been imprisoned. He let go of the rifle with his left hand and caught hold of the bars to steady himself and keep from falling. At the same time, he tried to bring the rifle up again with his right hand and fire. He was too late, though, because Major Cortez had shoved the dying third guard away and was now stalking toward him, ready to blast him again and again.

At that moment, Laura finally got the rear door unlocked and threw it open. She stepped aside and shouted, "Get out! Get out!" at the other girls. She looked toward the far end of the corridor, hoping to catch sight of Ricardo and see if he was still all right. There had been a lot of shooting up there.

The girls started to rush past her into the courtyard, and as the crowd thinned a little, she saw Ricardo slumped against the open door of her old cell, blood on his shirt, trying futilely to raise his rifle as Major Cortez closed in on him with a pistol ready to fire again.

He was about to kill Ricardo—and there wasn't a thing Laura could do to stop him. Ricardo had freed them, but he was going to pay with his life.

Laura screamed, "Nooooo!" and Cortez hesitated, turning his head toward her.

Ricardo finally succeeded in tipping up the rifle barrel. He pulled the trigger—

Cortez's head exploded in a spray of blood and brain matter.

Just as outside in the courtyard, the entire world seemed to explode in a huge ball of flame that shook the earth and engulfed the night in fiery, ravening destruction.

Thirty-seven

Flaming debris was still falling from the sky like drops of fiery rain when Sonia lowered the helicopter into the courtyard at the rear of the mission compound. Tom was out of the chopper before its skids even touched the ground. Elliott, Van Sant, and Lambert were right behind him. The rifles carried by the four men were ready to fire, but for the moment, there were no targets.

Tom's eyes widened in amazement as he looked toward the entrance of the rear wing and saw girls come pouring out of the open door. Most wore jeans and T-shirts; a few had lost their shirts and were clad only in bras above the waist. They were hysterical, panic-stricken, but somehow they were holding it together long enough to get out of the building.

Then he saw a girl bringing up the rear, prodding along the others, keeping them moving, her actions carrying an indefinable air of command. There was a man with her who appeared to be wounded. She had an arm around his waist, supporting him as they hobbled along. He carried a rifle in one hand.

The shock of recognition that went through Tom told

him that he was looking at his niece. That was Laura herding the other girls out of their captivity, and somehow Tom wasn't surprised. The family had a habit of doing what needed to be done.

Behind him, he heard Wayne Van Sant cry in a choked voice, "Michelle!" and knew that the man had spotted his daughter. Lambert shouted a name, too, but in the confusion Tom couldn't make it out. Some of the girls were screaming, and not far off men shouted in angry confusion. The rest of the Night Wolves would be arriving at any moment, drawn by the explosion.

Tom and his companions had to hold them off until the girls got away. He ran toward the fleeing former captives and shouted, "This way! This way! Laura! Bring them this way!"

The girls had no way of knowing what was going on, but they had to see the helicopter and the Americans and realize that somebody had finally come to help them. Several of them ran desperately toward Tom. He moved aside and waved them past.

"Outside!" he told them. "Get outside the compound! Stay on the road!"

It was possible that the terrain around the mission was mined, but the road wouldn't be, so the girls would be safe enough as long as they stayed on it. The way out was clear, because the rocket that had destroyed the machine-gun emplacement had also wrecked the gate. It hung crookedly open, and the girls had no trouble getting through it.

Van Sant and Lambert caught hold of their daughters and hugged them fiercely as both girls shrieked, "Daddy!" The reunion lasted only a few seconds, though, as the men then pushed the girls on toward the gate and told them to stay with the others and get out.

Tom was trying to reach Laura and the man with her.

He had no idea who the man was, but he was dressed like one of the Night Wolves, in black jeans and T-shirt. And he was carrying a gun, so Tom didn't trust him. But Laura wouldn't be trying to help him if he was one of their captors, he told himself. Finding out the details would have to wait until later. For now, Tom just wanted them out of here while they still had the chance.

"Laura!" he shouted again. "Laura, over here!"

She stumbled toward him, eyes wide with shock. "Tom?" she cried. "Tom Brannon?"

He grinned at her. "That's right, kid." As she came up to him, he threw an arm around her shoulders and gave her a quick hug. "We've come to get you out of here, so go with the others. Get outside the compound."

She glanced around, sizing up the situation, and he was proud of the way she obviously took it all in so quickly. "Four men can't hold off Guerrero's army," she said, "and one little chopper can't carry us all. How are we going to get out of here?"

Suddenly, a sound like a huge rushing wind filled the night air, and spotlights lanced down from above, illuminating the ground outside the mission and the frightened girls gathering there. Dust rose in the air as giant spinning rotors lowered three big choppers from the darkness.

Tom's grin stretched wider. "There's your ride now!" he told Laura. The other three helicopters had made it across the border somehow and reached the compound in time.

The man with Laura straightened, pulling out of her grip. "Go!" he told her as he gave her a little shove toward the gate. "Get out while you can! I will stay and help this man and his friends."

"No, Ricardo!" she said. "You're already hurt!"

Tom could see now that the left side of the man's shirt was sodden with blood. Ricardo leaned closer to Laura and pressed his lips to her forehead. "Go," he said, and the word was almost a whispered plea.

Tears rolled down her cheeks, but she nodded shakily and started to walk backward. Then she turned and ran after the other girls.

Tom and Ricardo exchanged a glance. "Ricardo Benitez," the young man said, introducing himself. "I work for the U.S. Drug Enforcement Agency."

"One of those deep-cover agents I heard about," Tom said as the light of understanding dawned.

Ricardo nodded. "*Sí*. And you are—"

"Laura's uncle. Tom Brannon."

"You risked your life to come get her out of this hellhole?"

Tom nodded toward Ricardo's wounded side. "You look like you risked your life to help her, too."

A savage grin creased his strained face. "And to get back at Colonel Guerrero for all the evil he has done."

"I hear you," Tom said.

At that moment, Wild Bill Elliott trotted up and said, "Hear this, Brannon—we got trouble comin'!"

Indeed, with a burst of gunfire, armed men ran out of the rising dust and opened fire on them. Tom and his companions scattered, returning the shots. Tom threw one glance toward the ruined gate and saw that the girls were still straggling through it. One of them stumbled and almost fell, hit by a stray bullet. But another girl caught her and held her up and helped her out of the compound.

Then Tom didn't have time to check on the fleeing former prisoners anymore, because he was too busy fighting for his life—and theirs.

Los Lobos de la Noche swept into the courtyard like a black tide, the soldiers of Colonel Guerrero converging on the rear of the compound and pouring lead into it. Four

men—five counting Ricardo Benitez—and one woman—
Sonia Alvarez, who fired a pistol from the door of the
helicopter—stood little chance of stemming that tide for
more than a few moments. But their hope was that those
precious moments would be enough for all the girls to
reach the other choppers and get the hell out of there.

Tom dropped to one knee. The butt of the rifle in his
hands kicked against his shoulder as he fired steadily into
the onrushing crowd of Night Wolves. Flying lead whispered all around him. From the corner of his eye he saw
Wayne Van Sant go to a knee, too, but the former tank
commander was hit. Van Sant stayed upright and continued firing, though. A few yards away, Craig Lambert's
face was pale with fear, but he stayed cool and the rifle in
his hands continued to bark.

Wild Bill Elliott was grinning and didn't seem to even
notice when a bullet kissed his cheek, leaving a bloody
streak. Just one more scar to go with all the others.

Ricardo had fallen, too weak to stand up any longer,
but he was still conscious and still firing toward the members of the gang he had infiltrated for the DEA.

A small but noble band of men—and one woman—but
unfortunately, Tom knew that they were about to get the
shit shot out of them. They had minutes, perhaps even
seconds, to live.

Worth it if the girls got away, he thought.

But he wished he could see Bonnie one more time.

It was chaos inside the old mission. Most of the men
who had come here tonight for the auction had brought
bodyguards with them, so at the sound of the explosion,
those hard-faced men jerked guns from under their coats,
grabbed their employers, and thrust the men behind them.

They were willing to shield those human vultures with their own bodies, which was proof positive that some men would do anything for money.

Willingham's guards were trying to reach his side as the Englishman clawed frantically at Colonel Guerrero's uniform jacket and cried out, "What is it? Oh, dear God, what's happening?"

The irony of a demon in human form like Willingham calling on God was not lost on Guerrero, but he had no time to reflect on it. Instead, he shoved the Englishman away and grated, "Stay calm, Sir Cedric. Whatever it is, my men will handle it."

But within moments, the sounds of gunfire began to penetrate the chapel. A battle was going on somewhere outside. Someone had dared to attack his sanctum, just as General Montero had warned him might happen. Rage filled Guerrero. How dare anyone do such a thing? He was Colonel Alfonso Guerrero, the leader of Los Lobos de la Noche! The yapping mongrels who nipped at his heels would soon learn the peril of their audacity!

He turned, again brushing off Willingham's frantic hands. The man's very touch made Guerrero's skin crawl. He strode toward the doors leading out of the old chapel, intent on finding out what was going on. He wanted to supervise the destruction of his enemies personally.

He could tell now that the sounds of gunfire came from the rear of the compound. That was where the prisoners were held. The Americans were trying to free them. Guerrero paused suddenly, feeling as if a fist had just punched him in the stomach. Angelina was back there! He had ordered her taken to the cells and put with the others—to teach her a lesson!

And now there were explosions and thousands of high-powered rounds filling the air, and she was back there in harm's way, where death might strike her down at any instant.

Cursing himself, his face grim, Guerrero broke into a run toward the rear of the compound.

It wouldn't be much longer now. The five men had pulled back toward the helicopter, Tom going to Ricardo's side to help him while Lambert gave Van Sant a hand. Elliott covered them as best he could. But as they came together, they all knew that this would be their last stand. They crouched behind rubble that had been blown off the wall, firing their rifles dry, slapping in new clips, firing again. But the Night Wolves were all around them, and within heartbeats they would be overrun and wiped out.

That was when Charles Long, Wally Chambers, Joe Delgado, and Frank Ramirez, all of them yelling at the top of their lungs, led reinforcements through the gate where the girls had fled, the rifles and pistols in their hands throwing slugs into the massed Night Wolves with deadly accuracy.

Elliott lowered his rifle for a moment and drawled, "Looks like the cavalry's here," as if there had never been any doubt in his mind that help would arrive in time.

There had been plenty of doubt in Tom's mind, but he felt hope surge within him as he heard explosions from the front of the compound. At least some of the rescue force had gotten here and was carrying out the frontal attack as planned. Long, Chambers, and the others had come around to help back here. That wasn't the way they had sketched it out, but Tom was damned glad to see them anyway. A good soldier had to be able to improvise, and even though in real life they were all civilians, tonight they were the best damned soldiers Tom had ever had the honor to serve with.

And now Tom and his companions joined in the charge as the reinforcements slammed into the Night Wolves. Vicious, hand-to-hand fighting filled the courtyard. When Tom emptied his rifle this time, there was no chance to reload it. He used it as a club instead, driving the butt into the face of a black-clad man who loomed up in front of him. Then he reversed it, burning his hands on the hot barrel but ignoring the pain as he lashed back and forth with it, shattering the stock. Night Wolves went down before the flailing frenzy, skulls crushed and blood sheeting over ruined faces.

Just like Davy Crockett at the Alamo, swinging Old Betsy as Santa Anna's minions closed in around him, Tom thought crazily.

Only this time Santa Anna—Colonel Guerrero—wasn't going to win.

Even though they outnumbered the Americans, the Night Wolves began to fall back toward the building. Some of them flat out turned and ran. Tom and the others pursued them, driving them along the corridor where the cells were located, catching up to some of them and dealing out the death they so richly deserved. Tom finally had to drop what was left of the rifle he had destroyed and pull the pistol from the holster on his hip. As he did, he caught sight of a tall man in some sort of fancy uniform, who had just run through the door at the far end of the corridor. Even though he had never seen the man before, Tom recognized him from Brady Keller's description.

Guerrero.

The colonel took one look at the bloody melee filling the broad hallway, then turned and went back the way he had come. Tom started after him. A gun exploded practically in his face as one of the Night Wolves lunged at him. The bullet whipped past Tom's ear, and the next instant he fired his own pistol and saw the man's head jerk back as the slug slammed into his forehead and bored through his brain. Tom shouldered the falling corpse aside and ran toward the door where Guerrero had disappeared.

It was time to settle the score.

Thirty-eight

Some of the rescuers had pulled back outside the compound to cover the girls as they climbed into the waiting helicopters. Laura stood by the open doors of one of the big choppers, helping her friends climb up into the aircraft. Men waited inside the helicopters, too, reaching down with outstretched hands to grasp the wrists of the girls and haul them to safety. The loading proceeded quickly and efficiently, especially considering the circumstances. Finally, one of the men in the chopper where Laura stood leaned out the door and called, "You're the last one, little lady! Come on!"

She hesitated, turning for a second toward the compound, where gunfire still racketed. Her uncle was in there somewhere, as was Ricardo, who had been wounded, perhaps seriously, while freeing them. She wanted to go back and see if she could help them.

But she knew that Tom and Ricardo would both be furious with her if she did, and she wanted to see her mother again, and despite everything, she was still just a seventeen-year-old girl. A very scared seventeen-year-old girl who wanted to go home.

She reached up, took the man's hand, and climbed into the helicopter. The door slid shut with a clang behind her.

Less than a minute later, all three of the big whirlybirds lifted off, soaring high into the night sky.

Guerrero was filled with rage. The sight that had greeted his eyes when he entered the rear wing of the old mission was shameful. His men, his Night Wolves, were being routed by a motley bunch of Americans! He had never dreamed that he would ever see such a thing.

Not only that, but he had caught a glimpse through the struggling mob of Cortez's body lying on the floor, obviously dead with most of his head blown off. That sent a spear of grief and anger thrusting through Guerrero. Eli had been his amigo, his *segundo*. Now he was gone.

That was just one more reason to crush the Americans, Guerrero thought. Cortez's spirit cried out for revenge.

He would rally his men in the chapel, he decided. There he would also have the help of the bodyguards who had come with the bidders for the auction. That was where they would put a stop to this attack and teach the Americans a lesson.

That thought reminded him of Angelina, and he grimaced. He didn't know where she was, but he hoped that she was all right. Those girls couldn't get away; there was nowhere they could run outside the compound where he couldn't track them down. He would find them, and he would find Angelina.

As he ran into the chapel, he heard explosions and gunfire coming from the *front* of the compound. The damned Americans were everywhere! He was caught between two forces, and most of his men had rushed to the back to deal with the threat there. That had been a mistake, one that might have doomed a lesser commander. But he would find a way to win yet, he told himself.

The Night Wolves on duty inside the chapel had stayed there, like the good soldiers they were. Guerrero called them together and placed them at the rear door. He gathered the bodyguards and over the strident objections of their employers, posted them at the front door.

"I say!" Willingham protested in his reedy voice. "My men are supposed to protect me!"

"They will be protecting you, Sir Cedric, by not allowing the interlopers in here," Guerrero explained, barely able to hold onto his patience. If Willingham got on his nerves much more, he was going to take his pistol and put a bullet through the man's brain himself, five million or no five million.

"I don't see how you could have let something like this happen, Colonel! Who *are* those men?"

"Fools," Guerrero said between clenched teeth. "Fools who will soon be dead."

Tom heard footsteps behind him and glanced back to see Elliott, Long, and several other men following him. They looked as grim as he felt, and he knew they wanted a shot at Guerrero, too. He didn't tell them to turn back. Everybody deserved a chance to make Guerrero pay for his crimes.

Again the role reversal with the Alamo struck Tom. They were heading for the interior of the old mission, the chapel where the place's defenders would make their last stand. As they ran down a vaulted hallway toward a pair of heavy wooden doors, he slapped a fresh clip into his pistol.

Those doors swung open, and Elliott barked, "Spread out!"

The warning came just in time. Automatic-weapons

fire sprayed through the corridor, knocking pieces of adobe off the walls. Staying low, Tom and his men returned the fire. Their coolly aimed shots took a toll, dropping a couple of the gunners and forcing the others away from the doors. Long tossed a flash-bang grenade. It bounced along the floor and through the doors into the chapel, where it went off with a burst of blinding light and deafening sound.

"Go! Go!" Long yelled as he came to his feet and surged toward the door. Tom and the others were right with him.

They opened fire again as they reached the doors. Bullets whined around them. Looking across the big room, Tom saw that another battle was going on at the front doors of the chapel. Guerrero and the Night Wolves were between a rock and a hard place, and they were about to be smashed.

The place was total chaos, filled with flying lead and angry shouts and the screams of dying men. Tom emptied his pistol, reversed it, and used it as a club, the same way he had used his lost rifle. After he had smashed the butt of the automatic between the eyes of one of Guerrero's men, he picked up the rifle the dying man dropped and used it. His feet slipped a little on the concrete floor, and he knew that was because he was splashing through pools of blood. Where the hell was Guerrero?

A tall, thin man came at him, shooting with a pistol he held awkwardly. The man didn't look like he knew how to handle the gun, but he was still a threat. The bullet that whined past Tom's ear proved that. Tom fired twice with the commandeered rifle, blasting a couple of slugs through the man's narrow chest. He went down hard, blood bubbling from his mouth as he thrashed for a second on the floor and then lay still.

Tom didn't know it, but he had just killed an English peer—and possibly the most perverted man in the Western Hemisphere.

He swung around, still looking for Guerrero, frustrated that he couldn't find the colonel whose colossal arrogance and evil had brought misery to so many people. The next instant, he was on his knees without quite knowing how he had gotten there, and the hot wet pain in his hip told him that he was hit. He pressed a hand to the wound and felt blood flowing over his fingers. He had no idea where the bullet had come from or who had pulled the trigger, but that didn't matter. His legs still worked and he still had a gun in his hand, so he forced himself to his feet and staggered on, still seeking the big, handsome man in the fancy uniform.

A flash of movement caught Tom's eye. He saw a figure diving into an alcove and recognized Guerrero. Stumbling a little, he ran after the colonel. Both of them left the main fight behind.

Guerrero must have heard Tom following him, or at least sensed the pursuit of an enemy, because he stopped suddenly, whirled around, and blazed a couple of shots from the pistol in his hand. Tom threw himself to the side, rolling and wincing in pain. The bullets screamed past him. From the floor, he fired the rifle and saw Guerrero's arm jerk. The colonel's pistol flew out of his hand. Guerrero didn't try to recover it. He just turned and ran again.

Tom pulled the trigger, perfectly willing to shoot the son of a bitch in the back if that was what it took to end his evil. But the rifle clicked futilely, out of ammunition. Tom scrambled to his feet and went after Guerrero.

The colonel's right arm hung uselessly at his side, and he staggered as he tried to run. Tom caught up to him in a few steps and left his feet in a diving tackle. His arms went around Guerrero's legs, and both men fell heavily. This was a deep alcove, and shadows lay thick in it. As the two men broke apart and rolled over to come to their feet, what little light that penetrated back here shone dully on the blade of the knife in Guerrero's left hand. He lunged at Tom, slashing with the blade.

Tom jerked back, but not in time to keep the knife from scraping across his stomach. The kevlar vest kept the blade from cutting him. Guerrero snarled and flung the knife at his face. Tom ducked. The knife glanced off his shoulder. He dove forward, tackling Guerrero again and knocking him back against a pedestal where a large ceramic statue of the Holy Virgin and Child sat. Left over from the days when this had been a real mission, the statue toppled and fell to the floor, smashing to pieces. Neither man noticed as they wrestled desperately. Both of them were hampered by their wounds, but each man knew he was fighting for his life.

Guerrero hooked a foot behind Tom's knee and jerked. Tom went over backward. Guerrero landed on top of him. His left hand, his only good hand, locked on Tom's throat, and the fingers squeezed like bands of iron. He slammed Tom's head against the floor a couple of times, stunning him. Tom went limp for a moment, unable to fight back as Guerrero's hand squeezed tighter and tighter, strangling the life out of him.

"Who are you?" Guerrero panted as he did his best to choke Tom to death. He didn't release his grip to let his opponent answer the question. He just asked it again. "Who are you?"

Tom fought his way back as consciousness tried to slip away from him. His right hand reached out, touched something sharp, and grasped it. Calling on all the strength he had left, he brought his arm up and around and brought the broken piece of statue across Guerrero's throat in a slashing blow that left a blood-spurting gash in the colonel's neck. Guerrero's eyes bugged out in shock and pain as crimson flooded across his chest. His grip loosened, and Tom was able to throw him aside.

Guerrero rolled onto his back and clawed at his ravaged throat with his good hand, but he couldn't stop the fountain of blood. His feet drummed against the floor. Tom pushed himself up and half crawled, half lurched over to the dying man, knowing that Guerrero was going fast. He looked down at Guerrero and grated out, "Who am I? *Just an American who won't be pushed around, you murdering, kidnapping bastard!*"

With a hideous, blood-choked gurgle, Guerrero died.

But not before the knowledge of what Tom had said showed briefly in his eyes.

Colonel Alfonso Guerrero had made the worst, last mistake of his life when he decided that he could invade the United States and get away with it.

Tom tried to get up but couldn't. His strength was gone. Most of the pool of blood on the floor had come from Guerrero, but a lot of it had belonged to him. He slumped to the concrete and stopped trying to fight the tide of blackness that tried to wash over him. This time he let it carry him away, and after that he knew nothing.

Laredo International Airport was closed tonight, shut down by order of the Federal Government. But that didn't mean it wasn't busy. Dozens of emergency vehicles screamed onto the tarmac, red and blue lights flashing. They lined one of the runways. Jet engines roared overhead, as well as the throbbing pulse of helicopter rotors.

Special Agent Sharon Morgan climbed hurriedly out of

one of the vehicles. Sheriff Phil Garza, Chief of Police Saul Jimenes, and John Holland from the State Department followed her. The men wore expressions of anticipation. Morgan just looked mad enough to chew nails, but at the same time, she seemed eager, too.

"Those bastards will never see the outside of a federal prison again," she said, as much to herself as to anybody else. But Garza, Jimenes, and Holland overheard the remark and exchanged worried glances.

The three helicopters descended from the sky, kicking up some dust from the runway as they landed. Morgan squared her shoulders, ready to stride forward and arrest everybody in the big choppers. Air Force jets had picked them up as they crossed back into American airspace and escorted them here, but it hadn't been a difficult chore. This seemed to be where the pilots of the helicopters wanted to go.

Something made Morgan glance over her shoulder. She stiffened as she saw a large number of headlights racing toward the runway from the direction of the airport's entrance. "Garza!" she practically screamed. "Your men were supposed to keep everybody out!"

Garza looked at the approaching lights and tried not to smile. "I'm stretched pretty thin these days as far as manpower goes, Agent Morgan," he said. "I must not have had enough deputies posted to stop whoever that is."

"Whoever that is!" Morgan repeated, her voice rising. "I'll tell you who it is! It's the damn media, that's who it is!"

"More than likely," Garza agreed under his breath.

"I don't care," Morgan insisted. "I'm still taking everyone in those helicopters into federal custody. By myself if I have to!"

She drew her gun and stalked toward the choppers. The doors slid back. The runway lights were on, and along with the headlights from the dozens of vehicles, they illuminated the scene brilliantly. Everyone got a good look at the young, blond girl who stepped into the open door of the first helicopter, shielded her eyes for a second with her hand, and then jumped to the ground. She walked forward calmly. Behind her, more of the former prisoners began to climb out of the helicopters.

Morgan leveled her pistol at the blond girl and shrieked, "You're under arrest! Get down on the ground and put your hands behind your head!"

The blond girl just ignored her.

Hearing a stampede of feet behind them, Garza, Jimenes, and Holland stepped aside to let a large group of men and women run past them. Seeing them coming, the girls who had gotten out of the helicopters screamed for joy and ran forward. The reunion was a glorious one, mothers and a few fathers embracing their formerly lost daughters, safe at last back on American soil. And all around them were reporters and cameramen, video cameras whirring as they recorded the reunion in scenes that would be shown hundreds of times all over the world.

Morgan just stood there, shaking with rage, ignored by everyone.

Except for John Holland, who closed the cell phone he had been talking into and walked over to the FBI agent. "You're not going to be arresting anyone, Agent Morgan," he said, raising his voice a little so that she could hear him over the clamor. "I've just been on the phone with the president herself. Whether any of us like it or not, the country won't stand for it if we jail American citizens for rescuing their own children from certain death. It's over."

"But . . . but they broke federal laws!" Morgan said in stunned anguish, as if she couldn't believe what she had just heard.

"And there will be a full investigation. . . ." Holland's mouth quirked. "Followed by a decision not to press charges. That will probably include Captain Rodgers, by the way." He shook his head slowly. "Let's face it, Morgan. There are some things not even we can do anything about, and one of them is the will of the American people."

"But . . . but . . ."

Holland just shook his head again and turned away.

A few yards away, Garza and Jimenes stood together and no longer bothered trying not to smile as they watched the celebration on the runway. "Who do you think alerted the media?" Jimenes asked.

An electric motor buzzed behind them, and they turned to see Brady Keller rolling toward them in his wheelchair. "That would be me," Keller said, "as soon as our boys radioed that they were on their way home. Your men didn't put up much of a fuss when we came in the gate, Sheriff."

Garza shrugged. "Wasn't really any reason to, was there?"

The left side of Keller's mouth lifted in a grin that the two lawmen returned.

And out on the runway, Laura Simms suddenly found herself in her Aunt Bonnie's embrace. Both of them started crying. "It . . . it was Tom," Laura choked out. "He saved us. He saved us, Bonnie. But I . . . I don't know what happened to him after that."

"We'll pray for him," Bonnie managed to say as tears rolled down her face.

"Wh-where's my mother?"

"She's waiting for you. I'll take you to her. We'll go right now."

"That lady over that said I was under arrest."

"That's no lady," Bonnie said, "and I don't think what she says means much anymore. Come on."

They turned and walked toward the cars, and behind them, the celebration continued.

Epilogue

Tom Brannon fought his way up out of the darkness. The feel of crisp, starched sheets underneath him told him that he was in a hospital bed, and the tightness around his lower torso confirmed it. He was bandaged up like a mummy.

He opened his eyes, the lids fluttering weakly, and his blurred vision took a few seconds to focus on the face smiling down at him.

But then he recognized his wife, and as he looked past her and saw the anxious faces of Laura and Kelly Simms, as well, he heard Bonnie say, "It's all right, Tom. You're going to be fine. Everything's all right now."

He believed her and managed to smile a little, too. Then, with a sigh, he went back to sleep.

Ten members of the rescue force had been killed during the fighting at the old mission, and a couple of dozen more were wounded, some seriously enough that they would be hospitalized for quite a while. But out of the forty captives, thirty-eight of them were returned safely to the United States. The only ones who didn't come back were Rosa Delgado and Billie Sue Cahill.

When Tom heard about that, he felt a pang of sorrow and sympathy for Rosa's father Joe and for her mother. He hadn't known the Cahill girl's parents, but he grieved along with them, too.

Many of the girls had been through a terrible time of it, of course, and no doubt some of them would need years of psychological help. Some of them might never fully recover from their ordeal. But they were alive and they had a chance. That was more than they would have had if Tom and the others hadn't come to free them.

Angelina Salinas and her mother moved to Chicago, far away from La Frontera.

Fueled by official complaints from Mexico, the investigation that John Holland had mentioned to Agent Morgan took a full six months . . . and in the end, no charges—state, federal, or local—were filed against those who had taken part in the rescue. That brought more protests from the Mexican government, which were largely ignored. A lot of high-level American politicians— including the one in the White House—secretly seethed at the idea that people could defy the Federal Government like that and get away with it, but what could they do?

Well, there were a few things. When he got back to Arizona, Tom Brannon found a letter from the Internal Revenue Service, informing him that his tax returns for the past seven years were about to be audited. The same thing happened to Roy Rodgers, Charles Long, Wayne Van Sant, and a dozen or so others. Although they were all taxpaying, law-abiding citizens, they had to go through the hassle of the IRS audits.

And when those proceedings were over, thanks to the counsel of a small army of tax attorneys provided by Hiram Stackhouse, the IRS was forced to conclude that, in fact, in each case they owed additional refunds to the people who had been audited.

That news got into the papers and onto the TV newscasts, too, and the higher-ups who had been so mortally offended by the very idea of American citizens doing the right thing on their own decided it just might be time to cut their losses. . . .

Tom was alone in the auto-parts store one afternoon when the bell over the door jingled. He looked up from the invoices spread out on the counter in front of him and saw a slender man using a cane come into the store. It took him a second to recognize Ricardo Benitez.

Tom came out from behind the counter and hurried forward to greet Ricardo. The two men shook hands and then embraced, slapping each other on the back, and Tom asked with a grin, "How are you doing?"

"Not bad," Ricardo said. "The wound in my side healed up without any trouble. What about yours?"

"I'm still a little stiff and sore every now and then, but usually just when it rains." Tom chuckled. "Down here in Little Tucson, we don't have to worry about that very often. Your leg still giving you problems?"

"The doctors had to give me an artificial knee. My own was just shot up too bad to repair. But I get around pretty good on it. I can't do any fieldwork anymore, of course, but I'm still with the DEA."

Tom's smile disappeared and was replaced with a frown. "What happened with the Night Wolves?"

"More than half of them were killed in the fighting that night, and the ones who survived scattered. I'm sure some of them have gone back to work for the cartel, but as a coherent fighting force . . ." Ricardo shook his head. "They're washed up. With Guerrero and Cortez both dead, there was nobody to pull them back together."

Tom rubbed a hand over his head. "The DEA sent you in to help bring the Night Wolves down, didn't they?"

"They did."

"I'd say you did a good job of it. I understand from talking to Laura that you're the one who killed Cortez."

Ricardo smiled again. "How is Laura?"

"Enjoying her senior year of school. She'll be graduating in another couple of months."

"I'll send her a card. And an apology. I should have done something to help those girls a long time before I did."

Tom shrugged. "If you had, likely you would have gotten yourself killed and wouldn't have really helped them. As it was, the timing worked out just fine, even though we didn't plan it that way."

"That was just good luck," Ricardo pointed out.

"Maybe." Tom thought about that broken statue and how his hand had happened to fall on the razor-sharp shard he needed to end Guerrero's life. "Or maybe sometimes things work out according to a higher plan that we don't know anything about."

The two men were silent in thought for a moment, and then Ricardo said, "Well, I was just on my way to California, and I thought I'd stop over in Tucson and drive out here to see you. Brady Keller's working for us again, as a consultant, and he and I have a meeting in San Diego with the local authorities. There are a lot of drugs coming across the border out there, and we're trying to figure out a way to stop them."

"You think you'll ever win that war?"

"I don't know," Ricardo admitted, "but we can't stop fighting and just let the bad guys win, can we?"

"No," Tom said. "We can't."

As he stood on the sidewalk in front of the store a few minutes later and watched Ricardo drive away, he looked around and saw life going on about its business in Little Tucson. People he knew smiled and waved at him, and even though they were average, ordinary folks, he knew there was a core of steel in each and every one of them. Just as Ricardo had said, they wouldn't quit and let the bad guys win. It might take a while, but they would rise to the challenge every time.

Because they were Americans, and that was what they did.

He heard the phone ring and turned to go into the store. Probably somebody looking for a carburetor or a fuel pump or a set of spark plugs.

Tom got back to work...

GREAT BOOKS,
GREAT SAVINGS!

When You Visit Our Website:
www.kensingtonbooks.com
You Can Save Money Off The Retail Price
Of Any Book You Purchase!

- All Your Favorite Kensington Authors
- New Releases & Timeless Classics
- Overnight Shipping Available
- eBooks Available For Many Titles
- All Major Credit Cards Accepted

Visit Us Today To Start Saving!
www.kensingtonbooks.com

All Orders Are Subject To Availability.
Shipping and Handling Charges Apply.
Offers and Prices Subject To Change Without Notice.